A COLD BETRAYAL

Sira was kneeling, getting her bedroll ready and thinking only of warmth and sleep, when her psi suddenly screamed a warning. Instinctively she cried out, "Rollie!"

It was too late even as she heard her voice ring across the *quiru*. She whirled to look at Rollie, and it seemed to her shocked senses that a fur-tipped arrow simply appeared in Rollie's bare throat. The rider's weathered face went slack as she fell backwards, sprawling off her furs into the snow.

Sira bit off another outcry. She could see no escape from the disaster. She straightened her back where she knelt, and was still. Her own arrow, bitterly punctual out of the darkness, pierced her body just below her collarbone. Obviously the assassins meant them all to die . . .

SING
THE
LIGHT

LOUISE MARLEY

ACE BOOKS, NEW YORK

This book is an Ace original edition,
and has never been previously published.

SING THE LIGHT

An Ace Book / published by arrangement with
the author

PRINTING HISTORY
Ace edition / November 1995

ISBN: 0-441-00272-2

ACE®
Ace Books are published by The Berkley Publishing Group,
200 Madison Avenue, New York, NY 10016.
ACE and the "A" design are trademarks
belonging to Charter Communications, Inc.

PRINTED IN THE UNITED STATES OF AMERICA

10 9 8 7 6 5 4 3 2 1

For my guys: Jake and Zack

ACKNOWLEDGMENTS

With deepest gratitude to the following, without whom there would be no book:

June Campbell, my first reader (and also my mother);
The most talented and generous writers' group on the planet, consisting of Brian Bek, Jeralee Chapman, Niven Marquis, David Newton, and Catherine Whitehead;
Phil Timmerman, computer genius, for saving my manuscript more than once from electronic oblivion;
Peter Rubie, agent and mentor;
My teachers and colleagues at Clarion West;
And most importantly, that great Spirit which is the source of all art, all music, all gifts. Thank you.

SING
THE
LIGHT

PROLOGUE

✲   THE OLD SINGER CONCENTRATED, HER PAPERY EYELIDS closed and the webbing of wrinkles etched on her pale face like cracks in the Great Glacier. On her *filhata* she played a simple, intense melody in the second mode, *Aiodu*, and reached far, far away with the thread of her thought, lengthening, narrowing, stretching it beyond all known limits. Past the thick stone walls of the Conservatory, across the great ironwood forests of the Marik Mountains she reached, following events by listening to the mind of Sira, her protégée, who was in the gravest possible danger.

The old Singer's psi, so often used to speed the motion of the tiniest parts of the air around her, to stir it into giving off heat and light, now carried her many days' ride away, to a lonely campsite where Sira, the youngest of Nevyan Singers, lay wounded, bleeding into the snow that covered her. The old Singer had followed the shadowed patterns that led to this, had sensed the lurking evil that pursued Sira from the safety of the great Houses out into the deadly climate of the Continent. She could feel, faintly, the cold that all Nevyans feared, that even now began to seep into Sira's body as night fell and the warmth of the *quiru* above the campsite waned. Around Sira was death and more death, and the old Singer could feel her shock and sadness, and her fear.

Then, as she listened with all her mind, the echo that was Sira's thought faded from her hearing. The Singer struggled to find it again, cast about in the darkness, her *filhata* flung aside on her narrow cot, forgotten. But try as she might, she could hear no more from Sira. In desperation, the old Singer prayed into the night for the Spirit of Stars to help her beloved student. As always, the unknowable Spirit sent no answer.

CHAPTER
ONE

✦ THE RIDERS CHATTED AND TALKED AROUND THE LITTLE softwood fire, and Sira listened to them in shy silence. So much talking aloud made her uncomfortable, but she supposed she would get used to it in time. Her *quiru* shimmered warm and secure above them all, the stars glittering icily beyond it, the huge ironwood trees around the campsite looming like ghosts in the night.

"Cantrix, would you like more *keftet*?" Rollie hunkered next to Sira, holding out the pot and spoon. "Or maybe you'd like to go out of the *quiru* for a moment?"

Sira hesitated, not wishing to make a mistake, but she did not understand the other woman's question. "Go out?" she asked softly. "Rollie, do you mean . . . do I wish to relieve myself?"

The rider laughed, her weathered face creasing. Sira blushed, and Rollie put out a hand as if to touch her, and then, remembering who she was, pulled it back.

"I'm sorry, young Cantrix," she said, chuckling, "those are just not the words I would have used."

"I am not much used to . . . conversation," Sira said.

Rollie laughed again. "I don't know if riders' talk can truly be called conversation," she said. She indicated the darkness beyond the *quiru*. "I'll take you out now."

The two women left the circle of riders in the warmth and

light of the *quiru* and stepped a few feet away to the privacy of the stand of irontrees. "Remember, now, Cantrix," Rollie said seriously, "we never leave a *quiru* by ourselves when we're traveling. Always in twos, at least. If I have to go out with one of the men, then I do it. Never alone."

"Why is that, Rollie?"

"More than one reason, Cantrix," Rollie replied, her voice soft and her face almost invisible in the vast darkness. "The cold, of course, can get you quick. You could fall, and no one would know until too late."

Sira nodded in the dark, then realized Rollie couldn't see her. Sira was not used to darkness, either, having lived virtually all her life in the light of Houses. "I will remember, Rollie," she said gravely. "Thank you."

"And don't forget the *tkir*, either, Cantrix," Rollie added. Her voice was deeper, harder, when she gave this warning. "They won't attack in a *quiru*, but they will in the dark. A person alone hardly has a chance."

Rollie kept behind Sira as they made their way through the darkness back to the *quiru*. It glowed in the starry, snowy night, an envelope of warmth and light, the little cooking fire a spark within it. Sira breathed deeply in appreciation of its beauty, and in satisfaction at having created it.

Rollie heard her sigh. "Something wrong, Cantrix?"

Sira shook her head. Her heavy, bound hair caught on her fur collar and she wished she could wear it cropped short as Rollie did. "Nothing, Rollie," she answered. "There is so much beauty, out here in the mountains."

The light from the *quiru* reflected on Rollie's leathery face as she turned to Sira. "Being outside is the best," she said. "We need our Houses, but the best life is out here, in the trees, in the snow."

Sira turned her own angular face up to the stars. "I have not seen the stars since I can remember," she said.

"Better get into the *quiru* now, young Cantrix," Rollie warned. "The deep cold season isn't over yet."

Sira obeyed, stepping back into the warmth of the *quiru* she had herself created a few short hours ago. It was like stepping into the warm water of the *ubanyix* on a cold day, and she shook herself with pleasure. She wondered how anyone who had never experienced the cold of outside could really appreciate a *quiru's* warmth.

The riders were rolling themselves into their bedfurs, and Sira saw two of them returning from outside the *quiru*, together as Rollie had said. She slipped into her own bedfurs, nestling down into their warmth, offering a little prayer of thanks to the *caeru* who had provided them. As she stretched her long legs under her furs, she felt the beginnings of the saddle soreness that would develop tomorrow, and she liked it. Today had been her first day as an adult, her first day on a *hruss*, her first day as a full Cantrix. The soreness was confirmation that it was all real, that what she had spent her short life preparing for was about to happen. She was Cantrix Sira v'Conservatory, on her way to the House of Bariken, her new House. These riders, this camp in the Marik Mountains, this very day, were all for her. She felt a rush of pleasure. Her whole life lay before her in a glow of hope.

Maestra Lu lay alone on her bed in her tiny room at Conservatory. Sleep would not come. She felt the absence of Sira in the House as a sharp wound, a feeling that some essential part of herself was missing.

Lu had said goodbye to many a young Singer in her years of teaching, but with Sira it was different. No student had ever affected her in the way Sira had, and as she watched the ceremony this morning, standing in the wintry sunshine on the broad steps of Conservatory, Lu had been overwhelmed with premonition.

As always, it had been a mostly silent ceremony. The riders, mounted and ready, provided a dark and restless backdrop as they waited to be on their way. Sira, tall and thin and so terribly young, sat high on the big, heavy-boned *hruss* Bariken had sent for her, shining-faced in her new furs, and with a newly made bedroll tied to her saddle. Her *filhata* was carefully wrapped and slung on her back.

For some minutes there was silence as the other students of Conservatory stood on the steps and wished Sira goodbye and good luck in their silent way.

Goodbye, Sira . . . Cantrix! This was sent by Isbel, Sira's best friend, who was better at a mental giggle than any student Lu had known.

Good luck, Cantrix Sira!

The Spirit protect you!

Congratulations, Cantrix!

One or two of the students sent nothing, but Lu knew that Sira was used to their resentment and would be unaffected by it. At least there were no taunts on this day.

Magister Mkel stood smiling at the top of the stairs, listening to the farewells. His mate, Cathrin, waited patiently for the part of the ceremony she could hear. She was fond of saying she was not burdened by the Gift, and preferred normal conversation. Maestra Lu, as the senior teacher, stood with Mkel and Cathrin, her face stiff and her eyes dry. Her own farewell she saved for last.

At length the mental chatter among the students ended, and Mkel cleared his throat and spoke aloud.

"Cantrix Sira," he said, and Sira's grave young face brightened at the sound of her newly earned title. "Every Singer's true home is Conservatory, and we will always await your return. Good luck. Serve well." He bowed, deeply and formally.

Sira's eyes shone darkly within the yellow-white *caeru* fur that circled her face. She bowed from her seat on the rough-coated *hruss*.

"Thank you, Magister," she said, and Lu treasured the sound of that deep young voice, knowing its power and the immense talent behind it. Then Sira turned her face to her teacher.

Thank you, she sent, her thought warm with affection. *Maestra Lu, thank you. I will miss you.*

Lu bowed, delicately and deliberately. *Farewell, Cantrix Sira. May the Spirit of Stars be with you always.*

And even as she sent her farewell to her protégée, the premonition struck her like a blow. She was quite sure, in that moment, that she would never see Sira again in this life.

As the party of riders made its way through the mountain passes toward Bariken, Sira rode in silent awe of the majesty of her surroundings. How different from the sheltered life most of her people lived, protected behind the thick stone walls of their great Houses. Only those whose work it was to ride between the Houses truly saw the magnificence of the Continent, she thought. The scattered iron-wood forests, the huge boulders that marked the landscape, the deep snowpack that never disappeared—all these were no less wondrous to Sira than the magic of her *quiru* was to the riders. To the south, she thought, there was Clare, where she had been born, where the thick paper all the Houses used was manufactured. To the north, Perl, where the people wove cloth and rugs. Northeast, four more days' ride, her new home of Bariken, known for its limeglass. For a moment, she envied the itinerant Singers who plied the mountain passes all their lives. They saw the glories of the Continent every day, every week, in all the seasons.

But for her, each day brought her traveling party closer to Bariken. Soon, the life she had always known, and had always sought, would be hers.

"Cantrix?"

Sira suddenly realized that Rollie was speaking to her. So lost in thought was she, and so unused to her title, she had not heard the rider.

"I am sorry, Rollie," she said. "What is it?"

"We would like to camp here, if it suits you."

If it suits me, Sira thought. She looked around at the riders, all considerably older than herself, and nodded. She knew nothing of campsites, of course. She knew only her music, her work, her duties.

Blane, who was the guide for the party, nodded back at her respectfully. "Rollie, thank the young Cantrix," he said. His face was brown and leathery like Rollie's. "Ask her if she would be so good as to raise the *quiru*, and we'll make camp."

Rollie jumped nimbly off her *hruss* and came to Sira to hold her stirrup, careful not to touch the Cantrix inadvertently. Sira had less than four summers to Rollie's six, but she was stiff and sore as she slid from the saddle. A small grunt of pain escaped her, and she gave Rollie a small and rueful smile.

"I am sorry," she apologized. "The Spirit did not pad me much."

Rollie chuckled. "Wouldn't matter, Cantrix. You're just saddle-sore." She untied Sira's bedfurs and spread them on the snow for her, but Sira shook her head.

"I believe I will stand," she said, and Rollie nodded.

Sira laid her *filhata*, still safely wrapped, on her bedfurs. Her *filla*, the little flute that was perfect for a traveler's *quiru*, she had been carrying inside her tunic. She brought it out now and put it to her lips.

The melody she played was a traditional one in the first mode, simple and bright. Her psi, focused and amplified through the music from her *filla*, reached into the air around her, speeding and warming its elements, brightening a column wide enough and tall enough to protect the people and the *hruss* from the deep cold of the Nevyan night. The small *quiru* needed for a campsite took only half her concentration, and she was aware, as she played, of the riders watching her. She embellished the melody a little here and there, making it as much a musical as a functional performance. The heat and light billowed out from where she stood, reaching up into the dusk of the evening and out to the shaggy *hruss* being fed. Sira had been warned beforehand that if the *hruss* were not included in the *quiru*, they would crowd into it, putting the riders at risk of being stepped on by their enormous hooves. She watched to make sure the animals were well inside the *quiru's* boundary before she stopped playing.

When she put down her *filla* there was a brief silence, which she took for appreciation. At Conservatory there would have been silent comments, criticism or praise. For the first time since leaving Conservatory, Sira became aware of her loneliness. There was nothing to hear in this place but her own thoughts. There was no Gift here but hers.

After dinner, the riders talked of the seasons.

"Softwood's almost impossible to find now," Blane said, and the other riders murmured agreement.

"My mate said they ate cold food from Bariken to Lamdon last trip," said one burly man. Sira was listening curiously.

"Rollie," she whispered, and Rollie, who had stayed close

beside her since they left Conservatory, and was the only rider to speak to her directly, turned to her.

"Why would they eat cold food?" Sira asked.

"The softwood trees are almost gone," Rollie explained. "If summer doesn't come soon, there will be nothing to burn."

Sira looked around their campsite, and saw that it was true. There were none of the thin, fragile softwood trees that sprouted only in the rare summers.

Blane spoke from where he sat on his bedfurs on the other side of the fire. "I have a son born in the last summer, and he's almost five years old. The Visitor better show up soon! Kel's driving us crazy wanting to know when he'll have one summer."

The group laughed together. The common practice of counting summers instead of years was cumbersome but popular. Sira smiled, too, thinking of her own brothers and sisters, and wondering how many summers they had counted up now. She had not seen them, of course, since she was seven, and she could hardly keep track. Communication between Houses carried no more information than births, matings, and sometimes deaths. Sira had had only one summer herself when she parted from her family. It seemed a lifetime ago.

"I can hardly remember what the Visitor looks like," she murmured to Rollie.

"I feel the same," said the rider. "But it shows up in the sky every five years anyway, thank the Spirit. Otherwise we'd all be under a hundred feet of ice by now."

"Is summer almost here, then?" Sira asked.

"So it is, Cantrix," Rollie told her. "This makes the fifth deep cold since last summer, and the days are getting longer. It's time, sure enough."

A little silence fell around the fire as the riders contemplated the inexorable cold that was their constant and unrelenting enemy. Sira could see one or two of them look up at the *quiru* above them, clearly appreciating its protection and comfort, and perhaps thinking of their homes. She was suddenly caught in a wave of nostalgia for the Conservatory, and she thought of the ironwood plaque that hung over its great double doors:

> Sing the light,
> Sing the warmth,
> Receive and become the Gift, O Singers,
> The light and the warmth are in you.

She remembered stumbling past that carved creed on her first day at Conservatory, in the company of all the other Gifted ones newly arrived. She had not wept, though many of the others had. But it was a day of parting from everything and everyone they had known, and no Singer ever forgot it.

Lost in memory, Sira reached for her *filla* and put it to her lips. As she looked above her *quiru*, where the mysterious stars wheeled in their mighty dance, a melody came to her mind. She used the fourth mode, *Lidya*, raising the third degree, and then shifted into the fifth, *Mu-Lidya*, dropping the third degree down in a subtle cadence. The stars seemed to shine brighter as she played, as if her Gift could reach into the very heavens, and the darkness beyond the *quiru* seemed to recede a bit.

Sira lost herself in the music. When she lowered her *filla* and looked around her again, she realized all the riders had ceased their conversation and were watching her. She blushed suddenly.

"I am sorry if I disturbed you—" she began. "I forgot where I was. . . ." She looked down at the *filla*, cradled in her long, thin fingers, and shook her head, shy once again.

"It was beautiful, Cantrix," Rollie said softly. "Does it have a name?"

Sira shook her head. "I was improvising. I am glad if you liked it."

"It should have a name," Rollie said. "So we can hear it again."

A faint smile lightened Sira's face. "I will name it, then," she said. "It is 'Rollie's Tune' from now on."

Rollie grinned around the circle. "Now, isn't that a nice thing to happen to an old mountain rider?" Her chuckle was comfortable, and one or two of the others ventured to nod respectfully to Sira. It was a moment rather like those Sira had dreamed of during the long years of her training. She tucked the *filla* back inside her tunic, enjoying the sudden sense of success and belonging. If this was being a Cantrix, she thought, she would like it very much.

CHAPTER
TWO

✷ Isbel had been Sira's closest, indeed her only, friend in their class at Conservatory. They were as different as they could be, Isbel plump and pretty, with auburn hair and flashing dimples, and Sira tall, thin, and solemn.

Isbel sought out Maestra Lu when Sira had been gone from the Conservatory for three days. She found her in the great room, in a rare moment of idleness, seeking the warmth of the sun as it filtered through the thick green windows.

"Excuse me, Maestra?" Isbel asked aloud. A student never sent thoughts to one of the teachers until invited to. Maestra Lu did not turn, but she smiled up into the weak sunshine.

Good morning, Isbel, she sent.

Isbel bowed. *Good morning*. Lu indicated a place on the bench next to her, and only turned when Isbel sat down.

The Maestra was looking more frail than ever, her pale, papery skin almost translucent over the sharp bones of her face. Isbel thought her own ruddy, freckled skin seemed extravagantly healthy next to Lu's. But she kept these thoughts low in her mind, not wishing to offend her teacher.

Maestra, I was wondering if you are following Sira.

Lu looked at her sharply. *And how could I be following Sira?*

Isbel dimpled, and the Maestra's lips twitched gently.

Maestra, we all know you have the longest reach of anyone. Maybe the longest ever.

Maestra Lu sighed a little. *And how do you all know that?*

We have heard the stories!

Maestra Lu turned to the window, gazing out, and for a moment Isbel thought she had forgotten she was there. It was the look of memory, Isbel thought, and Maestra Lu, who had twelve summers, must have many memories. She waited until the Maestra turned back to her.

Sira is fine, Lu sent. *That is all I can sense, but it is enough, is it not?*

Isbel nodded, content. *She will be a wonderful Cantrix.*

Indeed, I hope so.

Do you remember her first quirunha?

Very well.

Isbel leaned against the cool glass of the great window. *The others were so jealous.*

Lu turned to her with eyebrows raised, although this was hardly a revelation.

Well, yes, Isbel went on. *It was two years before any of the rest of us could perform a* quirunha. *At breakfast that day, they were teasing her.*

Tell me about it, Isbel.

Isbel loved stories, her own or anyone else's. No one knew more of them, or invented more, than Isbel. Sira had loved to listen to her tales, especially when the two girls lounged together in the *ubanyix*, floating lazily in the scented warm water. Now Isbel sat up, ready to make a story of Sira's first *quirunha*.

She was only fourteen.

Maestra Lu nodded, remembering that very well. Individual birthdays were put aside when the Gifted children entered Conservatory. Each summer, a class came from the Houses across the Continent, delivered by their families.

From then on, they all had the same birthday, the anniversary of their first day.

In the great room, the students were tormenting her at breakfast. One, in particular . . . Isbel looked sideways at her teacher, not wishing to cause trouble for one of her classmates. Lu pretended not to notice.

One was asking her if she was not nervous. She went on and on about how the whole House would be there, and how many things could go wrong. Sira was trying to eat—you always tell us to eat before we work. . . . Lu's lips twitched again. Isbel saw, and her dimples flashed once more.

Finally, I am afraid I lost my temper. I told them all to stop it. All around us the House members were calmly having breakfast, not noticing our argument. Sira could not eat her keftet, *and she stood up.*

She sent to me, so that everyone could hear, that I was not to worry, that she was not nervous. Then she turned to . . . to the one who was teasing her, and she told her she had better not miss the quirunha; *she might learn something!*

Lu was smiling to herself as she listened to Isbel.

Sira went striding out of the room—you know how she walks with her back so straight. Lu nodded, sharing the memory of her student's tall, narrow form pacing the halls of the Conservatory. *And of course you remember the* quirunha, *because you were her senior that day. It was beautiful.*

Lu took Isbel's hand. Only a Gifted one could touch another Gifted one, and the contact soothed and connected them, one to the other. *So it was, Isbel. And you need not have worried about your friend.*

I was still angry.

I know. But Sira would not have worried about what her classmates thought. She is always most critical of herself,

*and had she been disappointed in herself, that would have
been something to worry about.*

Isbel grew thoughtful. *I am sure she will be a great
success at Bariken.*

A shadow passed over the Maestra's mind and she
withdrew her hand. Isbel looked searchingly at her. The
rumors about Bariken were very disturbing. Isbel sensed
Maestra Lu push the worry very low in her mind.

She will be a fine Cantrix, Lu sent, and she smiled gently
at Isbel. *And so will you, my dear. Perhaps you should be
practicing now?*

Isbel giggled. *Yes, Maestra.* She jumped up from the
bench under the window and bowed. *Thank you.*

Lu watched her leave the great room and thought what a
pleasant student she was. Neither complicated nor difficult,
reasonably hard-working, and with such a pretty voice. Sira
had been her most challenging student, intense, talented,
driven. Her only weakness was in healing, but both Mkel and
Lu had thought her new senior Cantrix could continue training
her. In the end, Lu felt certain, Sira would be a better Cantrix
than she herself. She had not been a great healer either, but had
been renowned for her singing and, as Isbel and the other
students knew, the strength and reach of her psi.

She hoped Sira's great Gift was not wasted on Bariken.
She had protested the assignment, but the shortage of
Conservatory-trained Singers was critical. Lu sighed and
rose from the window seat. There was something not right
at Bariken, something hard for Conservatory and Lamdon to
identify. And now Sira, young and inexperienced, was their
Cantrix. It was out of her hands.

Because of the steepness of the mountains and the short
daylight hours, it took five days to ride between Conservatory and Bariken. Traveling had a rhythm of its own, Sira

discovered: riding, resting, meals. There was little talk
during the day. Sira often did not speak at all, and the odd
silence of being with unGifted people added to the strangeness of her new experiences. As her saddle-soreness began
to ease, Sira studied the riders to see how they sat their
hruss, how they handled their reins, how they used their
feet. In the evening, around the little softwood fire, the
riders would talk, telling stories and jokes. Never did one of
them speak directly to the young Cantrix. She was the
reason for their journey, and their protection, but it was not
for them to hold unnecessary conversations with a Gifted
one. Only Rollie, assigned to Sira for the trip, spoke to her.
Sira was grateful for Rollie's warmth and humor, Gifted or
not.

On their last day in the mountains they made their camp
rather late, in purple twilight. Blane found a spot that was
ringed by huge ironwood suckers. Sometimes the long thick
shoots that connected the great trees lay hidden under the
snow to trip the *hruss*. But tonight they were welcome, and
the riders leaned back against them in comfort.

Sira made the *quiru* rise swiftly, and Rollie sat next to her,
grinning in appreciation.

"I'll be sorry not to hear you do that anymore," she said.

Sira frowned. "I do not understand."

"We'll be at the House tomorrow, just after midday,"
Rollie said. "If the Spirit allows."

"I see." Sira tucked her *filla* into her tunic and smoothed
her bedfurs. "But you can attend the *quirunha*, can you
not?"

Rollie's tanned face changed subtly. "It's not my custom," she said carefully.

"But at Conservatory, even the Housemen and women
hear the *quirunha*."

"Things will no doubt be different at Bariken from what you're used to, Cantrix," Rollie said gently.

"But I would like you to attend the *quirunha*," Sira responded ingenuously. "I know no one else there."

Rollie looked out beyond the *quiru* into the deepening dusk. "I'll be around," she said obliquely. "If you want me, just tell that Housekeeper. He'll send for me. But he won't like it."

Sira wanted to know more, but with Conservatory courtesy, she did not press the rider. After a moment, Rollie went to the fire for Sira's tea and *keftet*. As the riders began their evening meal, the silence was broken only by the gentle crackling of the little fire. In the quiet, Sira's sensitive ears picked up a sound.

"Rollie!" she called softly. "There is someone approaching."

Rollie came to her. "Not likely, Cantrix." She stared out past the *quiru*, listening, then shook her head. "Why do you think so?"

"I hear it!" Sira turned toward the direction of the sound. "Out there, up the hill. *Hruss.*"

"Blane!" Rollie called, and gestured to him. "I don't hear it, but the Cantrix says there's a *hruss* up on the hill." She pointed.

Blane nodded. The possibility of anyone, or even just a loose *hruss*, being left out in the deep cold of the dark was unthinkable.

"We'll go see," he said. "I'll take Chang." The other man was already beside him. They both pulled on their heavy furs, and turned and left the *quiru* without further discussion.

Sira stood with her head bowed, listening to their progress up the hill. She knew it was serious, to send people out of the safety of the *quiru* into the deep cold. Following them with her ears, she opened her mind as well. She could sense fear, and sadness, in some poor man lost out there in the freezing dark.

Those in the *quiru* did not have to wait long. The sounds from the hillside grew until everyone could hear them, and as they watched, Blane and Chang led two *hruss* into the campsite. A man, stiff with cold, clung to the stirrup of one, barely able to keep his feet. He stumbled as he came into the *quiru* and fell clumsily to his knees.

Blane crouched beside him and dropped an extra fur over his shoulders. "Take your time," he said quietly. Everyone in the *quiru* was silent, aware that the stranger had been within heartbeats of freezing to death.

Sira, seeing that the man's *hruss* were still outside the circle of light, pulled her *filla* out of her tunic. She played briefly, and the *quiru* swelled to include the animals. Ice hung from the long hair under their chins and clogged their shaggy forelocks.

The stranger turned, with difficulty, to see who was playing.

Blane spoke again, saying, "We're a party from the House of Bariken. I'm Blane, the guide."

There was a long silence. Everyone knew that the man's lips and face were too cold to move. After some moments he mumbled, "Devid," through still-rigid lips. He managed his House name, "Perl," and then fell silent again. They all waited for the man's circulation to return, understanding that it was a slow and probably painful process. At last he sighed raggedly.

"My Singer . . ." he struggled to say, and although Sira had by now shielded her mind, his pain was unmistakable. "My mate . . . she died last night." Chang had brought the man's bedroll from his saddle and helped him to sit back on it. Devid pulled his hood back, uncovering a lined, weathered face and brown hair mixed with gray. "She was ill." Another pause. "We were going to Conservatory for help."

Rollie, stepping over from where she had built up the little fire, pressed a cup of hot tea into Devid's icy hands.

"We're bringing our new Cantrix to Bariken," Blane told him with a slight bow in Sira's direction. Devid stared at her, too exhausted for courtesy. "You can come with us," Blane went on, "and hire a Singer there to get home."

"I don't have any metal," the traveler said miserably. "My mate hasn't worked in some time."

Blane put up his hand, and Sira saw that his eyes shone suddenly. She knew he was moved by the man's plight. "It's not necessary," Blane murmured. "Nevyans help each other when they can."

"Thank you," Devid said. He turned his body and bowed then, stiffly, to Sira.

Sira nodded. She felt strange, being treated with such deference for doing only what every Conservatory student over three summers could do. "I am sorry about your . . . Singer." She stumbled over the word. It was unthinkable for a Cantrix or Cantor to mate, although she had known, in a rather distant way, that the itinerant Singers did so. Generally, the Conservatory students believed that mating was one reason that traveling Singers were less capable than they.

"We thought we could make it," Devid said to the riders, shaking his head. "Thought Conservatory could help. But she wasn't strong enough."

There was a long silence. Tragedy struck often on the Continent, and there were few whose lives had not been touched by it.

The deadly cold ruled the lives of all Nevyans. The snow and ice, which receded only once every five years, was as much a part of their surroundings as the sky or the rocks. Survival required almost all their energies.

At length Sira asked, "What was troubling your mate?"

Devid looked up at her, his face dark with grief. "She had a pain in her side," he said. "We were on our way home, in Deception Pass." He indicated the right side of his body. "Inside her, it was. It was terrible. We turned for Conservatory, but then she couldn't ride. She couldn't heal herself," he added obscurely.

"There's no road there," Blane commented.

"Right. We tried to make a shorter trip of it, but the irontrees are so thick, and the drifts are twice as tall as a *hruss* . . . Then, her pain got much worse. Thank the Spirit, at the end she couldn't feel it anymore."

"Your mate is with the Spirit of Stars now," Chang offered, almost whispering.

Devid nodded to him. "Yes. Yes. But our children will miss her. And I had to leave her there."

Sira took a breath. The thought of a Gifted one, with children . . . She had known it happened, but it was shocking nevertheless. Of course, this had not been a Conservatory-trained Cantrix, but an itinerant Singer, with far less ability, and infinitely less responsibility, as Sira had been taught to believe.

"You can go back in the summer," Chang suggested. Devid nodded again, numbly, and a wave of pain swept out to Sira.

"Better get into your bedfurs," Blane said gruffly, but not unkindly. "Warm up quicker."

Devid nodded, and obeyed, and the other riders also rolled into their furs. Rollie and Sira went out of the *quiru* briefly, and returned to find the others already sleeping, except for Devid. Rollie said good night, and Sira slipped under the warm *caeru* furs of her own bed.

Devid could not sleep, though, and Sira could feel his suffering, though she was carefully shielded against the random thoughts that so often flowed from the unGifted. She heard the small sounds as he turned and shifted under his furs. When she sat up, she could see his long hair tangling as he twisted in his bed.

"Traveler?" she whispered.

Devid lifted his head to look at her. He was exhausted, the skin around his eyes gray and worn.

"May I help you sleep?" she asked quietly.

He looked confused, and said nothing. She hesitated a moment, and then began to sing, softly, a brief and simple *cantrip* that the older Conservatory students had sometimes used for the young ones when they lay awake crying for their mothers. It was as familiar to her as the memories of the dormitory where the narrow cots of the first- and second-level students lined the walls, one after the other. She sang unself-consciously, using just the gentlest touches of her psi to soothe Devid into sleep.

It did not take long. Soon his fretfulness stopped, and sleep stole over him. No one else seemed to have been disturbed by her singing.

Sira was satisfied, thinking how simple her job was, really. Looking up, she saw her *quiru* warm and bright above the travelers. Reassured, she too lay down.

She was surprised to hear Rollie's voice saying, "Sleep well, Sira."

In her drowsiness, Rollie had forgotten her title. The omission, in a strange way, made Sira feel at home.

CHAPTER
THREE

★ THE RIDERS, WITH SIRA AND DEVID AMONG THEM, clattered over the clean-swept paving stones of Bariken's courtyard just after midday. Sira looked up at the big doors of the House, and took in the sweep of its wings that stretched east and west. It was smaller than Conservatory, but she could imagine the fullness of the life inside, the great room where the House members met for meals, the huge kitchens, the small apartments where families lived, their children tumbling over each other on the stone floors. At the very center would be the Cantoris, where she would do her work. The glassworks, she thought, would be between the wings in the back, perhaps behind the nursery gardens. Those were always kept close so the *quiru* that warmed the House could nurture the essential food plants.

One of the riders had galloped ahead to announce their arrival, and there were several people on the steps of the House awaiting them.

Rollie was close by Sira, and she murmured, "Perfectly natural to be nervous, Cantrix."

"Do you know my thoughts, Rollie?" asked Sira.

The rider chuckled softly. "You're the mind-listener, Cantrix, not me!"

"Rollie, I have not done so," Sira protested, and did not realize until a moment later that Rollie had been teasing her.

They had reached the front of the courtyard, and now Rollie slipped off her *hruss*. She came to assist Sira, but Sira had dismounted on her own, her young body already accustomed to the rigors of days in the high-cantled saddle. Rollie untied her charge's saddlepack, and a little, wrinkled Housewoman left the group on the steps to come and take it.

Rollie bowed quickly to Sira and stepped back. "Good luck, Cantrix." It sounded like goodbye.

"But I will see you, Rollie?" Sira asked. Her words hung in the clear air like those of a forlorn child, and she wished she could take them back. She would have liked to touch Rollie's arm, although she knew that would certainly be a breach of custom. Rollie bowed again without speaking.

"Cantrix, Rhia is waiting for you," said the old Housewoman. She was frowning impatiently and looking up at the steps of the House.

There were two men and two women waiting before the big doors. The Housewoman said again, "She's waiting, Cantrix. Better hurry."

Sira had no idea who Rhia was, nor did she know the identity of this little Housewoman who spoke to her so brusquely. Taking a deep breath, she pulled her wrapped *filhata* from where it hung on her back, and slipped it into its customary place under her arm, a badge of office to give her confidence. Then she strode quickly to the steps, her back arrow-straight. Blane, the leader of the traveling party, walked close behind her.

"Rhia," Blane said, and Sira saw that one of the women stood a little apart from the others who were waiting. Her face was as smooth and still as the ice cliffs of Manrus, her bound hair glossy and pale. She seemed to be measuring Sira with her eyes, and unconsciously Sira put a hand to the binding of her hair.

Blane went on. "This is Cantrix Sira v'Conservatory."

Sira, still unsure of who the woman was, bowed politely. "I am Rhia v'Bariken," she said. "And this is Cantrix Magret, and Cantor Grigr." There was no mention of Magister Shen, although Sira had fully expected him to be in her welcoming party.

The blond woman bowed the shallowest of bows, but Cantrix Magret, middle-aged and plump, smiled warmly at her new junior, cheerful eyes crinkling. Sira noticed, however, that she sent nothing.

"Welcome to Bariken, Cantrix," Rhia said coolly, her voice dry and crisp as a softwood leaf.

"Thank you," Sira replied.

"I hope you had a good journey," Magret remarked aloud, in the resonant tones of a Singer. "I can hardly wait to hear all about Conservatory."

"Welcome, Cantrix Sira," the old Cantor said. His hair was quite gray, and his face was lined and marked by illness. "We are so glad to have you here."

"You're very young, aren't you, Cantrix?" Rhia observed.

"Yes," Sira said matter-of-factly. Surely youth was nothing to apologize for. She regarded the woman curiously. Sira knew nothing of the ineffable concept of style, but she recognized it in Rhia; there was something extraordinary about every aspect of her appearance and bearing, the binding of her blond hair, the cut of her tunic. She spoke with authority, and yet she bore no title. It was strange, and Sira hardly knew how to respond to her.

The dark man standing next to Rhia spoke now. "Magister Mkel of Conservatory spoke very highly of Cantrix Sira," he reminded. Rhia nodded.

"Yes. Of course." Rhia lifted a graceful hand in the man's direction. "This is my Housekeeper, Wil. He will show you to your room." As an afterthought, it seemed, she added, "We all look forward to hearing you sing."

She did not sound as if she truly cared one way or the other, Sira thought, but she kept the thought low so as not to offend her new senior. Rhia went into the House, the elderly Housewoman trotting after her like a *caeru* pup after its dam.

Sira turned back to say farewell to the riders who had escorted her, but they were already leading the *hruss* out of the courtyard, turning to the back of the House, to the stables. The traveler Devid went with them. Only Blane still stood next to Sira.

"Thank you for escorting me, Blane," she said formally, and bowed to him, feeling suddenly too tall and awkward.

He bowed deeply. For a moment, he hesitated, and when he spoke, she sensed his sympathy for her youth and inexperience. "Good luck, young Cantrix," he murmured deferentially. "We're sure you'll be a great success."

Sira straightened her shoulders and looked up at the House awaiting her. "By the will of the Spirit," she responded, and started up the steps.

Sira had expected, once she had joined her new senior, the silent and easy communication she was accustomed to. It was a surprise to her that Magret persisted in speaking aloud as they sat together over their evening meal. The great room of Bariken was very like that of Conservatory, although on a smaller scale. The biggest difference between the Houses, Sira thought as she looked about her, was one of adornment. At Bariken it seemed that every surface was carved and molded into rich detail. The brightly colored clothes of the Housemen and women looked familiar, but the dark tunics worn by those of the upper class were heavily embroidered and decorated. Every wall bore hangings, and all the floors were laid with rugs. Conservatory had been austere, its hard surfaces left bare to enhance their resonance. The first thing Sira had to do tomorrow morning was to remove the extraneous adornments that cluttered her own room.

"We are so glad you are here at last," Magret was saying. "Poor Cantor Grigr was not sure he could cope much longer."

Sira looked down the table to where Grigr leaned on his elbows. His hand, as he lifted the wooden spoon to his mouth, trembled slightly. She felt a rush of compassion that the old cantor must have sensed, for he turned to her. She thrust the feeling down, sorry to have disturbed him, and bowed respectfully from where she sat. His answering nod was tired and full of understanding.

Since her senior was speaking aloud, Sira did so, too. "Can you not discover what is wrong?"

Magret shook her head. "Perhaps Nikei at Conservatory can help him. But you know, my dear, Cantor Grigr has eleven summers. He would have retired before this had there not been such a shortage of Singers."

Sira nodded. This, of course, was why she had been graduated so quickly. As a general rule, Cantors and Cantrixes did not step into a Cantoris before the age of twenty. Sira was only seventeen, not yet having four summers.

"Cantrix Magret . . . where is the Magister?"

Magret's customary smile faded. "I do not know where he is tonight, Sira. He may be hunting. He likes it very well."

Sira raised an eyebrow but remained silent. Her mind was open, waiting for closer communication from her senior, but Magret was looking around the room and sending nothing. Sira followed her glance.

There was a central table, just as at Conservatory, and Sira saw that Rhia, who she had learned was the Magister's mate, was sitting there deep in conversation with the

Housekeeper, Wil. At Conservatory there would have been people coming to the table, asking questions and advice and being given directions. No one approached Rhia's table. Wil lifted his dark, narrow head occasionally to scan the room, but he and Rhia were left in privacy.

Sira turned back to hear Magret say, "Would you like to bathe now? After all that traveling . . ."

Sira accepted gratefully. It had been a busy afternoon, and a long, warm bath would be a great pleasure.

She and her senior both fetched clean clothes, and Magret led the way to the *ubanyix*. Here, as elsewhere at Bariken, there was an abundance of decoration. The great ironwood tub was scrolled and sculpted all around its edge, and Sira marveled at the number of *obis* knives that must have been worn to slivers in its making. Scented flower petals floated on the water, and piles of woven towels from Perl, familiar to Sira, were set out on the benches.

The two women stepped out of their tunics and trousers, hung them on pegs above their furred boots, and then slipped into the tub. Sira stretched joyously, relieved to be clean and free of the heavy clothes she had worn for five days. Her body under the water was as lean and taut as a child's, while Magret's was curving and plump, her breasts and hips generous, softened by the passing of years and comfortable living.

There were bars of soap from the abattoir in carved niches around the tub, and the soap, too, was scented. The Housekeeper must be very good at his job, Sira thought, knowing that such details were the essence of that position.

"Cantrix Magret, shall I warm the water a bit?" she asked.

Magret nodded. "That would be very nice, Sira."

Sira slipped out of the tub to fetch her *filla*; they stood naked, unself-conscious, and played a little melody in *Doryu*, the third mode, commonly used for water. The temperature of the water rose sharply, until Magret held up her hand.

Very good, Sira, she sent.

Sira's solemn face lighted with a half smile. Perhaps now they could really talk to one another. She stepped back into the tub and began to unbind her hair for washing. *Maestra Lu sends her greetings to you,* she sent.

Is she well? Magret asked.

I think she is tired. And worried about me, Sira sent back.

Magret lifted her head and frowned suddenly. "We have a need to keep our thoughts private here," she said aloud. Sira looked up through the wet, dark strands of her hair. Her confusion made her abrupt.

"But why?" she asked sharply.

Her senior's frown softened and she reached out to push a lock of Sira's hair away from her eyes. "Everything is different here," she said carefully. "It is difficult to explain. But there are Gifted people in the House who can hear us."

Sira leaned back in the water to rinse the soap from her hair. She could only follow her senior's lead, of course. If Magret wished to explain to her, she would, and if not, Sira's duty was to accommodate her.

I know it is strange, Magret sent. *Try to be patient.*

Sira nodded, unsure what was expected of her. As they stepped from the tub to dry themselves and dress, she told herself she must simply wait, and watch. Surely her questions would have answers soon enough. Surely Magister Shen would attend her first *quirunha* tomorrow, and perhaps she would understand more then. In any case, she had only to fulfill her duties, and she was supremely confident in her ability to do that. The politics of the House could not possibly matter to her, she thought.

She was mistaken.

CHAPTER
FOUR

✳ ALONE IN A PRACTICE ROOM AT CONSERVATORY, ISBEL
labored over inversions in the fourth mode, trying
to drive away the loneliness created by Sira's absence. The
fingering was complex, and she did it again and again until
her fingers grew tired. She stopped to rest, laying down her
stringed *filhata* and stretching her arms. Her hair was
coming out of its binding. She reached back to refasten it,
and the sensation of her fingers in her hair triggered a
memory, a scene she had not recalled for some time. She
pulled the binding loose and let her hair fall about her
shoulders as she dwelt for a moment in the past. She felt that
her loneliness had begun then, in her babyhood.

Isbel had been born between summers, so that she had
been two and a half years old when she first stepped outside
into the summer light from Nevya's two suns. What she
remembered of that day most clearly was the look on her
mother's face at the day's end.

Isbel's mother, Mreen v'Isenhope, had smiled at her as
she ran back and forth over the smooth cobblestones. Isbel
squirmed when Mreen caught her up, laughing, and put her
fingers into the mass of curling hair that already fell down
Isbel's back. For a moment Mreen hugged her little daughter, then released her to run again.

Isbel was Mreen's only family. She had lost a child, a

little boy who never saw a summer, to a fever the Cantor could not control. Her mate had died of the same fever. Mreen sat with other parents who had brought their children out on this first warm day, and the courtyard was full of squeals and laughter.

When a woman began calling, "Karl!" with fear in her voice, the playing stopped. Then, more urgently: "Karl! I can't find Karl!" Isbel could remember how the bright afternoon seemed to go dim all around them.

The adults in the courtyard were on their feet, looking behind the benches, one hurrying off toward the back of the House where the stables were, some stepping up to the edge of the forest and calling between the huge irontrees. Isbel was unhappy that the pleasant afternoon was being interrupted. She ran to her mother and tugged at her tunic.

"Mama, Mama, play!"

Mreen had picked her up. "Not now, darling. Ana can't find Karl. I must help her. You stay right here and wait for me."

The House children were so unaccustomed to the freedom of outdoors, it was rare that one had the courage to walk away. Isbel recalled sensing the sharp fear in the air. She had held tight to her mother's neck.

"But, Mama," she said. "I know where Karl is."

"You do? Show Mama, then." Mreen put her daughter down and Isbel immediately trotted to the edge of the courtyard and into the woods.

"Isbel, where are you going?" Mreen called, hurrying after her.

"Show Karl, Mama." The beginnings of softwood shoots softened and greened the earth under the great ironwood trees in early summer. Isbel led Mreen without hesitation into the chill shade of the trees where the thick walls of the House were obscured from their view. Karl was asleep, curled up in the crook of an ironwood sucker, just out of sight of the courtyard.

Mreen swept him up in her arms, and the child was just waking as she handed him to his frantic mother, back in the sunny courtyard. The adults gathered round, laughing in relief and asking Mreen where she had found him. It was then that Isbel saw the look on her mother's face that would remain in her memory forever.

Mreen's eyes were wide and shocked. There was only one way Isbel could have known where Karl was.

Still Mreen searched for another explanation.

"Isbel, did you see Karl leave the courtyard?"

Isbel shook her curls impatiently. "No, Mama. I heard him."

"What do you mean, you heard him?" Mreen asked, her voice harsh with fear.

"I heard him sleeping," Isbel said, pulling her hand away from Mreen's. "I heard his dream. Didn't you?" She looked into her mother's face and watched the light go out of her eyes as surely as the suns would set a few hours later.

Mreen began, inexorably and deliberately, to withdraw from her daughter from that day forward. Isbel could not understand until much later that her mother simply could not bear the loss of another loved one. Mreen knew the pain that was coming as well as she knew her duty. Her little Isbel was Gifted, and that meant she belonged, not to Mreen's House, but to all of Nevya. And as her mother withdrew, Isbel suffered.

Isbel was two and a half that summer. There were five years until the Conservatory claimed her, and Mreen did what she had to do. But Isbel never saw her mother's smile again.

Eighteen-year-old Isbel, now a third-level Conservatory student, dashed tears from her eyes and bound her hair tightly. She picked up her *filhata* again with determination. Maestro Takeh would want to hear the inversions tomorrow, and that was what mattered now, she told herself. Her mother had long ago gone with the Spirit beyond the stars.

The evening meal in the great room cheered Isbel. She took comfort in the familiar routine, seeing Mkel and Cathrin at their table in the center of the room, with Maestra Lu and the other teachers next to them. The Conservatory students, Isbel's class and the two lower levels, all sat together at one side. Their tunics and trousers were drab, but their faces and eyes shone brightly. The air was thick with their silent chatter for those who could hear it. At the other side of the room, the colorfully dressed Housemen and women conversed aloud. The rich blend of Gifted and unGifted was the very nature of Conservatory.

Who is next, do you think? Kevn, one of the third-level students, sent to the group in general.

No one for a while, I hope, sent Jana, the youngest student in their level. *It is too soon.*

Not too soon for Sira . . . I mean, Cantrix Sira, Kevn responded.

Maybe it was, though, Jana sent back. *She is still not a strong healer. And not close to four summers.*

Closer than you! Kevn teased, and Jana grinned.

Isbel smiled, listening, but the sadness of the afternoon came back. She looked down the table at her classmates, her friends. *There are so few of us*, she mused. Kevn looked at her, his smile gone.

Only one for each House, he sent. *A heavy responsibility.*

They were all silent for a moment; only the first-level class was oblivious to the turn their conversation had taken. No one needed to mention that the newest class was even smaller, not even one young Singer for each of the thirteen Houses. Isbel felt, somehow, that her memory of her mother and the students' concern over the small classes were in some way connected, but she couldn't put her finger on it. She shook her head, frustrated, and saw that Kevn was watching her.

What is it? he asked.

I do not know, she sent back. *Something I was thinking of earlier, but it is gone now.*

Kevn turned away and returned to teasing Jana. Isbel tried to join in the general conversation, but as one of the oldest students, she felt she hardly fit in anymore. When she pushed away her *keftet* and rose from the table, she was surprised to see Magister Mkel's eyes on her. He smiled gently, and she bowed. She knew he understood that she missed Sira, and that she shared the concern over her friend's assignment. She felt heavy, older, as she left the great room, feeling the Gift as a burden that could never be put down.

She looked back as she reached the door. The students and the teachers in their plain tunics, together with the Housemen and women dressed in vivid red and green and blue, made a lively and beautiful scene in the bright light of the Conservatory *quiru*. They had gathered, almost all of them, for the *quirunha* earlier, and after the evening meal some would go to their family apartments, others to the *ubanyor* or *ubanyix* for bathing. Some would stay here to talk and tell stories, one of Isbel's favorite pastimes. She hoped Sira found the atmosphere at Bariken as congenial, but she was sure that however pleasant Bariken was, Sira would feel as they all did, that Conservatory was home. It was now lost to Sira for years to come, and before long it would be lost to all of them.

Sira, her hair carefully bound and her *filhata* impeccably tuned and shining with fresh oil, waited expectantly outside the Cantoris at Bariken for Magret to join her for their first *quirunha* together. Many memories of Conservatory *quirunhas* rose in her mind. She smiled as she recalled the Conservatory Cantoris, an austere room with its rows of plain ironwood benches filled with students, teachers, and visitors who came to hear the finest Singers on the Continent. They would be silent, concentrating, preparing to support the Cantors in their work.

Usually two Singers worked together in the Cantoris, although there could be more. At Lamdon, the capital House, there might be as many as four at the daily *quirunha*. Lamdon was famed for the intensity of its House *quiru* and the abundance of Singer energy it could expend.

Cantrix Magret appeared now, smiling at her junior, and led the way into the Cantoris, which Sira had not as yet seen. She looked around curiously, and was intensely disappointed.

There was only a scattering of people seated on ornately carved benches, and they were chattering and laughing as if this were a social occasion. Their clothes were dark. The vivid colors of the working Housemen and women were conspicuous by their absence.

Since Magret was clearly neither surprised nor dismayed, Sira had to assume this was a typical *quirunha* gathering at Bariken. She kept her mind open, but her senior sent nothing, and had in fact only sent to her once since her arrival. Sira followed Magret up onto the dais, her *filhata* under her arm. She must clear her mind now, she told herself, and think of these things later, when the ceremony was accomplished.

As was customary, those attending the *quirunha* rose and bowed to the Cantrixes as they stepped onto the dais. The chatter subsided, and the atmosphere grew solemn at last. This was the most important function of the Cantor or Cantrix, after all. Without the *quirunha*, the House would grow cold and dark; first the plants and animals would suffer, and then the people. This was why Gifted children were dedicated at the age of seven, turned over to Conservatory to learn to safeguard their people against the deep cold of Nevya. The *quirunha* demanded respect and concentration.

Magret bowed briefly to her junior, sat, and began the

ceremony with a quick strumming of the *filhata* strings. Her high, delicate voice had a slight vibrato, a fragile sound like the chiming of icicles striking together. Sira's own dark, even tone contrasted dramatically with Magret's. The heavy, stringed *filhatas*, schooled in the same tradition, made an effortless and disciplined counterpoint beneath their voices.

Sira followed her senior's lead easily, thinking perhaps that Magret, by using only the first mode, was keeping things simple for their first *quirunha* together. Lacy drifts of melody rose to fill the high-ceilinged Cantoris as they concentrated their psi together, and the room grew visibly brighter and warmer. Sira's mind reached out to the glass-works, the family apartments, the stables, and the nursery gardens that lay enclosed by the long wings of the House, places she had not yet seen with her eyes. She imagined each seedling and plant in the gardens stretching out its green leaves to receive the blessing of warmth.

When the *quiru* was strong and warm once again, and Magret had laid down her instrument, Sira looked out into the faces in the Cantoris. She could see Wil, the House-keeper, seated at the end of one of the benches, his long legs stuck into the aisle. Cantor Grigr sat close to the dais, tremulously nodding appreciation. Rhia was absent, nor was there any man present who looked as if he might be Magister Shen. Sira's pride was hurt and her hopes dashed. How could both the Magister and his mate ignore her first *quirunha* in their House?

Magret rose then, and Sira did too, bowing formally to her senior as the assemblage rose and bowed toward the dais. Together they chanted the traditional prayer:

> Smile on us, O Spirit of Stars,
> Send us the summer to warm the world,
> Until the suns will shine always together.

The ceremony was completed then. Magret sent, *Thank you, Sira. You are as talented as Maestra Lu said you were.*

Sira was relieved to be able to send to her senior for a moment. *You are very kind, Cantrix Magret. It was a lovely* quirunha.

Magret made a little deprecating face. *Future* quirunhas *will be more interesting, perhaps.*

Sira caught a flash of wordless feeling, and understood suddenly that Magret, in keeping their music simple, was protecting Cantor Grigr's feelings. Sympathy for the old Cantor welled up in her. She could think of no loss heavier than that of the Gift. She thought of Maestra Lu, aged and yet still musically and mentally so strong. Perhaps Maestro Nikei really could restore some of Grigr's health. She sent a brief prayer to the Spirit that it might be so.

The Housekeeper came to the dais and stood by as first Magret and then Sira stepped down. He was very tall, half a head taller even than Sira, and he looked down at her with narrow, dark, unreadable eyes.

"A charming *quirunha*, Cantrixes," he murmured as he bowed. His face was properly respectful, but there was an undercurrent of laughter in his voice. Whatever could be amusing him? Sira wondered. When she glanced up at him, his thin mouth curved, and she looked away quickly. She felt suddenly tall and awkward and childish, not at all the way she wanted to feel. She tucked her *filhata* under her arm, hugging its weight to her body.

"Thank you," Magret said to Wil, and put her hand firmly under her junior's elbow. "Come along, Sira, and I will show you the gardens before the evening meal. Grigr and I had Cantoris hours this morning, and for now I am free."

Sira, glad to escape Wil's intense gaze, bowed goodbye to him quickly, and went with Magret out of the Cantoris. Several House members bowed from a distance. Sira could still feel the Housekeeper's eyes on her back as she walked away.

Just outside the doors of the Cantoris they were accosted by the wrinkled little Housewoman who had been on the steps with Rhia when Sira first arrived. She stepped up to Magret with a sketchy bow.

"Cantrix Magret," she said. "Rhia wants you to come and warm the *ubanyix* for her."

Sira drew breath quickly to offer herself for the task instead, but Magret had already nodded to the Housewoman and turned toward the hall that led to the *ubanyix*. Sira opened her mind, but Magret sent nothing. Uncertainly, Sira followed her, expecting some instruction. The little Housewoman trotted busily ahead of Magret. Sira sensed neither resentment nor anger from her senior, only resignation.

Finally she called out, "Cantrix Magret, allow me this small task. You are senior now."

Magret looked back in surprise. "That is very kind, Sira," she said aloud, "but I think it is better if I do it today. We will have our walk in the gardens later." Her voice had gone rather flat but her face gave nothing away. She hurried down the hallway, following the old Housewoman.

There was nothing Sira could do but turn and walk on alone, wondering. Magret had accepted a peremptory, even discourteous command, and she had complied without demur. Sira did not understand why a senior Cantrix, with her heavy responsibilities, should be treated in this way. Naturally, customs would differ here, but such disrespect went against everything Sira believed in.

She wandered down the long, broad corridor. The intricate carvings that lined the walls reflected the yellow *quiru* light richly from curved and faceted surfaces. It was distracting, she thought—so much to look at everywhere. It must have taken many summers to decorate every inch of

Bariken in this way. Several people passed her, and they bowed, but of course did not speak. There were no voices to be heard in her mind, no friendly, if respectful, smiles as there might have been from the Conservatory Housemen and women. Sira felt terribly isolated and restless.

A wide staircase opened up invitingly before her, with a carved banister that rippled and flowed under her hand. It was beautiful, she had to admit, if extravagant. It made her wonder about those who had carved it. Mere *obis* knives, in the hands of simple craftsmen, were not enough. Such a piece of work would have required psi to accomplish. What Cantor or Cantrix in these times would have energy enough for such endeavors?

She climbed the stairs, admiring the wavy limeglass window above the first landing. The glassworkers also had much to be proud of.

On the floor above, the hallway was similarly wide, and the apartment doors spaced far apart. Sira was sure not all the apartments at Bariken could be so large. She must have come upon the Magister's wing, since he and his staff would have the largest rooms. There was a quiet murmur of conversation and ongoing family life behind the doors she passed. It was a homely and familiar sound, and she enjoyed hearing it as her fur-booted feet whispered across the stone floor of the corridor.

She was sure she must soon come to another stairwell that would return her to the first floor. As she paced the corridor, she heard a door open behind her.

"Cantrix Sira!" The voice resonated in the hall. It sounded, in fact, like the voice of a Singer, the soft palate lifted and the vowels open. When Sira turned, she saw only a pretty, middle-aged woman in the dark tunic of House rulers standing in the doorway of one of the apartments. A child's voice could be heard behind her.

"Yes," Sira said, wondering how this woman had known she was passing.

"I believe you have lost your way," said the woman. She closed her door and came to Sira, a curving, soft-looking woman as ample in her proportions as Sira was spare. She bowed rather casually. "I'm Trude. May I show you back to your room?"

"It is not necessary. I will find it."

"Very well. At the end of the corridor, turn right down the stairs and then right again." Trude smiled, her expression reminding Sira of Wil's half-suppressed amusement. "I enjoyed your *quirunha* today. Certainly a relief after listening to old Grigr's wobble."

Sira was immediately offended by this casual insult to a colleague. She frowned. "I am sure he gave long and distinguished service," she said stiffly.

"Too long, Cantrix. You're a refreshing change." Trude seemed undisturbed by Sira's disapproval, and looked her up and down as if she were a *caeru* hide for sale. "You certainly look like a Singer. No danger of you going astray, is there?"

Sira's eyebrow lifted. "I beg your pardon?"

Trude laughed richly, and Sira heard again the overtones of Conservatory in her voice. "Never mind, young Cantrix. I'll leave you alone. If you really don't want a guide, then . . ." She bowed again, still amused at her own joke, whatever it had meant.

"Thank you." Sira spoke coldly, and made a bow of her own, a deliberately shallow one. She turned her back on the woman as she stood there smiling. Sira was some way down the hall before she heard Trude's door close behind her.

Shrugging off her irritation, Sira went looking for the stairs. Bariken had some unusual members, she decided, who would never be known for their manners. She took her *filhata* from under her arm and stroked its glowing surface, remembering the wonderful Housemen at Conservatory who had so painstakingly carved and polished and tuned it, then ceremoniously presented it to her. At Conservatory, the House members took pride in the work of the young Singers, and Sira had never had reason to question the respect they showed her. She hurried now, to find her way to her own room and relieve her confusion and loneliness in the best way she knew, through her music.

Sira was always an early riser, preferring to put in an hour of work before breakfast. On her third day at Bariken she rose even earlier than usual and gently searched for Magret with her mind, careful not to intrude but only to discover her whereabouts. When she had determined that Magret was still in her room, Sira went out. She carried her *filla* in her hand, and moved quickly among the few people who were in the halls at that hour. When she opened the door to the *ubanyix*, she saw with satisfaction that the great carved, scrolled tub was empty. The air was redolent with the fragrance of herbs left to soak overnight.

Her little melody in the third mode, with its plaintive raised fourth degree, floated out across the water, and Sira played until she could see curls of steam rising from the water's surface into the yellowish light.

Magret startled her by coming in just as she was about to leave. A Housewoman was behind her, carrying a stack of woven towels.

"Sira? Are you bathing so early?"

Sira bowed respectfully. "No, Cantrix. But a senior Cantrix should not have to perform this small task."

"Ah, I see." Magret's cheeks curved with her smile, making her look younger than her seven summers. "Thank you, Sira." She hesitated for a moment, eyes half-closed, clearly listening to something. The Housewoman was on the other side of the room, busy with towels and cakes of soap. Magret opened her mind briefly to Sira.

There are problems here, as you have seen, she sent. *You are very thoughtful. But please be cautious.*

Sira raised one eyebrow, and waited for an explanation, but Magret shook her head, and her next communication was verbal. "Let us have breakfast before Cantoris hours."

Sira nodded, suppressing her curiosity. She would follow her senior's lead, of course. On the point of leaving the *ubanyix*, Magret turned back.

Keep your thoughts shielded, she sent briefly. *Always.*

Sira's eyes widened, but she nodded once again. It was strange advice, she thought, as she followed Magret through the door. At Conservatory, she and her fellow students always observed the courtesy of mental privacy, obviating any need for shielding. Only first-level students intruded on each other's thoughts, and then inadvertently. She drummed her fingers against her *filla* in frustration. Were these trivial things the lessons that could not be taught? They seemed a waste of a Singer's time.

At breakfast Sira ate in silence, with a healthy appetite for the nursery fruit and spicy *caeru* stew. She and Magret sat alone at a table, basking in the bright light from one of the thick windows. Mealtime at Conservatory had been a time of community and friendship. The great room here at Bariken, although filled with people, seemed cold and foreign to Sira. She wondered what Rollie would be doing on a sunny morning like this. Perhaps she was outside, riding after the *caeru* in the sunlit hills. Sira could not help wishing, just for the moment, that she could go with her.

CHAPTER FIVE

CANTORIS HOURS BEGAN RIGHT AFTER BREAKFAST. SIRA and Magret, *fillas* ready, seated themselves on carved, wide-seated armchairs at one end of the room, and those House members seeking healing lined up before them. Sira knew her role would be mostly one of observation at first, but she felt some nervousness just the same. This was the weakest part of her Gift, although the small bumps and ailments of the dormitory had been within her scope. She knew that Maestro Nikei, who was a master of healing at the Conservatory, had been frustrated with her. But Maestra Lu had thought that the skill would come, with practice. As with everything else, Sira had practiced, and practiced hard, but still the knack of sensing the physical state of others eluded her.

The first few patients were easy, a bruised elbow and one or two mild colds. One infant, held by a sweet-faced, tired young mother, had a toothache, and Magret allowed Sira to treat it while she watched and supported her with her own psi. Sira played a simple, soothing melody, and the baby stopped crying, distracted by the music. Then, still playing, using the gentlest nudge of psi, Sira eased the gum tissue away from the tooth where it was making its slow way into the baby's mouth. It was easy to slip past the little one's unformed mind and find the pain. Magret showed Sira how to soothe the tiny nerves with her psi, and the baby let out a breath of relief. Sira did, too, and was glad of Magret's help.

"Oh, thank you, young Cantrix," the young woman whispered. She was no more than four summers old, Sira was sure, but her eyes were smudged and swollen from lack of sleep.

"You are welcome," Sira said. "You need rest, House-woman."

The young mother sighed and shook her head. "You've never raised a baby, young Cantrix," she said tiredly.

Sira raised one eyebrow and Magret spoke sharply. "All right, Mari," she said. "You may go now."

Mari blushed and put her hand over her mouth. "I'm sorry," she said in confusion, glancing hastily at Cantrix Magret.

Magret looked stern as Mari hurried off.

I do not think she meant to offend, Cantrix Magret, Sira sent.

We must discourage familiarity, Magret responded quickly. *It hampers our work.* Sira shielded her thoughts quickly as she wondered why disrespect was tolerated from some and not from others. It would bear thought, she told herself, when she had time.

The baby was sleeping as its mother carried it from the Cantoris, and Sira felt a rush of satisfaction. She kept her face impassive, but she felt like an adult at that moment . . . like a professional. She had much to learn about Bariken and its ways, but she was delighted with this first small success.

She sat back in her chair, her *filla* loosely cradled in her long fingers, and found Wil watching her. Outrageously, he winked one narrow eye. Sira flushed, and looked quickly away to the next patient. The Housekeeper's very presence disturbed her. Surely his behavior could be called disre-spectful. Sira breathed deeply. It was all very confusing.

A man with his arm in a sling was next in line, but a Housewoman stepped in front of him. Sira expected Magret to tell the woman to wait her turn, but although she gave a long and audible sigh, the senior Cantrix said nothing. Her pleasant face was unreadable and her mind carefully shielded.

"Cantrix, Trude wants you to see her boy upstairs," the woman said to Magret. Sira turned to her senior in sudden protest. Working Housemen and women were waiting for treatment, and in her experience, no House member re-ceived consideration above another. Magret did not return her glance, and she rose without comment to follow the Housewoman. The young Cantrix opened her mind, but Magret sent nothing. Sira was suddenly exasperated.

Without stopping to consider what she was doing, she spoke. "A senior Cantrix is not summoned like a cook or a stableman." Her deep voice rang out in the Cantoris with authority beyond her years, beyond even her own intent. The people in line looked up in surprise, and she sensed Wil's sudden movement, but she could not stop. "I am junior, and if the boy cannot come to the Cantoris, I will go to him."

The Housewoman looked bewildered. "Trude said Can-trix Magret," she blurted stupidly.

Sira saw Magret was about to speak, so she hurriedly stepped forward. "Let us go," she said firmly, "so that I can return to assist Cantrix Magret here. People are waiting."

The Housewoman hesitated, looking about for guidance. There was the sibilant hissing of people whispering to each other, and Sira strode from the Cantoris before Magret could demur. Wil was grinning openly as she passed through the door. Remembering where she had encountered Trude, she walked quickly in that direction, her long legs moving too fast for the fat Housewoman, who hurried after her with little puffing noises. Wil caught up with them at the stairwell.

"Cantrix," he said, matching his own long stride to hers. "Are you sure about this?"

Sira did not look at him. She was afraid of losing the sense of purpose that had carried her out of the Cantoris, and unwilling to show a lack of confidence in her ability to heal the child. She used the energy of her anger to quell dismay at her own rashness. "Of course I am sure. Cantrix Magret has great responsibilities."

"But customs at Bariken . . ."

"Are different, so I have been told," Sira finished for him. The fat Housewoman was far behind them now. "But some things do not change. A senior Cantrix must be respected."

"Perhaps I can smooth this over, however," Wil said, with the sardonic smile still on his lean face. "Without offense to your senior, of course."

Sira slowed her walk a little. She knew she had acted impulsively, but she was sure she was in the right. A slight doubt assailed her then, and she turned her *filla* over in her hands and looked down at it, suddenly self-conscious. "If I cannot heal the boy, naturally I would call on Cantrix Magret."

"Naturally." They had reached the upper hall, and Wil stepped ahead of Sira and knocked on Trude's door. His smile vanished, leaving his dark face carved and smooth, although his eyes still twinkled. The door opened, and Trude stood there, looking quite composed. Sira watched curiously as the woman's eyes met Wil's directly, as if they knew each other well.

"Is Denis ill?" asked Wil. "Your Housewoman said you needed one of the Cantrixes."

Trude saw Sira behind the Housekeeper and frowned. "I asked for Magret." Sira frowned, too, at the omission of Magret's title. The Housewoman came panting up behind her.

"Cantoris hours were busy this morning," Wil answered. "Cantrix Sira offered to come and help."

"A child to heal a child?" Trude turned away and went back into the apartment. Sira sensed a wave of irritation from her, and wondered at the strength of it. Usually unGifted people did not broadcast their emotions so strongly.

Wil beckoned to her to follow him, and they stepped inside to find a boy of about two summers, perhaps nine or ten years old, playing on a *caeru* rug on the floor.

"Is this Denis?" asked Sira quietly, and she knelt beside the child. He looked up at her suspiciously. Sira sensed Trude behind her, still angry. When she looked around for permission to proceed, she saw a glance pass between Wil and Trude, and saw the Housekeeper shake his head. Sira turned her attention back to the boy.

"What is bothering you?" she asked him.

"My ear hurts." His face and voice were sullen, although he had seemed happy enough when Sira came in. She was relieved; earache had been a common complaint among the little ones in the dormitory.

"Please sit very still," she told him. He looked up at his mother, and then put down his wooden toy. Sira raised her *filla* to her lips and began to play.

The music carried her quickly out of herself, and she could easily see Denis' inner ear with her mind, the slight redness deep in the curving recesses, the swelling that would give the child pain. It was a matter of moments only, a melody in the healing third mode, and a gentle probing of psi to release the congestion and diminish the swelling. From the pocket of her tunic she drew a scrap of soft cloth and fashioned a small cushion which she put in the boy's ear.

"What's that for?" he asked curiously. Sira smiled at him, and got a small, knowing smile in return.

"It is to keep the cold from your ear," she told him. "Take it out when you think your ear is healed."

Sira stood, her *filla* by her side, and looked at Trude. "This was not serious. Denis could have come to the Cantoris," she said firmly.

Trude's temper grew, palpably filling the room with its energy. Sira could feel it as clearly as if Trude were one of her Gifted classmates. Wil's face was impassive, but Sira could see laughter in his eyes once again.

"When we need healing, young Cantrix, the Singer comes to us," Trude retorted, biting off the words. Her soft face looked harder, older, in her anger. "Denis is the Magister's son, after all."

Sira raised an eyebrow, surprised, but said nothing. She waited a moment. When no thanks or explanation were forthcoming, she bowed the briefest of courtesy bows, and turned on her heel. The door shut with satisfying sharpness behind her, and she paced down the corridor as quickly as she could.

Wil caught up with her at the top of the stairwell. She flashed him a look, but did not stop walking.

"Trude can be temperamental," he said, grinning broadly. Sira said nothing as she started down the broad stairs.

"She was Cantrix, you know," he went on conversationally. "Before Denis' birth."

The revelation stopped Sira in midstride, with one foot on the landing. She was thunderstruck. "Her voice . . ."

"Yes," Wil said. "She was Trude v'Conservatory. She came here as a girl of four summers."

Sira felt shock. A Cantrix . . . who had a child. She

knew what that meant. Wil, watching her thoughts cross her face, nodded.

"It was almost a disaster. Cantor Grigr saw what was happening, of course, and the Conservatory sent Cantrix Magret before it was too late." He gestured with his long arm, and they resumed walking, more slowly now. "Perhaps you can understand that Trude is somewhat . . . sensitive."

Sira shook her head with profound disapproval. "She, especially, should know better."

Wil chuckled. "Ah. So young, and so sure. We'll see, young Cantrix." They had reached the door of the Cantoris once again. Wil bowed elegantly. "Well done, Cantrix Sira." He straightened, and looked directly into her face.

Sira felt the rising flush on her cheeks, and she stiffened. She was no Trude, to be dallied with and seduced. She was a full Cantrix, to be respected by any who were unGifted. She turned her back on him, hearing his soft laugh as she went through the door.

In the Cantoris, Magret looked up, a worried expression on her face. Sira felt a fresh surge of anger that a senior Cantrix in the midst of Cantoris duties should be bothered by such things.

But she calmed herself. There were still people who needed healing. It was their work that mattered most, after all. Let Trude and Wil play their games, Sira thought. It meant nothing to her.

She sat once again beside her senior, ready to help in whatever way she could.

The Cantoris hours went quickly, and Sira was surprised when it was time for the midday meal. The *quirunha*, after the meal, filled the early afternoon. When it was completed, with no more House members attending than the day before, Sira addressed the problem of her room.

It was situated in the same wing as the Magister's

apartments, but on the lower level, and close to the Cantoris. It would suit her well, she was sure, once the fussy hangings and rugs had been removed. The Houseman who came to take away the offending decorations was carefully formal.

"What can I do for the young Cantrix?" he asked. He was thin and far shorter than she, having to turn his brown, wrinkled face up to look at her.

Sira wondered briefly if the word "young" were to be forever attached to her title. But she thrust the thought aside as unimportant, and said only, "These hangings. They dampen the resonance."

The Houseman nodded blankly, and she doubted he understood. She wanted a live acoustic in her room, of course, for practice. When he had pulled down the hangings and rolled up the rugs, he bowed to her deferentially.

"Will there be anything else, Cantrix?"

Sira shook her head. As he bowed again in the doorway, she realized that, besides herself, this Houseman was the only person who had been in her room since she had arrived.

"Excuse me," she said before he left. "Do you know where Rollie might be today?"

The man looked quizzical. "If you need something else, Cantrix, I've been assigned to help you."

Sira shook her head again. "No. Never mind." She could hardly say she only wished for company. It would be beneath her dignity, and perhaps it would only make Rollie uncomfortable if she asked to see her. Sira thrust the idea aside. "Thank you," she said formally to the Houseman, and closed the door after him. She picked up her *filhata* and began to work.

She was deeply immersed in a melody that combined the fourth and the fifth modes, searching for the perfect modulation from one to the other, when there was a sharp knock on her door.

Automatically, she cast her mind out to discover who was there, but she did not recognize her caller. She opened the door with the *filhata* still under her arm. Her visitor was the elderly Housewoman, white-haired and round-shouldered, who attended Rhia. Sira had never been introduced to the woman.

"The Magister wants to see the young Cantrix," the woman said, with a quick bow. She did not exhibit the Houseman's deference.

"Oh, certainly," Sira said, more quickly than she might have had she not been searching in her mind for the woman's name.

The Housewoman's faded blue eyes sparkled with malice as she regarded Sira. "Trude's been to see him," she said with obvious satisfaction. "Something about you."

Sira stood still for a moment, realizing that this summons meant she would meet her new Magister at last. She put down her *filhata* and followed the Housewoman out, closing the door behind her. The Housewoman looked up at her sharply.

"Your hair," she said briefly. Sira put her hand up to her head to feel her thick hair coming loose from its binding. She tucked the errant dark strands back, and straightened her tunic. She had to shorten her steps to match the Housewoman's pace as they walked.

"Do you know about Trude?" the woman asked.

"We have met," Sira said.

The woman cackled dryly. "You want to be careful with her. Denis is the Magister's only child."

Sira was resolved not to be drawn into gossip. She wondered if the Magister were angry about what she had done, but she disdained to ask. Nevertheless, it was not the first impression she had hoped to make.

"Rhia has no children," the woman went on. "Not one."

She grinned, making deeper wrinkles in her thin cheeks. "Nice for Trude."

Sira remained silent. Except for Rollie and Blane, she had not been impressed by the House members at Bariken. She was completely unaccustomed to secrets and gossip and rudeness. She could not think how to reprimand the woman, but she kept her eyes forward and walked with her back very straight, towering over her, and glad of it.

They went up the same staircase Sira had found on her own, with the intricately carved banister and the beautiful limeglass window. Sira could see that the glow of Bariken's *quiru* shone beyond the window, fading the sunshine that was visible through the glass. In the upper corridor, they walked past Trude's apartment, and the Housewoman stopped at the very next door. She opened it without knocking, ushering Sira into a room with furs and tapestries everywhere—on the chairs, on the walls, on the floor. Sira had never seen a room so full of furniture and decoration. She had not known there were so many colors of thread for weaving, red and purple and blue and lavender all worked together.

"Magister?" the woman called, and Sira noticed that her tone was polite now.

"Here, Dulsy." A stocky man of middle height with thick, graying hair and beard emerged from a back room. When he saw Sira, he grunted and dropped quickly into a big carved chair. She knew intuitively that her height bothered him; he sat so that he wouldn't have to stand looking up at her. Carefully, she bowed. When Dulsy only stood to one side, watching her in silence, she introduced herself formally.

"Magister Shen, I am Cantrix Sira v'Conservatory."

Shen nodded a curt greeting, murmuring "Welcome," or something like it. He stared at her for a moment. "How old are you?" he asked. His face was weathered and creased as if from exposure, making him look more like Sira's father, the hunter, than Mkel, the Magister she knew so well.

Sira was weary of this question. As much as she wanted to make a good impression on her new Magister, she was exasperated. "Almost eighteen, and fully qualified as Cantrix," she said shortly.

"How many summers is that?"

"It will soon be four." She met his eyes steadily, and after a moment he turned his gaze away.

"Well, young Cantrix," the Magister began, "I need peace in my House. I don't want these women coming to me with their problems. Listen to Rhia, and don't cross Trude, that's all you have to do. That's all I want."

"Is that all?" Sira said softly. Her temper rose like a softwood blaze, and the air around her began to glow. He had not met her, had not bothered to hear her sing, and yet he called her here . . . ordered her here, just to scold her! Was she supposed to respect and serve a man like this?

She clenched her fists behind her back, feeling the muscles of her shoulders hard against her tunic. Shen seemed unaware of her reaction.

"Do you suggest, Magister, that your mate should supervise your Cantrixes?"

The man's face clouded and his eyes grew dark. "Now, listen—" he began.

Rhia forestalled his answer by walking gracefully into the room.

"Magister," she said, giving the title an odd, exaggerated inflection that Sira heard clearly, "I did not know you had met our young Cantrix yet."

"Trude complained about her," was his curt answer. Sira saw a flash of unmistakable satisfaction on Rhia's face, replaced quickly by her usual icy demeanor.

"Trude interrupted Cantoris hours," Rhia said smoothly. "I think Cantrix Sira handled the situation appropriately."

"Wouldn't hurt Magret to go see Denis," Shen said.

"Cantrix Magret is senior now," said Rhia, "and Cantrix Sira was perfectly able to take care of Denis."

"Denis was not seriously ill," Sira put in. She had meant it to be a reassuring remark, but she saw with sudden alarm that Magister Shen's face was flushing darkly. The woman Dulsy stood by with arms folded, almost grinning with enjoyment. Rhia noticed, and gestured her to leave the room. She obeyed resentfully, with neither bow nor ceremony, banging the door shut behind her. At the sound, Shen's temper snapped.

Smacking a heavy fist against the carved arm of his chair, he shouted, "By the Six Stars, Rhia! Can't you keep this women's business out of my hair?"

"House business," Rhia said, her voice very low and even. She touched her glossy hair, momentarily hiding her eyes with her hand.

"I'll take care of House business," the Magister roared. "Trude, and her boy . . . you take care of them! And these silly Cantrixes!"

Sira sucked in her breath as if she had been slapped. A rush of anger flooded her, and the air around her sparkled with its power. She struggled to hold her temper. Had she let it go, something in the apartment would surely have broken from its force. Shen, oblivious, sprang out of his chair, his muscular vitality out of place, wasted, in the heavily decorated apartment. He stamped out of the room.

Rhia stood frozen in her graceful posture by the big chair. Her face was still, but when she lifted it to Sira, her eyes glittered and her breathing was shallow and quick.

"The Magister—" she began tightly, then stopped. Sira could almost see her take control of her anger, as if she were reining in a rebellious *hruss*. Her breathing grew deeper and her face relaxed, but her eyes were on fire.

Rhia began a second time. "Magister Shen . . . has no patience."

Sira's own anger evaporated as she watched the other woman's attempt to regain her composure.

"He has no idea that he has just insulted you," Rhia said. "Other things occupy his mind."

The atmosphere in the apartment was charged with emotion. Sira could feel it like waves of heat and freezing cold, something she had never experienced before in her sheltered life. Rhia certainly sounded as if she were trying to protect her mate, and yet Sira was sure that beneath her anger there was satisfaction at the scene Shen had created. Her disappointment at the Magister's reaction to her was overridden by her wonderment at the strange relationships these people had.

"You may go now," Rhia said in dismissal. Sira raised an eyebrow at the older woman's curtness. She thought that Rhia and her mate were both ridiculous.

"And Trude?" she asked curiously.

Rhia looked sharply at Sira. "I can handle Trude," she said, and Sira was washed in a wave of her fresh anger and that other, complicated reaction. "You will find I am the one who handles it all," Rhia added, and then turned abruptly away.

Sira folded her hands together, and bowed.

"I'll call someone to show you back to your room," Rhia offered.

"It is not necessary," Sira replied. "I know the way."

Rhia nodded, and bowed quickly. A muscle jumped in her jaw, marring its smooth line. Sira turned to leave the elaborate apartment.

In the doorway, she met a Housewoman whose bow was

hindered by the stack of ledgers in her arms, and as Sira closed the door, she saw Rhia and the woman sit down at a large desk with the thick books between them. If Rhia managed the inventories and the Cantoris, settled disputes and acted as intermediary for Shen, then what did the Magister do? It seemed that it was Rhia, disciplined and self-possessed, who did the Magister's job. Sira wished she could find it in herself to like her.

CHAPTER
SIX

✳︎ ISBEL, LIKE ALL THE CONSERVATORY STUDENTS, LOVED
to see travelers ride into the courtyard. No matter
who they were, travelers seemed to bring with them the very
essence of the mountains and glaciers and irontree forests of
the Continent. For the students, as for most of the people of
Nevya, life was bounded by stone walls year in and year
out. Only in the brief summers did their world expand to
include the sky, the earth, the smell of fresh breezes. Riders
coming in from the great outside seemed somehow glam-
orous—adventurous and free. For Isbel, the storyteller, they
were also mines of information.

When word passed among the students that travelers were
riding into the great cobbled courtyard, Maestro Nikei
released Isbel from her third-mode exercises so that she
could join her classmates in the window seat and watch the
party dismount.

They were a bedraggled-looking group from Perl, the
poorest of the northern Houses. There were three rather
small, thin men, and one who was big-shouldered and
strong, with a shock of curling blond hair, worn short in the
manner of those who travel for their livelihood.

That is Theo, one of the students sent. Without turning,
Isbel recognized the voice of Jana, and she remembered that

Jana was from Perl. *He is a Singer, an itinerant. I have met him.*

What is that fur he wears? asked Kevn.

Urbear, Jana sent with a shiver. It was silvery-gray, with dark gray beneath. *Be glad they do not leave the coast.*

Who are the others, Jana? sent Isbel.

I only know one, the one with gray hair. He is House-keeper at Perl.

What do you suppose they want?

No one had an answer yet. The party were now off their *hruss* and were coming into the hall, shrugging off furs and stamping their cold feet. The young Singers untangled themselves from the window seat and reluctantly went back to their lessons. In the hall, Isbel watched Cathrin greeting the travelers and inviting them to bathe and eat. The broad-shouldered itinerant, Theo, looked up and met Isbel's eyes. He recognized her, no doubt by her dully colored tunic, as one of the students, and bowed carefully, but when he straightened he caught her staring and smiled. Isbel dimpled and ducked back out of sight, hurrying up the stairs toward the students' wing.

By the time the House gathered in the great room for the evening meal, all the students knew why a party had come from Perl. Perl, as Bariken had been a few weeks before, was in need of a Cantor. At Perl, as at most of the Houses, two Cantors or Cantrixes shared the Cantoris duties. Now Cantor Evn, who had only eight summers and should have been able to work for some years yet, had something wrong with his fingers. His junior had been unable to relieve his disability. Unable to play either the *filla* or the *filhata* with ease, his effectiveness had been seriously diminished. At the Magister's table, the students saw Perl's Housekeeper and Magister Mkel looking across at them, and shivers of excitement went through their ranks.

Cantor Evn must be very worried, came from a second-level student. *What if he can never play again?*

That would be disaster, Kevn sent. *No one can sing that way.*

So it will be one of us. That was Arn.

I am ready, boasted Kevn.

We are all ready, sent Arn, but several of his classmates shook their heads in doubt.

Perhaps they'll send Jana, someone put in. *It is her home, after all.*

Jana sounded forlorn. *The Conservatory is my home, just as it is yours.*

There was a long moment without communication. The first- and second-level students looked with wide, respectful eyes at their seniors, who were so close to adulthood and professional life. All the older students knew that the day of their departure was close, whether this year or the next. Now it appeared that someone, besides Cantrix Sira, would be leaving early.

Isbel looked around at them—tiny Jana with the dark eyes, Kevn tall and thin and craggy, Arn plump and slow-moving but with quick fingers on the strings of the *filhata.* There had been thirteen, and now there were twelve. Soon they would be only eleven. They were her family, as indeed were all those at Conservatory. Cathrin herself had given Isbel more affection than she had received from her own mother.

Looking around the great room, Isbel discovered Theo, the itinerant Singer, seated at a table with several stablemen, but watching the students with a strange expression. Daringly, Isbel opened her mind to see if he would send to them. She heard nothing. Still, his eyes seemed full of longing as he gazed at the students' table. Isbel wondered what he might be thinking. She was curious about him, about a life spent forever traipsing back and forth between the Houses. He was tanned and muscular, everything about his appearance speaking of the outdoors and constant exposure to the sun and wind, and the deep cold. Maestro Nikei, at the Magister's table, was white and slender and as fragile-looking as Maestra Lu.

Isbel turned away at last, back to her friends. She hoped she would have a chance to speak to Theo before he escorted the Perl party back to their House. He must have many stories to tell.

When the evening meal was over, the youngest of the students begged a story from Isbel, and they clustered around her in one of the broad window seats. The first-level students were a very new class, having been at the Conservatory only a few months, and sometimes they still cried for their mothers at night. Isbel and the other third-level students indulged them at every opportunity, prompted by poignant memories of loneliness and heartache during their own first year at Conservatory.

With one child on her lap and others leaning against her, their little hands on hers, in her hair and tugging on her tunic, Isbel told them the story of how the Spirit created the thirteen Houses. Because the story was one of the legends, she chanted it aloud, on three scale degrees of *Mu-Lidya*. Her voice was pure and sweet, and she sang the old, old words without embellishment.

> "The Spirit of Stars, the great Sower of seeds,
>   Looked down at the empty world,
>   And lamented its barrenness.
>   The Spirit reached out with Its great right Hand
>   And gathered thirteen stars from the abundant sky.
>   They sparkled in Its Palm.
>   The Spirit breathed on the burning stars

To cool their fire,
And then It threw them across the Continent.
At Manrus they fell, and at Arren,
At Perl, and Isenhope, Amric, and Conservatory,
At Lamdon, Bariken, Soren, and Clare,
And Tarus and Trevi and Filus."

The children sighed, each having waited to hear the name of his or her own House as Isbel chanted it. One, with tears in her eyes, put her cheek in Isbel's hand, and she stroked it as she sang. Looking up, she found the itinerant Singer watching from a respectful distance.

"The stars took root, and the Houses grew,
And the Spirit breathed on them a second time,
To fill them with new life.
The people came, and the *caeru*, and the *hruss*.
The Spirit looked down and saw the emptiness filled,
And was content with Its creation.
But the people cried out to the Spirit
That the world was cold, and their seeds would not
    grow.
And the Spirit of Stars grew dim and sad
That Its people were dying.
A third time the Spirit breathed,
And from Its own fire created the Gift,
The spark that would warm the world."

That is us, sent one sleepy child.

Isbel ceased her chant for a moment. *You are quite right, Corin,* she responded. *That is us.*

Go on, please, sent several of the others. One small girl was already asleep, leaning on Isbel's shoulder. Softly Isbel finished the chant.

"The Spirit of Stars, the sower of seeds,
Looked down on the world with its Houses
  and Singers,
And smiled to see it.
And when the Spirit smiled,
The summer came,
The last and greatest of the Gifts."

One or two of the children, who remembered the chant, joined in the last lines, the prayer that was said at the end of every *quirunha*.

"Smile on us, O Spirit of Stars,
Send us the summer to warm the world,
Until the suns will shine always together."

There was a silence when the chant was ended, and the Housemen and women who cared for the young ones came forward to gather up the sleepy children. The Singer Theo waited until they had all left the room.

"That was beautiful," he said to Isbel.

"Thank you," she replied.

He looked about to say something else, but was interrupted by several House members coming in to set the long tables for the morning meal. Isbel bowed to him, her mind open for him to continue his thoughts, but still he sent her nothing. He only bowed in return. She knew no other way to invite his friendship, and so she left the great room to go to her own bed.

Magister Mkel and Maestra Lu had to make a decision quickly, and the students knew it. They were breathless with anticipation. Within two days, they learned that it was to be Arn who would become full Cantor at Perl. Although by common reckoning, the students were all the same age, in actuality Arn was the oldest of their class. Nevertheless, he had not quite four summers, being just short of twenty years old. His ceremony and departure would take place in a few weeks. His classmates congratulated him, touching him and encouraging him. He was smiling, but naturally anxious. Cantor Evn, however, would remain at Perl to smooth the transition, since except for his stiffening, painful fingers, he was healthy. His continued presence would lighten Arn's burdens considerably.

In the *ubanyix* that night, the third-level girls stayed long in the water, so long they had to warm it twice. They clustered at one end of the great ironwood tub, trailing their fingers and their long hair in the water, talking and laughing, treasuring these moments of leisure and each other's company.

Even Arn will grow thin at Perl, sent Olna, who was plump and fair, and they chuckled.

No, he will make them improve the kitchens, was the response from Ana.

I am afraid they are beyond help, Jana sent, somewhat disloyally, but they laughed together just the same. Then a silence grew among them.

Soon we will all be saying goodbye, Isbel sent unnecessarily.

There were nods, and their young shoulders seemed to bow with the weight of their great responsibility. One by one, they climbed out of the bath and dried themselves, helping each other to rebind their hair.

Isbel was the last to leave the *ubanyix*, and as she pulled the door closed behind her, she saw Theo, the itinerant Singer, coming down the corridor from the *ubanyor*. His blond hair was damp, and a bit of metal on a thong around his neck shone in the *quiru* light. She nodded to him.

"Good evening," he said aloud.

"Good evening, Singer," she responded, also aloud out of courtesy, but wondering why he did not simply send to her. She kept her mind open, but again he sent nothing, although they walked together down the long hallway to the stairs. She glanced sideways at him, appreciating the bright blue of his eyes and the vigorous curl of his hair. He caught her glance and smiled.

"I'm Theo," he offered.

She smiled back. "I am Isbel," she said. They walked a few more steps. "Why do you speak aloud so much?" she asked bluntly, like a curious child.

Theo laughed, the resonating laugh of a Singer. It made Isbel laugh, too.

"My talents are different from those of Conservatory-trained Singers," Theo said then. He was still smiling, but Isbel was sensitive, and she heard pain in his voice. She wondered what it was.

"Oh," was all she said. "I did not know."

He lifted his broad shoulders in a shrug. "It's a big Continent. There's much to know."

They had reached the stairs, and impulsively Isbel asked, "Would you like to see our nursery gardens?"

Theo bowed, smiling. "A pleasure, Isbel. It's not too late for you?"

She shook her head, smiling back at him, and led the way down the long corridor to the back of the House, where the seedlings and plants of the nursery filled a huge, steamy space with a thick glass roof. The smell of rich earth and melted snow-water met them even before she opened the door.

"We are especially proud of our gardens," she told Theo as they strolled down a path between flats of plants just starting to grow. A gardener stepped out between them and bowed deeply to Isbel. She bowed in return. "We have more fruit trees even than Lamdon," she said, pointing to the southeast corner where small trees in raised boxes were lined against the outer wall. The kitchens of the House were on the other side of the wall, so that no breath of the deep cold should penetrate into the gardens and harm the fragile trees or their fruit.

There were benches here and there, and Isbel chose one. They sat, the itinerant keeping a careful distance from Isbel.

"It's wonderful here," he said. "I rarely see this part of the Houses I visit."

"What House are you from?"

"No House," he said, and sensitive Isbel heard the pain in his voice again.

She said gently, "How is that possible, Singer? Who on Nevya has no House?"

He chuckled. "The son of two itinerant Singers has no House," he said.

"But other itinerant Singers have Houses," she protested. "I know a story about one, Tarik v'Manrus. Every Nevyan should have a House."

"Perhaps you're right, Isbel," he said. "But not everyone does."

"I never knew that."

"So there are some things they don't teach you at Conservatory!" Theo said, laughing. He lifted the thong that held the bit of metal around his neck and showed it to her. It was strangely marked, and she could not read it.

"This belonged to my mother, and her father before that," he told her. "We come from a line of Singers past remembering. Healers, cutters, itinerants. Perhaps this makes up, in some way, for having no House."

"I have only seen metal once before," Isbel said. "Do you earn great amounts of it?"

Theo laughed again. "There is no great amount of it on the whole Continent! I earn enough to keep me supplied. A few bits for each traveler, a few more for healing. It's enough."

Isbel felt suddenly tired. She was unused to so much talking aloud, and the quiet of the nursery made her aware of how late it must be. Theo seemed to sense her feeling immediately.

"It's very late," he said quietly. "You should surely be in your bed by now."

She nodded to him. Evidently his Gift was intact, though apparently he could not send. She wondered why he could not, but only said, "You are right, Singer. I must go up." They rose and walked back through the gardens, down the deserted corridor to the stairwell that led to the students' wing.

"Will you wait here at the Conservatory for Arn?" Isbel said before going up the stairs.

"No. Magister Mkel has arranged a party for me to Arren."

Isbel's eyes widened in respect. "So far," she breathed. "All the way to the Southern Timberlands."

He grinned at her, his eyes ice-blue, like the sky in winter. "It's my specialty," he said. "I know the southern Houses better than anyone."

"Sometime you must tell me about them," Isbel said. She had to stifle a yawn with her hand.

He bowed. "With pleasure. Sometime when you're awake!"

She showed her dimples, and bowed too. Experimentally, as she turned into the stairwell, she sent, *Good night, Singer.* But although he waited there politely and watched her climb the stairs, there was no response.

CHAPTER
SEVEN

✳ THE LONG-AWAITED SUMMER WAS BEGINNING AT LAST. The distant speck of the Visitor, the wandering sun, could be seen just above the southern horizon, and the firn had begun to diminish on the lower slopes of the Mariks. Children who had never been out of doors in their lives scrambled over each other to peer through the rippled window glass at the pale disc of the Visitor. They squealed with delight as the snow that seemed eternal now dropped from the trees in large, mushy chunks.

Sira, who had only seen three summers herself, was almost as excited as the little ones at the coming season. She came into the great room before Cantoris hours and watched the children at the window for a few moments before sitting down to her breakfast. Several House members bowed to her from a distance. Sira would have liked to crowd into the window seat with the children, to have them sit in her lap or lean over her shoulder as they watched the changes outside. She knew they would not, though. If she sat in the window seat, they would pull back, careful to keep their distance, wary of sharp words from the other adults, perhaps even fearful of her power. As Cantrix of Bariken, Sira had only her senior for real company.

She looked around the great room as she drank her tea. By now she could distinguish between the House members and their guests. There were some here to trade for limeglass, perhaps with carefully worked leather goods from Amric or *obis*-carved ironwood implements from southern Tarus. In the far corner of the great room, two itinerants sat negotiating with the Housekeeper for work. Summertimes, Sira knew, could be difficult for the itinerants; for a few short weeks, Nevyans could move between the Houses without hiring Singers to protect them. Itinerants had to find some other work to do while both the suns shone. The daylight was long and abundant during the summer, with the sky growing dark for just a short period of the thirty-hour cycle.

Sira leaned her head on her hand, remembering the brief visit her family had made to Conservatory during the last summer, five years before. They had found little to say to each other. Her mother had been silent and worn-looking; even her father was awkward and formal. Although Sira had not yet reached full Cantrix status, they did not touch her, keeping an uncomfortable distance from her as if she had become something alien and awesome. She had been relieved when they departed, leaving her to her music and the company of the other students. Since then, as before, she had received one message a year, carried by some traveler for the price of a small bit of metal, on the anniversary of her entrance to the Conservatory.

Sira was not sure how many children her mother had. When she had left for Conservatory, there were already three older than herself, and two younger. Of all her family, only her father seemed vivid in her memory, full of energy after a hunt, striding into the family's apartment with a joy in life that her mother had never shown. Sira had not liked the rough-and-tumble of her siblings. Her mother, she recalled painfully, had accused her of thinking herself better than her brothers and sisters, because of her Gift. The memory was painful because there was a substantial amount of truth to her mother's criticism.

Good morning, Sira, Magret sent, sitting down opposite her at the table.

Good morning, Cantrix. Sira was glad of the interruption to her thoughts.

Summer at last. Magret and Sira had fallen into the habit of sending their everyday pleasantries, and speaking less trivial thoughts aloud.

Sira nodded, and looked again at the children crowding against the big windows. She knew a few of them by name, and she could see Denis, Shen and Trude's son, in the thick of them. Magret followed her gaze.

In a few days, they will be playing outside. Magret sipped her tea, and looked again at the children. Now she spoke aloud. "Last summer," she said softly, "Denis ran off into the woods, and Trude had the whole House looking for him." She shook her head ruefully. "The Magister treated it as a huge joke, but Rhia was furious. None of the children were allowed out again for the rest of the summer."

"That was hardly fair to the other children," Sira remarked.

"Certainly not. And it still did not change Denis' behavior."

Sira had finished her breakfast, but waited politely, in silence, for her senior. It was burdensome to have to speak aloud with another Gifted one. Seeing Trude at the Magister's table, however, she understood Magret's wish for privacy. It should not be necessary, Sira thought indignantly, but she kept the thought low in her mind.

The *quirunha* went on as usual, since the thick stone of the House walls shed the warmth of summer as effectively as it did the more persistent cold of the long winter. The daily ceremony was Sira's chief pleasure, the more so as she and Magret grew to know each other's musical inclinations.

Cantrix Magret seemed to be almost without ego; she allowed Sira to dominate the *quirunhas*, enjoying the freshness of her ideas and the effortlessness of her technique. Sira enjoyed each opportunity to perform, although the sparse attendance was still a disappointment. Magret, one day, had seen her searching the listeners when the music was over.

"You know, Cantrix Sira, it is only important to sing; it is not so important for whom you sing."

"I am sorry, Cantrix," Sira said quickly, abashed. "Of course you are right." It was not wasted on her that Magret had kept the rebuke private, so that Trude should not hear.

Magret put her soft hand on Sira's arm. Sira was surprised, and realized it had been many weeks since she had felt the touch of another's hand. "I am not angry with you, Sira," Magret said gently. "It has not been so long since I was a junior Cantrix, you remember."

"So I do, Cantrix," Sira said. "And you are generous with me."

Magret shook her head lightly, as if it were not important. Sira marveled at the older Singer's ease with her Gift. She seemed . . . tranquil, content. In Sira's own breast the fire of ambition burned so hotly. She wanted applause; she wanted to be presented in concert as Maestra Lu so often had been, simply for the sake of her beautiful music. She cared very much what her listeners thought of her work. Cantrix Magret seemed only to care about the work itself.

The summer came on quickly, as it always did. In a very few days, Magret's prediction came true, and the children were playing outside in the courtyard, with a few Housemen and women watching over them and enjoying the suns on their faces.

Sira was lingering over breakfast again, looking out into

the courtyard, when she saw the man ride up, two long-legged boys on *hruss* beside him. In only a moment she recognized Devid, the man her traveling party had encountered on the last day of her trip to Bariken. The boys were so like him, hair and eyes and build, that she had no doubt these were Devid's sons. She pressed against the casement to watch them, putting her cheek to the cool glass. They all dismounted, and Devid sent the taller boy around back to the stables with the *hruss* while he and the other boy turned into the entrance.

After the *quirunha* that day, Sira saw the younger son once again, in the back of the Cantoris, on the bench furthest from the dais. His eyes were intent on the two Cantrixes as they stepped down. Sira tucked her *filhata* under her arm and strolled toward him.

He rose as she approached, his brown eyes shining up at her in awe.

"You are Devid's son?" Sira asked.

He nodded, and a sudden flood of feeling swept out of him and over Sira as he stammered his compliments. "It was a beautiful *quirunha*, Cantrix. It was wonderful! Your voice is so beautiful . . . your melodies . . . Do you change them? I don't know that many modes, but . . ."

Sira, almost laughing, had to put her hand up to hush him. His thin cheeks flushed red and he stopped talking, but the tides of emotion did not recede. There was elation, and pleasure, and a spate of longing that was unmistakable.

"What is your name?"

"Zakri, Cantrix." He ran nervous fingers through his brush of brown hair and bowed awkwardly.

"Your father did not mention to me that one of his children is Gifted."

The boy gaped at her. "Can you tell? How did you know?"

"Why, Zakri, your thoughts flow out of you like spilled water, going in all directions at once."

Zakri blushed again, helplessly. "I'm sorry, Cantrix! My mother was trying to help me with that . . . but she died. She was a Singer." The last he said with youthful pride and sorrow.

"Yes. I am very sorry about your mother." Sira looked about her, realizing that the Cantoris had emptied of people. "Zakri . . . how old are you?"

"This summer makes three."

"But in years, how old?"

He frowned, concentrating. "I . . . I think I am twelve."

"You should have been at Conservatory long ago!" Sira blurted without thinking. She knew she had blundered when she saw the tears well up in Zakri's eyes. He dropped his head, not answering, and Sira wished the words unspoken.

Devid's bulky form came up beside them. "Zakri, your brother needs your help in the stables." The boy looked up at his father, and his eyes flashed. His father stepped back suddenly, holding up a warning hand.

The boy took a deep, audible breath, then bowed stiffly to Sira and rushed out of the Cantoris. It made Sira's heart ache to watch his thin back as he hurried away. She could feel the undisciplined emotions that poured from his mind until he was out of her sight. She turned to Devid. He had bowed, and was turning to leave when she spoke to him.

"Your son needs training." She spoke as a full Cantrix, with the authority of her position.

Devid turned back. "His mother was teaching him," he said. "Now I must find someone else to help him."

"Why did you not send him to Conservatory?"

"There was no need for that." Devid's face closed, with a stubborn set to his mouth. "His mother was a Singer. And we didn't want to part with him . . . We needed him at home."

"But he longs to be a true Singer," Sira said thoughtlessly.

An old anger sparked in Devid's eyes. "He will be! I will apprentice him to an itinerant Singer and he'll learn all he needs to know, just like his mother did."

Sira frowned. "It is very late for him, but you could still send him to Conservatory. I can send a message to Magister Mkel."

Sira was so intent on her purpose that she was caught by surprise when Devid suddenly punched one big fist into his other hand, making her jump. She had not realized he was losing his temper.

"Why do you Cantors always think yours is the only way?" he asked, anger making him forget the respect she was due.

Sira had no answer, because of course he was right. For a Conservatory-trained Singer, there was only one way. She stood tall and kept her eyes steadily on him. For a frozen moment they stared at one another, and then Devid suddenly remembered himself. He looked down at his furred boots.

"Forgive me, Cantrix," he mumbled. "You saved my life, and now I've offended you."

Sira turned away from him, to look up at the dais where she had so recently sat and played. She tried to keep the anger from her voice. "Nevya needs every Gifted person to be fully trained and capable. My class at Conservatory had barely one Singer for each House. We cannot afford to waste any."

"We love our children," Devid said softly. "To send one away so young . . . we couldn't do it."

"But a Gifted child suffers without training," Sira said swiftly, turning back to him. "If he hears other thoughts and feelings, and cannot direct his own, he will go mad. He will be dangerous to those around him."

"It's been hard on him since my mate died," Devid said. "But I'll find someone else. He'll be all right."

Sira could think of no further argument. She bowed to Devid in grim silence, and turned to leave the Cantoris. Poor Zakri, she thought. If his father could feel his emotions as she did, he would know the child wanted nothing more than to go to Conservatory to train, late or not. What kind of life could he make for himself, she wondered, as an itinerant?

Sad and thoughtful, she went to her room and spent her emotions in long, painstaking practice with her *filhata*. Later she heard from Magret that young Zakri had stood in the hall outside her room for an hour, listening.

The brief weeks of summer passed quickly. Sira noticed the children growing brown and strong with running in the woods around Bariken. They laughed and chattered at dinner, and ate prodigiously, making the adults smile. The hunters ranged far, bringing back many *caeru* to be skinned and dressed, preserved for leaner times. One trip netted them a *tkir* pelt, and the entire House gathered to exclaim over its tawny, speckled richness, and to praise the hunters who had brought it down. They had brought its great serrated teeth, too, to be made into cutting tools valued by the abattoir. The children clamored to touch them, and were allowed to do so under careful supervision.

In the forest around the House, the softwood shoots sprang up, growing visibly every day. Even the children were careful with them, never stepping on them or pulling them, knowing how much they were needed.

Sira had time to spare after the *quirunha* each day, and she took to spending it in the courtyard, enjoying the sun on her face, and playing little tunes on her *filla* for the children and the adults watching over them. Zakri sat near her one afternoon, and she smiled at him. She offered him her *filla* to play, but he shook his head, embarrassed, and a leather ball lying near his feet suddenly rolled away over the cobblestones, bouncing sharply against the side of a bench. Sira watched, trying not to show her surprise.

Zakri, it seemed, possessed a powerful Gift that would cause serious problems if not harnessed soon. She tried to open her mind to him, but he didn't know how to respond. This was a surprise for Sira; she hadn't realized that untrained Singers could not listen with their minds. She remembered, from her first days at Conservatory, how the dormitory had grown quieter and quieter as the young Gifted ones, surrounded by their own kind, began to talk with their minds and not their voices. She had thought all Singers learned to do it.

The next day Zakri and his father and brother were gone, in search of the mother's body to take home for burial. Every summer brought burials, but it meant more sadness for Zakri, Sira thought, and she sent up a prayer for the boy. It was all she could think of to do for him.

Another day, when the summer had passed its zenith, Sira sat in the courtyard in the long afternoon playing a lively melody on her *filla* for a little girl who danced, laughing, on the rough cobblestones. Denis and several other children were watching and applauding, laughing in the sunshine. Sira was startled to suddenly find Rhia standing over her, her smooth face creased and frowning.

"Must you play here?" Rhia said sharply.

Sira abruptly broke off the music and stood. She was deeply offended that her musical offering should be treated as a nuisance. The little girl who had been dancing dashed away, and Denis and the others stepped back, watching warily.

Rhia was elegantly dressed, as usual, but her jaw was set and she was pinching the material of her tunic, over and over. Even as Sira searched for some response, Rhia turned and called to one of the Housemen who had been nearby a moment before.

"Bors! Bors! Come here!" Her voice was harsh in the bright air.

Sira was silent, fascinated and repelled. Rhia was angry, and clearly the other House members were afraid of her.

"Bors!" The Houseman came around the corner of the House, and bowed quickly to Rhia. "Where is the Magister?" she snapped.

"I believe he is away from the House," the man offered, with distinct hesitation. "There was a report of a *caeru* den . . ."

"Hunting. Just when he is needed, naturally!" Rhia said bitterly, and waves of her deep and helpless anger swept over Sira.

Deciding that this situation had nothing to do with her, Sira turned to walk away.

"Cantrix." Sira turned back. Rhia's eyes glittered at her, and Sira knew that her anger was out of control. "Don't play out here again," she said.

Sira looked down at Rhia, her own composure secure once again. "I see no reason not to entertain the House members with my music," she said slowly.

"They have no need of entertainment," the older woman retorted. "There is work to be done."

Sira? Do not argue with her. Come in, please.

It was Magret, sending clearly and swiftly to her junior.

Sira, of course, obeyed immediately, but she was furious at being called away like a child. With her mouth firmly shut and her back arrow-straight she turned and went into the House. Just inside the door, Cantrix Magret was waiting, and she gestured to Sira, drawing her toward their apartments.

Sira, I am sorry, but . . . Magret looked up quickly, and Sira saw that Trude was leaning against the doorjamb of the great room, an amused expression on her face.

"Did Rhia find the Magister?" she asked lazily. "The Committee member is waiting."

"I do not know," said Magret quickly. Sira was lost in the currents of anger, fear, and envy that swirled around her.

"Don't mind Rhia, young Cantrix," Trude went on, straightening and turning toward the stairs. "It's hard for her. She can't win either way." She did not bother to shield her enjoyment of the conflict, and Sira's temper grew.

As Trude's generous figure vanished up the stairs, Sira turned to Magret.

What is happening here?

"It is better we speak aloud," Magret said softly. "The mind's ear extends far beyond the physical one. Come to my room, and I will explain as best I can."

Sira followed her senior, but her fury made the air around her glitter with energy. It was not a long walk, but her jaws ached with clenching them by the time she sat down on Magret's single chair and tried to breathe out her tension.

"A member of the Magistral Committee is making the rounds of the Houses to arrange a congress," Magret told her. "She expected to talk to Magister Shen, and Rhia is embarrassed that she cannot find him."

"But, Cantrix Magret, what does that have to do with my playing in the courtyard?"

"Nothing, of course, Sira. But Rhia is not kindly disposed toward Singers in general. Trude and Denis constantly try her patience. It is one reason the House members avoid the *quirunhas*. She was angry, and you were there . . . that is all. But she can be dangerous. When she loses her temper . . . she abuses her power." This last remark Magret whispered.

"In what way?" Sira asked.

Magret kept her voice very low and her eyes averted. "She has banished one or two Housemen who crossed her, and they and their families had to go begging for another House. And through the Housekeeper, she controls privileges certain families receive. Some of them are essential, and families suffer."

"But what could she do to me?"

"I do not know. But she is a clever and determined woman. And not a forgiving one."

Sira looked down at the fists she had made in her lap, and released them, stretching her long fingers. "This is a strange House."

Magret nodded. "Yes. But all Houses have their strangenesses. Do not worry. You will become accustomed to it."

Sira looked up at her senior again, her face set and stubborn. "We have trained and worked all our lives to serve our Houses. I do not think I will become accustomed to disrespect."

"We have no choice, my dear. Where the Conservatory sends us, we go. And serve." There was a pause, and Magret sighed. "Choice is a luxury beyond a Cantrix's reach."

Sira said nothing more, but she could not accept that thought. There would be more to her life than compliant obedience. There had to be.

CHAPTER
EIGHT

★ THE SOFTWOOD SHOOTS HAD SPRUNG UP IN ABUNDANCE around Bariken during the weeks of summer, their tender green needles flourishing under the light of the twin suns. The dark, thick ironwood trees looked heavy and ancient among them.

Now the summer was fading away. The faraway disc of the Visitor dropped closer and closer to the southern horizon, and the air cooled sharply. The steady trickle of summer guests at Bariken dwindled, and itinerant Singers began to offer their services to those who had stayed late, to ensure their safe journeys home.

It was on one of these last summer days that the Housekeeper Wil bowed charmingly to Sira after the *quirunha* and asked her to come to the Magister's apartments. "Rhia wishes to see you, Cantrix," he said, adding with a deprecating smile, "at your convenience, of course."

Sira nodded, although quite sure her convenience had little to do with the summons. She followed the House-keeper out of the Cantoris. They were two tall, slender people, passing through the corridors among other House members. The pair drew many glances, and Sira tried to look oblivious to the attention they received. For once she felt graceful, not awkward in her great height.

Rhia was waiting for them with tea and a tray of

refreshments. Trude was also present, sitting near the window and selecting tidbits from the tray with her plump hand, in the manner of one long familiar with her surroundings. It was odd to see the two women together. What a strange relationship they had: Trude the former Cantrix, mother of the Magister's son, and Rhia, the mate of the Magister.

Rhia bowed nicely, and Sira's answering bow was careful but shallow, asserting her importance. Rhia's attitude toward her was quite different today from the last time they had met.

"I won't keep you long, Cantrix," Rhia said. "I want to discuss something with you." She gestured to the refreshments, but Sira shook her head. The Housekeeper stood behind Rhia's chair. Sira, watching the woman sink elegantly into her seat, felt suddenly and distressingly gauche. Rhia's dark tunic and trousers were simple but impeccably draped. Sira tried unobtrusively to smooth her own plain tunic, then stopped as she saw Wil watching her with a slight smile. She straightened and composed her face, determined not to look at the Housekeeper again.

"The Magister will be making a trip to the capital, to Lamdon," Rhia was saying. "There is to be a meeting of the Magistral Committee. I . . . that is, we would like you to accompany him. It will be a three-day ride, and he needs a Singer."

With Trude so close, Sira kept her thoughts low. She could indulge in her excitement later. But Lamdon! Lamdon, with its eight Cantors, and people coming to the Cantoris from all over the Continent. She was so delighted she almost forgot an important question. When it occurred to her, her spirits sank as quickly as they had risen.

"Why me?" she blurted.

Rhia smiled, and reached for her teacup. "We would

prefer Cantrix Magret to stay here, to sustain the House *quiru*. Now that Cantor Grigr has retired, we are again shorthanded. Naturally, Cantrix Magret has managed it alone many times, and we feel there is less risk that way."

She did not mention the possibility of hiring an itinerant Singer, and Sira did not want to bring it up. Perhaps they felt an itinerant was not adequate protection for the Magister. Knowing that Trude was watching her from the window, Sira refused to let her elation show, feeling like a child hoarding a sweet.

"In that case I will be happy to travel with the Magister," she said rather stiffly. Rhia nodded.

"Good," she said. Her smile was gracious. Sira could hardly reconcile this charming, capable woman with the one who had insulted her in the courtyard not many days before. "Thank you, Cantrix. You leave in a week, then, and you'll be gone eight days. The Magister only expects to be at Lamdon two nights."

Sira nodded. Rhia rose, signaling the end of the discussion. The Housekeeper and Trude stayed behind, and Sira went quickly back to her own small room, her step light and her eyes sparkling with anticipation.

Magret found her later in the *ubanyix*, lazing in the warm, scented water.

"Well, Sira, this is unusual for you, isn't it?" Magret smiled at her junior as she hung up her tunic. "Is the water hot enough?"

"It is fine, Cantrix," Sira said, returning Magret's smile. Magret eased herself into the warm water with a pleasurable sigh. There were only two other women in the deep ironwood tub, washing each other's hair at the far end, giving the Cantrixes privacy.

Magret reached for the soap at the edge of the tub. "What did the Housekeeper want?" she asked casually.

It would have been so much easier to describe the meeting mentally, but Sira spoke aloud as her senior did.

"Rhia wanted to see me." Sira tried to be casual about it. "They want me to go to Lamdon with Magister Shen."

Magret dropped her eyes, and Sira feared she was upset, perhaps resentful. She opened her mind, hoping for some sharing of Magret's inner thoughts. She was relieved to feel neither anger nor envy, only a brief moment of warm concern before Magret shielded her thoughts once again.

Abruptly, Sira spoke. "It should have been you, should it not? So I said to Rhia."

Magret looked up, the lines around her eyes deepening. "Perhaps. In another case it might have been I, or more likely an itinerant. Perhaps because of your youth . . . perhaps they hope the journey will give you experience."

Sira knew that Magret did not believe this was the reason. There was something else. She waited for her senior to explain, but Magret just sighed. "I do not know, Sira. I do not know what might be in Rhia's mind." She cast a careful glance at the other women in the *ubanyix*. "I beg you to be cautious."

Sira nodded. "I will, Cantrix. Although I do not know what to be careful of."

Magret chuckled. "I do not usually hear any doubts from you, Sira. And I cannot tell you exactly what to be on guard against. Perhaps I just mean for you to be aware of everything.

"You will meet Cantrix Sharn, senior Cantrix at Lamdon. She is a wonderful Singer and an old friend," Magret went on. "Give her my regards. And enjoy yourself!"

"I will." Sira stretched her long arms above her head in joy, pushing away any doubts that might cloud her pleasure. Lamdon! It was a dream come true!

*   *   *

The sight of her old friend Rollie in the traveling party was an added delight for Sira. The rider, her lined brown face swathed in the yellow-white fur of her hood, quickly came forward to secure Sira's furs and saddlepacks and to help her mount. Patting the *hruss*'s heavy neck, she winked at Sira.

"So here we go again, young Cantrix!"

A joyous smile lighted Sira's face. "I am glad to see you, Rollie."

Sira would not soon forget Rhia's angry countenance as she forbid her to play in the courtyard, and she could understand some of the working Housemen and women not wishing to risk that sort of confrontation. But now a great adventure lay before her, and here was Rollie to share the enjoyment. Not even the Magister's gruff presence could dim Sira's pleasure. And unless he chose to freeze to death, he would have to hear her sing, something he had not done in all the months of her sojourn in his House.

It was a small traveling party, only two riders in addition to Rollie. Big-shouldered men, who looked even larger in their *caeru* furs, they rode ahead of the group in stolid silence. The last halfhearted days of the summer were a week past, the Visitor having disappeared into the southern skyline, and the travelers were in full cold-weather gear.

"Alks is the one on your left, Cantrix," Rollie whispered, "and Mike is the other one." She winked again, and grinned. "Not too sociable, you'll find."

Sira loved the feel of the saddle, although she knew that after all these months she would be saddle-sore once again. The cold air was exhilarating, and the prospect of Lamdon filled her with energy. Having Rollie to ride beside her made everything perfect. There would be news of Maestra

Lu at Lamdon. . . . Lamdon had everything. Sira hummed contentedly to herself as she rode.

As the day wore on and the party climbed swiftly into the Mariks, snow began to fall. The Magister, boisterously cheerful, and clearly in his element out here in the mountains, told Alks to make camp as soon as they dropped into Ogre Pass. Sira lifted her face and caught a snowflake on her tongue, then blushed when she realized what she had done. Rollie chuckled and Sira smiled at her. She supposed that just for the moment, with Rollie, she could forget the dignity of the Cantoris.

Ogre Pass was in itself exciting to Sira, as she had never traveled through it before. In fact, she had never been further north than Bariken. A wide canyon with steep, wooded sides and a flat floor, Ogre Pass wound north and south through the Mariks, with Lamdon and Isenhope at the northern end and its southern mouth pointing to the Houses on the Frozen Sea. There were no Houses to the east, unless, as legend had it in one of Isbel's favorite songs, the Watchers had their House there. Sira looked eastward to the fierce jagged peaks on the horizon; it didn't seem possible that anyone could build a House in that terrain.

Shen chose a campsite in a hollow between stands of immense irontrees. Conscious of the Magister listening, Sira created her warmest and swiftest *quiru* that evening. As the melody in the second mode wafted from her *filla*, the envelope of warm, brilliant air sprang up vigorously around them, tall and bright, but Shen gave no sign that he noticed.

Drifts of snowflakes tumbled past the *quiru* as Rollie and Mike built a cooking fire with softwood from their packs. Everyone's furs sparkled with tiny, transitory jewels as the snowflakes, dropping through the light, quickly melted. Alks and the Magister were already seated on their bedrolls, and Alks had pulled a big leather flask from his saddlepack.

Sira saw Rollie roll her eyes at Mike, and she wondered why. But when the hot food and tea were ready, she soon understood that the Magister was more interested in the flask than the food. His face began to flush the dark red she had seen once before.

"Never mind, Cantrix," Rollie muttered from her place next to Sira. "Alks knows how to handle him. They've traveled together many times."

Mike leaned back against his bedroll, eating in silence, while Alks and Shen handed the flask back and forth between them. Rollie finished her own meal and rose.

"Magister, would you like more *keftet*?" she asked, bending to take his half-empty bowl. Shen grinned up at her, and seized her legging with his free hand.

"You've got something I'd like better, Rollie!" he said loudly, and he and Alks and Mike roared with laughter. Rollie frowned at them, pulling her leg free and nodding in Sira's direction.

"Oh, I know." Shen laughed. "Our very young Cantrix! Too young for my jokes, you think, Alks?" He laughed again, and took another pull on the flask. Then he held it out to Sira. "Want some, young Cantrix? I'll swear by the Six Stars you never had this at Conservatory!"

Sira had no idea what to say. She hid her confusion behind a frozen countenance, feeling the firelight warm against her face, and Shen bridled.

"Too high and mighty, hmm? Well, then . . . you're my Singer, aren't you? Sing, then!"

Sira turned her head to look at Shen. She thought of refusing him. She thought of spilling his wine flask with a burst of careless psi. Instead she reached into her tunic and slowly drew out her *filla*. Her long fingers caressed its smooth surface even as she kept her gaze on Shen's face, and she put it to her lips. She turned her eyes away from him only when she began to play.

It was not the way Sira had pictured her first performance for Shen. In the haven of her *quiru*, with the snow drifting down around them, she played the merriest tune she could think of, a jaunty fifth-mode melody with a dance rhythm. After the first statement of the tune, she toyed with it, never satisfied to play the same piece twice in the same way. She embellished and modified it into something that fit the mountain campsite with its fluttery curtains of falling snow.

Then, in the middle of the music, the Magister abruptly rose and went outside the *quiru* to relieve himself. Alks quickly followed, and Sira, staring after them, stopped playing. Rollie swore under her breath, and Mike kept his craggy face averted, gazing down at the snow slowly melting under his bed of furs. Where Shen had been sitting, Sira saw the flask lying flat and empty.

Shen reeled back into the *quiru* a few moments later, brushing roughly past the *hruss*, who huffed and stamped nervously. "Sing!" he cried loudly. Alks stood behind him, holding his arm as he collapsed, laughing, onto his furs. "You're my Singer . . . Sing!" And he laughed harder, belching and thrusting his booted legs out toward the fire.

Sira found him revolting. She bowed ironically from her cross-legged position. Her control was absolute. There was a feeling of sympathy around her, and she wondered why. Surely no one could think the behavior of a boor like Shen could hurt her? But of course, they could not know.

Sira let her *filla* rest on her knee as she began to sing. She did not trouble to disguise the lullaby, one she had heard as a child at Conservatory, and had later sung to the new little ones as she tucked them into their cots. Her voice, so dark and smooth, rolled over her audience, and Rollie's weathered face relaxed, her frown peacefully smoothed away.

Both Mike and Alks were still and silent, watching and listening.

Sira wove a sleep *cantrip* into her song, delicately and accurately directing it straight at Shen.

> "Little one, lost one,
>   Sleepy one, small one,
>   Pillow your head,
>   Dream of the stars,
>   And the Ship that carries you home.
>   Little one, sweet one,
>   Drowsy one, lost one,
>   The night is long
>   The snow is cold,
>   But the Ship will carry you home."

Shen's eyes grew heavy and his face slack, and he nodded quickly into snoring sleep, still sitting fully dressed on his bedroll.

Sira concluded her song, and looked up to see that Rollie was smiling and shaking her head, eyes wet with some emotion. Alks had rolled himself in his furs and turned away from the fire. Mike was watching Sira, his rugged face set as if to resist her, as if she had been trying to invade his thoughts. It seemed an odd reaction.

"Beautiful, Cantrix," Rollie whispered. "We'll have peace now. And he'll never figure out what hit him. Tomorrow I'll ask you for 'Rollie's Tune.'"

"Thank you, Rollie," Sira said. "I will be glad to play it for you."

In the quiet, Rollie murmured, "I knew you would do well at Bariken, Cantrix."

Sira laughed a little. "I am not so sure that I have, Rollie. I think Rhia is not fond of me."

Rollie turned to glance at Mike. He, like Alks, had rolled into his bedfurs, his face turned from the fire. "Rhia's a disappointed woman," she said softly. "I came with her when she was mated to the Magister. She grew up thinking she would be Magistrix at Tarus, and then a younger brother was born when she already had three summers."

"Were you born at Tarus, then, Rollie?"

The rider nodded. "It's very different on the coast. Sometimes whole islands of ice appear overnight. Once one crashed against the cliffs when we were sleeping, and we thought the House was coming down around us." She chuckled a little. "Bariken's been a big change, but after three summers, I'm used to it."

Their talk dwindled, and Rollie began to yawn. She said good night, and went to see to the fire before retiring. Sira crept into her bedfurs, feeling spent, and listened as Mike got up to cover the Magister and Rollie banked the fire. The irontrees creaked, groaning in the deepening cold as Sira closed her eyes.

Just before dawn, Sira woke from a vivid dream of being trapped under an icy cliff with icicles sharp as knives crashing down around her. It left her with an overwhelming sense of dread. A warning, she thought. I have had a warning, but of what?

She sat up quickly to assure herself that the *quiru* was holding. It shimmered securely about all of them, undisturbed by any wind, and would probably stand for hours after they had moved on in the morning. The quiet snow continued to fall.

Uneasily, Sira lay down again. The dreams of a Singer were never to be ignored. There was danger somewhere, of some kind, but it was impossible to identify. She pondered it, but without success. Eventually the fatigue of her long ride in the fresh air crept over her, and she slept again as the night faded slowly into icy dawn.

Maestra Lu, six days' ride to the southwest, could not capture sleep again at all that night. Awakened by the same alarm as Sira, she lay on her cot at Conservatory, trying to fathom what danger hung over her protégée.

CHAPTER
NINE

✱ SHEN WOKE THE NEXT MORNING COMPLAINING OF A HEAD-
ache, and the party could not break camp until Sira
had treated him.

"Do whatever it is that Grigr used to do," the Magister
said gruffly. His breath was sour with wine and his beard
and hair uncombed. Sir pressed her lips together tightly, but
she brought out her *filla* despite her revulsion. He was her
Magister. Nevertheless, she wondered what Maestro Nikei
would think about this use of her Gift. Mike and Alks and
Rollie squatted around the camp, quiet, while Shen lay on
his furs and Sira knelt beside him with her *filla*.

It was a simple enough thing that Sira played, a melody
in the third mode, straightforward and brief, directing her
psi to relieve the constriction of the tiny channels that
carried blood around the body and into the head. For once
she added no refinements to the music. Her playing and her
healing were unsubtle and direct.

The Magister grunted as the pain eased and the blood
flow grew easier. She heard him, and gooseflesh rose on her
arms. As she put down her *filla*, her lip curled in disdain.
Shen did not notice.

"You're a handy one, Cantrix," he said jovially, sitting up
and running his fingers through his bushy hair. "Now that's
a useful skill!" he added with a laugh. Sitting so close to

him, Sira saw the broken red lines in his cheeks and nose, and knew why his face grew so dark when he was excited.

"You should not indulge so much in wine, Magister," she said. "Your health will suffer."

He laughed again, louder. "Hear that, Mike? We should not indulge so much! Ha! We should be like those fancy Cantors, no mating, no wine, no hunting!" Mike joined in the Magister's laughter, and Sira rose from where she was kneeling.

"You should have known my father, Cantrix!" Shen called after her as she turned her back on him and went to fasten her saddlepack on her *hruss*. "He drank twice as much as I do, and never suffered for it!"

Rollie came to help Sira, and winked at her across the *hruss*'s back. "His father never saw twelve summers," she whispered. Alks and Mike and Shen were laughing together as they mounted up.

They rode out of camp with the rumps of the *hruss* draped with bedding furs, wet from melted snow. They would dry in the cold air. Mike and Alks went ahead, large and stolid as the mountain *hruss* themselves, and the Magister followed. Sira and Rollie brought up the rear, their hoods pulled well forward to hold in warmth. Snow fell intermittently all day, frosting their furs with white, freezing on the opened bedfurs. Ogre Pass was cruelly cold, even in daylight. The *hruss*'s big hooves plodded silently in the soft powder.

They stopped just before dark to make camp. The season was one of long days and short nights, and they had ridden far. They were so close to Lamdon that they could see the glow of its *quiru* on the mountain slope ahead, a distance of about four hours' ride. The snow-bleached sky and the pale peaks melded into one indistinguishable landscape at this hour, and the circle of Lamdon's warm light seemed to float in the air, as if suspended above the ground. As their own *quiru* grew around them, the larger one sparkled vividly beyond and through it like the first star of evening.

Alks's wine flask had been emptied the night before, and their camp was quiet this night. Sira lay on her furs wondering what Lamdon would be like, and listening to the Magister reminisce with Alks and Mike about their boyhood years. Several stories included Shen's father, usually with Shen on the receiving end of some rough joke. Sira thought of her own father. It had been such a long time since she had seen him. She recalled most clearly the familiar smell of him when she was tiny, the odors of *caeru* and softwood smoke and snow that clung to his furs when he came in from the forest.

She had no more night terrors, but instead dreamed a soft, persuasive dream in which the Housekeeper Wil unaccountably appeared. This dream was no less confusing to her than the menacing one of the night before, and she was glad to be moving in the morning, shaking it off.

By the middle of the next day, the travelers rode into the great courtyard of the capital House, the *hruss*'s hooves clattering on clean-swept paving stones, a startling sound after three days of snow-muffled hoofbeats. Sira sat straight in her saddle, trying to see everything at once. Lamdon was even larger than the Conservatory, perhaps twice again as big, and its great doors looked as if they would take four people to open. Its *quiru*, lavish and large, sparkled and gleamed in the snowy setting.

Their approach had been noted, and a formal welcoming party was assembled on the broad front steps. Their *hruss* and saddlepacks neatly disappeared into the hands of several Housemen, and a bewildering variety of people were introduced. Sira was grateful when a small man with a merry expression bowed and seemed ready to take charge of her.

"Greetings, Cantrix," he said, his voice startlingly deep for a person of small stature. "I am Cantor Rico. Welcome to Lamdon."

Sira bowed in return, a much deeper bow to honor a senior Cantor. Rico gestured to the big doors.

"Please come in, and meet the other Singers who have gathered here. They are all in our senior Cantrix's apartment at the moment, talking Conservatory talk, I should imagine."

"Thank you, Cantor Rico," Sira said. The riders were going off to the back of the House, and Magister Shen had been formally received by some Committee official. She followed Rico, almost forgetting to watch her step as she gazed in wonder at this largest House on the Continent. Its *quiru* was so warm that people were wearing sleeveless tunics and no fur at all indoors, not even on their feet. Sira had never seen a sleeveless tunic before. The unaccustomed heat made her feel breathless.

As Rico led her down a long hall to the right of the big front doors, she caught a glimpse of the great room to the left, and the Cantoris, which she noted was in the usual place, although much, much larger than any she knew of. They crossed to the north wing, and made their way to an apartment at the end of the hall.

There were eight Singers for Lamdon's Cantoris, Sira knew, and the senior Cantrix was a person of significant influence, second only on the Continent to the Magister of Conservatory. At least so Sira had been taught. The senior Cantrix at Lamdon served as advisor to the Magistral Committee and was also liaison between Conservatory and Lamdon. If a Cantor or Cantrix was recalled, it would be by her order. If one was reassigned, the decision was made jointly by her and Magister Mkel of Conservatory. Such issues were grave responsibilities, matters of life and death, and the shortage of Cantors was their most vital concern.

Cantrix Sharn's apartment was as big as Rhia's at Bariken, and now it was crowded with at least twenty Singers of all ages and sizes. It was absolutely quiet.

Cantor Rico, please take Cantrix Sira's furs for her; she will be so uncomfortably warm.

Sira turned to see a slender white-haired woman of about twelve summers. Rico helped her with the heavy furs, and then introduced her. *Cantrix Sharn, this is Cantrix Sira v'Bariken.*

Sire bowed deeply. *Cantrix Sharn, I am to give you my senior's greetings.*

Sharn smiled warmly at Sira. *I have greetings for you as well. From your teacher.* For a moment, the image of Maestra Lu, created by their joined memories, filled Sira's mind with an intensity that made her close her eyes.

Sharn, sensitive to Sira's feelings, waited until the moment passed, then indicated two chairs close together. They sat side by side, and Sira looked around the room for the first time.

The apartment was almost as bare as Sira's own, although there was of necessity much more furniture. But it looked like a room one could practice in, Sira thought. She looked back at the senior Cantrix and saw her smiling.

Indeed it is, my dear, and I do it every day, even now.

Sira smiled, softening the sharp angles of her face. Sharn gestured to a passing Housewoman, who brought a tray of refreshments to them. Sira took a piece of dried fruit containing a kind of nut she didn't recognize, and she sipped thirstily at a cup of tea. She watched Sharn as the senior nodded to the Housewoman, noticing her very long fingers.

Good hands for the *filhata*, Sira thought, and hoped she would have the chance to hear Cantrix Sharn play.

Again Sharn heard her idle thought, and turned her attention back to Sira. *Actually, Sira, I was hoping you would play for us.*

Sira nodded, suddenly shy. Rico had returned and stood at her elbow.

We are all very curious to hear how things are at Bariken, Cantrix Sira, he sent.

All is well there, I think, Sira responded carefully, keeping her mind as clear as she could.

And how do you find working for Magister Shen? he pressed.

Sira was disconcerted to realize that all of the other Singers were listening for her answer. She took a moment to collect herself, thrusting her doubts down as far as she could, then nodded politely to Rico.

The Cantoris is a good one, with Cantrix Magret as senior. She is very helpful, and a fine Singer.

Rico surprised her by chuckling aloud. He patted Sira's shoulder lightly with a small brown hand. *A diplomatic answer, friends! Our young colleague should be a great success!* There was general, friendly laughter. Several Singers close to Sira sent warm wishes to her. Uncertain as to what Rico had meant, Sira turned to Sharn for guidance.

Do not let Rico's teasing disturb you, my dear, she sent. Sira was relieved to see that Sharn was also amused. She went on. *He is searching for crumbs of gossip to offer round for dinner company!* There was more laughter.

We all knew of your early assignment to Bariken, offered a middle-aged Cantor in the group. *We have all been thinking of you.*

Sira was touched, and she bowed to him. *You are very kind.*

There were nods and bows all around, and the Singers turned to the topic of the Committee meeting. It had not occurred to Sira to wonder why the Magistral Committee had been called together. It seemed they were here to discuss the shortage of Cantors and Cantrixes, and the failure of many families to dedicate their Gifted children to Conservatory training. Penalties were being proposed.

Magister Shen, Sira thought privately, would have little interest in such a discussion. He clearly was not concerned about Singers or Conservatory, or anything except that which gave him pleasure. It was a most disloyal thought, and she kept it low.

One of the Singers, a young man of about five summers, nodded coolly to Sira from across the room, and she recognized him. He had been a third-level student when she was technically second-level, although they had done much of the same work. She basked in the glow of their mutual history and profession, and felt at home in a way that was not yet possible at Bariken. Perhaps she could discuss the situation of her Cantoris with Sharn, as she might have talked it over with Maestra Lu. If the chance presented itself, she would. She sighed happily. Sharn reached out with her white hand and patted Sira's arm.

I could send a message to Maestra Lu, Sira sent.

Yes, you should do that, Sharn sent, not as a command, but as a friendly urging of one colleague to another.

I have no metal at all. Will it matter?

Sharn shook her head, smiling. *I will see to it for you. Now, I will tell you all the news I have from Conservatory, and you tell me all about Magret, and anything else interesting!*

Sira thought that next to Maestra Lu, Sharn must be the most wonderful woman on the Continent. In her turn, Cantrix Sharn examined Sira's face, with its sharp-boned planes and dark eyes, alight with the intensity of her feelings. She looked even younger than her eighteen years, and it was Sharn's turn to thrust her thoughts low so that her doubts would not be heard.

In Sira's guest room at Lamdon there were several nursery flowers gathered into a little stone vase, serving no purpose but a decorative one. At Conservatory, herbs were grown, but no flowers. Bariken grew flowers, she knew, because she had come upon them when walking through the nursery, but they were not used like this. It seemed to her an extravagance worthy only of Lamdon.

After a brief bath in the large *ubanyix*, where the other women left her in privacy, Sira rested, waiting for the evening, and thought about Cantrix Sharn. The older woman's charm had drawn more out of Sira than she had offered to anyone in a long time. Still, Sira had been careful. For all their strangeness, Magister Shen and Rhia were her employers, and she did not wish to seem disrespectful to them. She had told the senior Cantrix the story of Shen's drinking and her treatment of its aftermath, however, and Sharn had not seemed surprised. She had only commented, *We were not really trained for that, were we, my dear?* and then gracefully turned their conversation to lighter subjects.

Sira drew her spare tunic over her face to shut out the brilliance of Lamdon's light, trying to sleep for a little while. Lamdon seemed a magical place. In a short time, she would observe the *quirunha*, and this evening there would be a concert given by Lamdon's own Singers. And she was a part of it all, one of them, the Singers of Nevya. How satisfying it was! She found herself wishing Wil had come along to observe how she was treated in this exalted company. He would not laugh at her if he saw her in private conversation with the senior Cantrix of Lamdon!

*   *   *

The *quirunha* at Lamdon was elegant and polished. Cantrix Sharn presided although she did not play. A Cantrix named Becca led, with a fluting soprano and small, quick fingers on the *filhata*. Two Cantors assisted her, one of them particularly skilled in the use of harmonics, pressing his fingers only lightly against the strings of his *filhata* to make the sympathetic overtones ring out an octave and more above the melody. The walls and ceiling of the Cantoris resounded until the room itself became a musical instrument. The Cantoris had such a live acoustic, in truth, that without the audience it would have been overwhelming.

Sira floated on the tide of music and psi, sitting as straight as if she were on the dais herself, forgetting everything else for the space of the *quirunha*, and unaware that her own fingers lifted and danced in her lap, following Becca's leads.

Cantor Rico had escorted her to the Cantoris, and noticing the flush on her cheeks, had chuckled and assured her that someone would lend her cooler clothes. *It is our little conceit*, he sent. *Abundant warmth.*

When the prayer had been said and the *quirunha* was complete, Sira had an opportunity to tell Cantrix Sharn how beautiful she thought it was.

Thank you, Sira, Sharn sent, smiling. *I have an idea that a compliment from you is an honor.*

Sira blushed, hoping she had not been effusive. She had been thoroughly sincere. Indeed, she reflected, she was always sincere. That could be a fault here among these sophisticated people. She hoped they did not think her naive.

Rico, true to his promise, sent a Housewoman to Sira's room with a cooler tunic. The Housewoman held it out to her, and Sira saw it was embroidered in green and yellow thread and had no sleeves.

"I am not sure I can wear it," she said shyly.

The Housewoman tilted her head to one side. "Oh, yes, Cantrix, I think it will be fine. May I help you?" She waited for Sira's nod of permission before reaching out to help her remove her heavy tunic and replace it with the lighter one. She smoothed it down over Sira's trousers, saying, "I am sorry we have no cooler trousers for you, but your legs are so very long."

Sira nodded, looking down at herself. "I know."

"No matter." The Housewoman pulled a brush from some pocket, waiting again for Sira's consent before she began to brush and rebind her hair. Having someone else dress her hair felt very strange to Sira, as strange as wearing a sleeveless tunic. Self-conscious, she held her bare arms down by her sides.

The Housewoman bowed deeply when she left, and Sira thanked her. For just a moment she wished that she did not always stand a head taller than everyone else. But when Cantor Rico came to fetch her for the concert, she forgot everything but the treat ahead.

The after-dinner recital was a formal program in the Cantoris, with the Magister of Lamdon, all the members of the Magistral Committee, the assorted guests who had come for the congress, the visiting Singers, and a number of House members making up a large audience. From the way in which everyone was dressed and the elaborate preparations, Sira gathered that even for Lamdon this was an event of note.

She was thoroughly enchanted. She sat on a bench between Rico and a Cantrix from Tarus, and the audience around her preened themselves and looked around, seeing and being seen. It was amusing to Sira, but she also rather enjoyed it. Once or twice she saw people looking at her and whispering to each other, and she lifted her head, pretending not to notice. It would seem that everyone knew who she was, the youngest full Cantrix on the Continent.

When the music began, Sira was ready to lose herself in it as she had lost herself in the *quirunha*. But with an ear meticulously trained by Maestra Lu, she found there were faults. Surely that cadence was a little rushed, and one of Lamdon's Cantrixes had a tendency to sharp on rising melodic lines. After the concert her compliments to the performers were modest. Fortunately no one seemed to notice, and other members of the audience were effusive in their praise.

When refreshments were served afterward, Sharn approached her. "How did you like the music?" she asked. Sira had noticed that Sharn usually spoke aloud when non-Singers were present.

"I enjoyed it very much," Sira said truthfully, keeping her thoughts low.

Sharn's smile told her that the senior understood her very well. "Yes, there were some nice moments," was all she said. "I would be very pleased if you would play for us while you are here."

Sira felt a thrill of pleasure and anxiety that tingled just under her borrowed, embroidered tunic. She bowed politely to Sharn. "I will if you would like me to."

"I have been looking forward to it. May I lend you my *filhata*?"

"Thank you, Cantrix," Sira said. "You are very generous, and I am sure I will play better on your instrument than my own."

Sharn nodded, approving her formal courtesy. "I thought perhaps after the evening meal tomorrow. Will that suit you?"

Sira murmured assent, glad of the day to practice. Sharn signaled to a Housewoman, and took from her a *filhata* that was beautifully wrapped in a piece of Perl's best fabric. Sira accepted it from her hands with another bow.

"Would it be rude of me to excuse myself now?" she asked Sharn.

The senior Cantrix shook her head. "Of course not. I am sure you are tired. Let me call Rico to escort you."

Sira allowed her to do that, not sure she could have found her way back to her room alone. She did not correct Sharn, either; she was sure Sharn knew it was not fatigue that sent her to her room. She wanted to play.

She cradled the borrowed *filhata* carefully under her arm as she walked next to Rico, trying to reply to his social chatter. The instrument felt warm and heavy and full of history, and she could hardly wait to feel its strings under her fingers.

Sira had no appetite for the delicacies offered at the evening meal the next night. She had not felt so nervous since her very first *quirunha*. She let the feeling flow over her, experiencing the quiver in her stomach and the tremble of her fingers, using the excitement as energy. Cantor Rico, sitting near her, smiled in understanding but said nothing.

Cantrix Sharn had invited all the Singers in the House, except the itinerants, to her apartment after dinner, and there were more than thirty of them, the most Sira had ever seen in one room. When they had all been served an after-dinner cup of tea, Sharn beckoned to her, and Sira paced the length of the room, already concentrating on the music she had in mind, oblivious to all the faces that smiled at her so pleasantly as she passed.

The guests saw a long-boned young woman who, in her reserve, seemed poised beyond her years, her borrowed *filhata* held with unconscious grace beneath one arm; but Sira felt too tall, and too young, and awkward. She was aware of her former schoolmate, and she felt his critical eye on her, the tingle of resentment coming from him. She was accustomed to this; it was a familiar, almost comforting feeling. She thrust it aside as she always had; she could not help others being envious. She must think only of the music.

Her anxiety disappeared the moment she sat and took up the *filhata*. She sat quietly for a long moment, shaping the first phrase in her mind, breathing in its mood and the attitude of her listeners, and then she began.

It was a piece she knew very, very well, and had studied and polished with Maestra Lu herself. It began slowly, with an instrumental line. When the voice entered, the meter changed, and then changed again, without ever marring the fluid legato. She had chosen a nostalgic text, and its appropriateness for this audience was in its own way a triumph:

> "Sing the light,
> Sing the warmth,
> Receive and become the Gift, O Singers,
> The warmth and the light are in you."

Her dark, even voice rose and fell, embellishing and modifying the melody. When she finished, there was a long silence. Looking up, she saw several Singers with glistening eyes, and one gray-haired Cantor who had covered his face with his hand.

Sharn rose and came to her, holding out both hands. *Thank you, Cantrix Sira,* she sent, her eyes glowing. Each of her many summers seemed imprinted on her face at that moment. *I think I may speak for all of us?* she inquired of the other Singers, who nodded assent. *If you are representative of the students coming out of Conservatory in these*

*difficult times, we are all honored. The House of Bariken is
most fortunate in their newest Cantrix.*

Sira stood, her face as still as she could keep it, trying to
temper her elation. She knew it had gone well. She bowed
to Sharn, and handed back the *filhata* with careful thanks.
There was a wave of approbation from the company, and
she bowed to them all.

It was only later that Sira had time to wonder why, as the
Cantors and Cantrixes clustered around her, Cantrix Sharn
sat again in her chair and did not smile. She looked almost
angry.

As a last celebration of their time together, the Cantors
and Cantrixes retired to bathe before beginning their journeys home the next day. In the *ubanyix*, Sira marveled at the
Singer-energies it must take to keep the huge tub of water
warm. Forty people could recline in this tub at one time,
although now there were just seven or eight Cantrixes. Sira
folded her long form on the bench next to the senior Cantrix,
her legs tucked under her. Dried flowers floated on the water
that lapped gently about their shoulders.

Sharn looked at Sira warmly, and opened her mind.

*Sira, I must tell you of our concerns about your assign-
ment.*

Sira watched the older woman, wide-eyed and waiting.

*We at Lamdon feel that something political may be
happening at Bariken.*

Sira shook her head slightly. *I am sorry, Cantrix. I have
heard nothing.*

I have met Rhia, Sharn went on, *and sensed her desire to
rule Bariken.*

She already does in many ways, Sira ventured.

Sharn nodded slowly. *Yes, so I understand. But I believe
she does not find it satisfying.* She leaned back wearily

against the side of the tub and closed her eyes. *She wants to be Magistrix.*

Sira looked away into the gently rolling clouds of steam that floated from the pool of water to the ironwood ceiling high above. Sharn had broken the psi connection, but Sira understood perfectly what she had been told. Sharn had trespassed on Rhia's thoughts at some time. Sira could guess that Rhia had accompanied Shen to Lamdon on some occasion, bringing her into Sharn's range, and perhaps Sharn had even received instructions from her own Magister.

Sharn was warning Sira, and Sira had already had a warning from her own instinctive mind. Should she tell Sharn of her dream? What could it mean? And how, Sira wondered finally, could these circumstances be any threat to her, a Singer?

Sharn's eyes were still closed, her lashes as pale and delicate as the rest of her body. She sent very faintly, *Your first responsibility is to protect yourself, whatever happens. Nevya needs its Singers. It is possible for some to forget that.*

Sira felt a sudden chill, and she rubbed her cold shoulders.

Come, Sira, you are getting cold. Let us get something hot to drink. As if their enigmatic conversation had never taken place, Sharn led Sira to the stack of linens, and they dried and dressed themselves.

Later, as they said good night, Sharn appeared perfectly serene, as always. Sira moved away from her down the hall, tired after an exciting day, and preoccupied. She had no idea that, like Maestra Lu before her, Sharn watched her with a heavy heart, regretting the need for such young Singers to bear the burdens of a troubled world.

CHAPTER
TEN

★ IT WAS A DULL GROUP OF TRAVELERS THAT HEADED BACK
into Ogre Pass on the return journey from Lamdon
to Bariken. Snow fell heavily, and a nasty wind snapped at
them. Even the middle hours of the day were shaded and
gloomy. Sira huddled in her furs, rocking with the *hruss*'s
movements, deep in her own thoughts.

Shen, debilitated by too much of Lamdon's wine two
nights in a row, was also withdrawn. He had not mentioned
either the Magistral Committee meeting or its subject. Alks
and Mike rode ahead, and Rollie, cheerful and talkative but
getting little response to her occasional tries at conversation,
also lapsed onto silence.

They had left Lamdon very early, and they rode until late
that day, covering half again the usual distance for a day's
travel. Sira's *quiru* in the evening took a few extra moments.
The cold was invasive, reaching frigid fingers inside their
furs to chill any skin it touched. Sira's lips were stiff with it,
and it was difficult to play.

The *quiru* bloomed above them at last, and Mike started
the cooking fire. With the *quiru* glowing about them, the
party was more relaxed. Alks and Shen gossiped about
Lamdon and its people, and Rollie prepared the *keftet* and
tea. Only Mike remained impassive and silent. When Sira

looked at him, she felt the prickle of her psi. She thought there must be something troubling him.

As the group settled down for the night, Sira spoke to Shen. "Magister, I think this *quiru* may need replenishing before morning. It is very cold tonight, and the wind may break it down."

In fact, the snow was falling slantwise, and the tops of the irontrees soughed and danced above their campsite.

"All right," Shen said. "Rollie, you waken the Cantrix mid-night, then sleep."

Rollie nodded and propped herself on her furs to take the watch. Mike and Alks had already gone outside the *quiru* with the Magister to relieve themselves, but now they stepped outside for the second time that evening.

Sira was kneeling, getting her bedroll ready and thinking only of warmth and sleep, when her psi suddenly screamed a warning. Instinctively she cried out, "Rollie!"

It was too late even as she heard her voice ring across the *quiru*. She whirled to look at Rollie, and it seemed to her shocked senses that a fur-tipped arrow simply appeared in Rollie's bare throat. The rider's weathered face went slack as she fell backwards, sprawling off her furs into the snow.

Sira turned swiftly to Shen and another atrocity, as an arrow and then a long-handled knife pierced the Magister's furs. His shock of graying hair suddenly reddened as blood leaped across it. He fell to the side with a long groan, and then was silent.

Sira bit off another outcry. She could see no escape from the disaster. She straightened her back where she knelt, and was still. Her own arrow, bitterly punctual out of the darkness, pierced her body just below her collarbone. Obviously the assassins meant them all to die.

Sira knew instantly her wound was not a mortal one. By instinct, just the same, she let its impetus carry her to the ground, like the other victims. The point of the arrow went through her flesh and dug into the freshly fallen snow. She lay still, as if her spirit had fled beyond the stars with those of Magister Shen and her friend Rollie.

Hushed, tense voices came to her from outside the *quiru*, and she understood the killers were coming to assure themselves that everyone within was dead. The cold would have driven them into the warmth in any case. Assuming it was Alks and Mike, how were they planning to save themselves once her *quiru* dissipated?

All this she thought in a heartbeat, lying utterly still. She knew that when her body's reaction to the danger had worn off, she would experience the true pain of her wound. In the meantime, she would do what she could to save her life. Shen and Rollie she knew were dead; their minds were past her hearing now. She must convince those coming that she was dead as well.

To her surprise, four people moved into the *quiru*, and she knew them all when she heard their voices. Mike was the one who came to confirm that the three victims no longer lived. Sira could sense him leaning over Shen, with his double wounds, and poor Rollie, who had at least died instantly. As he came toward where she herself lay, she drew over her mind the darkest veil she could imagine, and Mike, leaning over her, convinced himself she was dead. He could not bring himself to touch her within her *caeru* furs. She could sense, even through the veil, his inability to overcome the tabu, and with it his repugnance for the task he thought he had accomplished.

Sira's will was very strong. She lay absolutely still, not allowing even her breath to move the furs that swathed her, and she listened to the voices.

Alks and Mike crouched around the fire with the two new arrivals. Wil, Housekeeper of Bariken, was speaking now with the other traitors. The second new voice was more shocking. There was no precedent as far as Sira knew for a traitorous Singer, but she was there: the former Cantrix, plump, sly Trude.

Sira thickened the veil over her mind, denying herself the luxury of any reaction to the double betrayal. Trude, despite the years of undisciplined living, would pick up her thoughts if she did not bury them. So Sira lay as if dead, and smoothed the waves of her mind until they were as flat and opaque as the lifeless rock beneath the snow.

Sira's discipline had always been exceptional; now it was phenomenal, and the success of her effort to shroud her thoughts caused Maestra Lu, wringing her hands in fear and grief as she paced her tiny room in the Conservatory, to believe that Sira was indeed dead.

Wil was speaking. "We'll cover the bodies as soon as we've had a chance to get warm. This campsite is enough off the trail, I think."

"What about their things?" This voice was Trude's.

"Their gear stays," Wil said. "If the story is that they got separated in the storm, their *hruss* and possessions would be lost, too."

"It's just . . ." Trude's voice dropped lower, almost to a whisper. "Her *filla* . . ."

"Everything," Wil said harshly. "No exceptions."

There was silence. So deeply had Sira forced herself below conscious thought that she heard their voices in a dream, a slow nightmare of cold and pain and shock. She hardly noticed as Alks and Mike piled loose snow over her body and those of Rollie and Shen. Even Trude, who might have known, was unaware that Sira still lived. Sira suppressed even the feeling of hope at the knowledge that her *filla* was to be left with her. It was in her tunic, tucked beneath her furs.

Through her blanket of snow, she heard the mountain *hruss* that had carried her being slaughtered and, like herself, buried in the snow. It seemed an unnecessary cruelty. The *hruss*, after all, could survive the cold on their own, although all *hruss* preferred the company of people. But Sira could not risk a reaction to this, either, nor allow herself to experience her pain or the deep cold of the snow. Her infrequent breaths kept a pocket open above her mouth, but otherwise she perfectly mimicked the corpses whose grave she shared.

A few hours before dawn she heard Trude playing a *filla*, competently enough, apparently, to strengthen the *quiru*. Some deep level of Sira's mind knew her body was getting dangerously cold, but her reactive mind could not be allowed to respond. She waited.

Dawn came, and the insurgents broke camp. There were shuffling and brushing sounds as they obliterated traces of the campsite. As if at a great distance, Sira heard Wil ask Trude something.

"It will be gone in two or three hours, in this wind and snow," Trude said, and Sira knew they meant the *quiru*. Still, she could not react, could not feel, did not dare even to think. She had been feigning death for fourteen hours.

The sounds of the *hruss* and riders faded away above the snow. Sira thought she could wait an hour before attempting to break through her snowy tomb, but when she began to feel warmer, she knew she did not dare. All Nevyans learned as children that the illusory sensation of warmth was the first symptom of freezing to death, and she feared her spirit might drift away after all if she did not move soon.

The snow that had been piled over her was the dry, powdery snow of the mountain passes, and her searching arm reached air quickly. It hurt to move, but she forced herself to dig in reverse, to make a hole upwards through the drift until she could see the remains of the *quiru* through it. Mike's arrow was an obscenity impaling her, crusted with snow, and she could not decide yet what to do about it.

It took her half an hour to free herself, gradually flaking away the snow cover with her numbed right hand until her torso, and at last her legs, were released. Her left arm, the side where the arrow was, caused her too much pain when she tried to use it. She was too cold to know if she was still bleeding.

Her *quiru* faltered around the site, having been renewed rather clumsily by Trude, and she thought she had perhaps an hour before it dissolved. The remnants of fire had been covered up, along with any other signs of human or *hruss* presence.

Sira feared using her *filla* now. Her betrayers could not be more than an hour's ride away, and Trude's ears, although dulled by years of abuse in everyday House life, might still be sharp enough to hear its bright timbre at a distance. The *quiru* was cooling, but warm enough to sustain her for a little while. Falling snow obscured the sun, which she supposed must be well overhead by now. Sira turned her thoughts to the problem of her wound.

As she began to warm, the pain caused by the offending shaft sharpened and grated, and the position of the arrow inhibited movement. If she were to escape, it would have to be removed. She felt fairly strong, leading her to think she could not have lost too much blood.

Casting about for a way to extract the shaft, she found a long thong that had been used to tie her pack on her saddle. Rollie had fallen closest to her, and Sira reached, shuddering, into the snow that covered her friend's body to take the long-handled knife from her belt. She paused a moment with her hand on Rollie's cold one, offering a silent prayer for her safe passage beyond the stars.

This prayer, sent in passionate sincerity and sorrow, reached Maestra Lu's questing mind. Hope for the life of her young protégée blazed suddenly in Lu's heart. As Sira went about ridding herself of the arrow, Maestra Lu was raising the alarm at Conservatory.

It took some minutes of sawing on the shaft of the arrow to cut through it and remove the furred flight. The movement made the wood chafe against bone and flesh, and Sira had to rest several times until the pain subsided. Perspiration trickled over her body and she gasped for breath. At last the knife broke through the wood, the flight falling at her feet and resting on the snow.

She tied the thong around the smallest of the trees near her. The hardest part of her task was then to reach behind her with her right arm to try to secure an end of the thong around the arrowhead protruding from her back. She tried to stretch her arm over her shoulder, and then down and behind her back, but the pain forced her to stop each time short of her goal.

Finally she made a loop like a *hruss*'s noose in the thong, and holding one end, turned her back to it and tried to catch the arrowhead in the loop. She twisted and writhed, trying to find it, panting and gritting her teeth against the pain when the arrowhead scraped the wood of the tree. It was like trying to thread a needle in the dark, but she finally succeeded.

She pulled the noose tight on the arrowhead, not wanting to chance its slipping out of the loop. When it was as tight as she could make it, she stood for a moment, effectively lashed to the tree behind her, and calmed her breathing and her mind. The last step in the extraction of the arrow would take mental as well as physical strength.

When she was ready, Sira took one deep breath, tested the noose once again, and then, pushing off with all her strength, sprang away from the tree. The arrow jerked out of her body and hung by the thong, grisly and broken. Sira lay face down in the snow, sobbing with pain and relief. She could feel fresh blood soaking her back, but was too glad to be free of the awful arrow to care at that moment.

She rested for some time, until she noticed that the air was growing colder around her. Carefully raising herself on her arms, she saw the last bits of the *quiru* dispersing in the wind and snow, and she knew she had to do something soon or her efforts thus far would be wasted.

She was stranded halfway through Ogre Pass, with no *hruss*, little food, and no guide. The snowstorm swirled around her, obscuring landmarks. Blood still leaked from her wound.

For today, anyway, she thought, what she needed was a *quiru* and a chance to stanch her wound and rest. She recovered her saddlepack from the spot where she had lain under the snow, mentally bade farewell to Rollie and even to Shen, and began her difficult trudge through the deepening snow to find a spot where she could rest away from the fatal campsite. She did not trust this place.

The wind was rising, making it difficult to listen for *hruss* and riders at any distance. Her pack was not heavy, but as she slung it over her shoulder, she winced with the pain from her wound. She would walk, she decided, for one hour, and then call up a *quiru* and rest. When she was rested, she could think clearly again and decide what to do, and how to get somewhere safe.

Maestra Lu was haggard from a night spent first in grief and anxiety, then a rush of hope. She leaned tiredly on the doorjamb of Magister Mkel's apartment and knocked weakly. Cathrin opened the door almost immediately, and drew a sharp breath when she saw Lu.

"Maestra!" she cried gently. "Why, whatever . . . You should have sent your Housewoman to us!"

"No, I am fine, Cathrin," Lu said. "And there was no time. Please get Mkel for me, would you?"

"Of course, of course I will," Cathrin fussed, leading Lu to a soft chair near a window. She did not actually touch her, but her warmth was almost tangible as she hovered over Lu. "But let me get you some tea."

"After," Lu said. "I must see the Magister immediately."

Cathrin disappeared into another room and returned in a moment with Mkel, still arranging his dark tunic. He carried his furred boots in his hand, and sat to pull them on.

"Mkel, something has happened to Sira," Lu said without preamble.

"Maestra?" he said, and waited, one boot still in his hand.

"Last night, something took place . . . I felt it. I thought she was dead." Cathrin gasped, but Mkel held up his hand.

"Where was she?" he asked.

"I cannot tell," Lu said wearily. "Far away."

"There was a congress at Lamdon," Mkel said. "It is possible she was there. But that is too far for you to hear her, surely."

Lu shrugged that off. "Something happened to her, and through the night I could not feel her at all. Then, this morning, at first light, I heard her clearly for just a moment. There has been a tragedy of some kind, and she is involved. We must send riders to Bariken immediately."

"But how could you hear anything so far away, Maestra?" whispered Cathrin.

Lu shook her head. "I have learned not to question my Gift."

"And so have we," Mkel said, with a little smile. He thrust his foot into his boot and stood up. "I will dispatch riders to Bariken immediately."

"They will need a Singer, someone strong," Lu said urgently. "No time must be wasted."

Mkel nodded, and Cathrin wrung her hands. "Now will you drink some tea, Maestra?" she asked. "And then you must rest. You look exhausted."

Lu leaned back in her chair, her strength ebbing. "Tea, yes. I will rest when the party is on its way."

A Housewoman brought Lu some tea and *keftet* while she waited for news. Magister Mkel went immediately to the great room, where the House was assembling for the morning meal, and was back soon after with two riders and a burly, blond itinerant.

"Maestra, of course you know Jane, and Gram," Mkel said. The two riders bowed to Lu. "And this"—Mkel indicated the itinerant—"is the Singer Theo."

Theo bowed also, and Lu inclined her head to him.

"Something is happening with Cantrix Sira at Bariken," Mkel told the three. "The Maestra has heard something, and feels the Cantrix is in great danger." Jane and Gram simply nodded. Theo frowned, not really understanding, but he was silent, waiting.

"There is no time to lose," Maestra Lu said in a low voice. "Jane, Gram, please do all you can to find her."

"We will ride immediately," Jane said. "To Bariken, then?"

Lu nodded. "I do not know where she is. You will need to begin at Bariken." She turned to the itinerant, who was watching her, waiting for information that would make sense to him. "Singer Theo," Lu said. "This is of the greatest importance. Will you help us?"

He bowed as elegantly as any Cantor. "Of course I will help, Maestra," he replied, and she found his voice resonant and reassuring. He then turned to Mkel for instructions. "Magister?"

"Yes," Mkel said, leading the way out of the apartment. "We'll make arrangements now for provisions and mounts."

A moment later the room was empty except for Cathrin and Lu. Lu leaned back weakly in the chair and closed her eyes. Cathrin watched her for a moment, and then brought out a soft-cured *caeru* rug and draped it around the Maestra. Lu took a deep, sighing breath, and fell asleep.

CHAPTER
ELEVEN

✳ SNOW AND WIND HARASSED SIRA AS SHE STRUGGLED TO put some distance between herself and the campsite. Her muscles strained, and blood trickled steadily down her back where the arrow had been. Her skin was cold and clammy, and she felt as if her head were floating free of her body. As if from another lifetime she remembered Maestro Nikei talking about the effects of bleeding. The remedies circled vaguely through her mind as she pressed on. None of them were available to her now.

When she judged she had waded through the powder for an hour, working her way off the main road into the forest, she finally allowed herself to collapse against an ironwood tree. Weakly, she reached into her tunic for her *filla*, feeling that she could go no farther until she was warm all the way through.

Sira's Gift almost failed her at that difficult moment. When she took a breath to play, her injury stunned her with pain. Her lips were cold and shaky, and her mind fluttered with fatigue and weakness. Her psi felt as distant as the safety of the Conservatory, and for one terrifying moment she could not think of the mode she needed.

She stiffened her resolve. "I have not come this far," she muttered aloud, "to let my body get the better of me." The iron will that had got her through the nightmarish hours under the snow cleared her thoughts. She bit at her lips to increase the circulation, and began to play. No emotion, no physical sensation, did she allow her mind to register until a slender, intense *quiru* was born about her, as warm as she could make it under the circumstances.

Then, while her body warmed, she gave in at last, and sobbed under the furs for her pain and fear and betrayal.

Several hours passed while she rested and the heat of her *quiru* did its work. As her mind cleared, she remembered that she should drink, and she used her *filla* again, the briefest *Doryu* melody, to melt snow in a hardwood cup from her pack, and she drank the icy water that tasted of wood and rock. She had a little food, a gift package of dried fruit and nuts that Cantrix Sharn had pressed on her when she departed Lamdon. It had been only two days ago, but it seemed almost past remembering.

She chewed some dried fruit and some of the nuts, and began to feel stronger. She could think of no way to bandage her wound, but the steady trickle of blood seemed to have ceased for the moment. She pressed some cloth from her pack between her back and the tree, thrusting it down inside her tunic as best she could. The wound in front, below her collarbone, was already closed and scabbing.

She decided to rest the night through before setting out. It seemed to her that Lamdon was the only safe place for her to go, and it was the closest House she knew of. Perhaps if she went back to the road and took her bearings, she could find the way.

It was hard to take in what had happened. Mike and Alks had been part of a plan to assassinate Magister Shen, she knew, and neither they nor Wil or Trude had cared who died with him. Sharn, and even Magret, had tried to warn her, but she had been too stupid to see how bad the situation was with Shen and his House. What had she missed? What evidence had she, in her eagerness to go to Lamdon, ignored?

A picture rose in her mind of Rhia, now a beautiful, pale widow, Magistrix at last, flanked by Wil and Trude. Perhaps it had been Wil who conceived the intrigue. Surely Trude was not so clever. And Alks and Mike? They would straggle in to Bariken, no doubt, with a dramatic story of storm and separation, a not unheard-of tragedy in the Mariks; so sad, everyone would say, the loss of the brilliant young Cantrix.

Sira shook her head. There was no way for her to know, now, what was happening at Bariken, or whom she had most to fear. She was convinced, however, that she must hide the fact of her survival until she reached safety. Cantrix Sharn, she thought, will know what I must do. Until I can reach her, it is up to me to protect myself.

Shen's party had come one long day's ride by *hruss* from Lamdon. Sira thought that it would probably take her three days to cover the same distance on foot. Accepting the necessity, she rolled herself in her furs and settled down to a healing sleep for her first night alone in the mountains. Outside her solitary *quiru* the snowflakes performed a menacing dance in the cold and wind.

I can do it, thought Sira. One step at a time, I can do it.

It did not occur to her that Maestra Lu could have heard her thoughts at such a great distance, and that it would make all the difference.

While Sira was trying to sleep and mend high in Ogre Pass, the riders from Conservatory, having pressed hard all day, were halfway to Bariken. Jane and Gram, longtime members of Conservatory, were completely dedicated to the Singers. Maestra Lu and Magister Mkel had been very sure that something unthinkable had occurred, and they were determined to wrest information from Bariken and to rescue

Sira. Because they had no details, only Lu's incredible report of Sira's crisis, they would go bravely and blindly into Bariken and reveal just what Sira desperately needed to conceal: that she was still alive.

Lu was at that moment telling Isbel: *I have heard Sira's thoughts, and I know she lives, but it is hard to follow her. I keep trying. Mkel sent two of our most loyal riders to Bariken when I heard her last night. We must save her. Nevya needs her; and I need her.*

Isbel gripped Lu's frail hands in her own, and she wept as she prayed for her friend's safety.

Sira rested well that night, under the circumstances. She was eighteen, and sleep came easily, without regard for her pain and fear. She woke once to replenish her faltering *quiru*, the wind having torn at it through the night, and then she slept again. It was bright day when she woke, the *quiru* looking faded and tired in the light of morning. Sira woke with her wound stiff, but manageable, and she rolled out of her furs quickly.

She made a brief meal of dried fruit and nuts, and put away what little was left. Then she hoisted the pack to her shoulders again and set out. The danger, she thought, was in getting lost. She could manage without food for a while, if need be, but if she failed to find her way back to Lamdon, she could eventually starve. Food was not easily come by in the Mariks.

The road they had followed to Lamdon and partway back again was one established mostly by tradition and landmarks, and very little by any improvements. Once in a while trees that blocked the way had been cut down, or rocks moved aside. But constant snowfall shrouded Ogre Pass most of the year and footprints rarely lasted more than a few hours. In places, the steeply sloping sides of the pass were invisible from the road.

Still, Sira knew that Lamdon was northeast of Bariken, and with a rough idea of that in her head, she was fairly confident she could find her way. She could not allow herself any doubts, and fashioned images in her mind of her welcome by Cantrix Sharn at Lamdon, making mental beacons to guide her to safety.

She intended to start her trek by returning to the campsite where Magister Shen and Rollie still lay entombed in the snow. The landmarks there she knew she would recognize, and she thought she could take more accurate bearings. Though it meant retracing an hour's worth of steps, it seemed the most prudent beginning.

The wind had died down with the coming of day, which gave her the added protection of her acute hearing, to detect the approach of any riders. By this time, she was sure, Wil and Trude and the two riders with them had reached Bariken, and were perhaps even now sending messages about the untimely accident that had taken the lives of Bariken's Magister, its junior Cantrix, and one faithful rider. She felt a pang, thinking how grieved Maestra Lu would be, believing her dead.

Sira was correct in most of her assumptions. Alks and Mike had dragged themselves into Bariken at dusk the night before with the tale of three of their party lost in the snowstorm in the Pass. No one at Bariken, with a single exception, even knew that Wil and Trude had ever been out of the House. Late that afternoon, the riders from Conservatory and the messengers from Bariken bearing bad news would meet each other on the road. By afternoon of the next day, the Conservatory riders would be at Bariken insisting on a search party.

Sira, unlike the Bariken and Conservatory riders, did not

make good time. Her injury was beginning to heal, but the bleeding had weakened her, and the deep powder was difficult to negotiate in many places. Her visual memory was good, though, and she found the campsite easily enough, remembering the configuration of the clearing and the ironwood trees around it.

The bodies were even more deeply covered by snow, but Sira, after several moments of straining her ears for signs of life in the surrounding mountains, uncovered them to retrieve what food they had in their packs. It was a tiny cache. Rollie had a little dried *caeru* meat, and Shen a very small flask of wine which Sira disdained. A Cantrix, even in a desperate situation, must never touch wine. Almost as an afterthought, Sira took Shen's long-handled knife to thrust through her belt next to Rollie's. She had never used one except to rid herself of Mike's arrow, but she thought it might be useful. She intended to survive.

With a last glance around the site, she decided there was nothing else to be done there, and she turned her back on its horrible memories and began plowing her way back up the road to Lamdon.

CHAPTER
TWELVE

✳ THE SINGER THEO FEARED THAT HIS TIRED MUSCLES
would fail him by the time he and the two
Conservatory riders galloped wearily into the courtyard at
Bariken. He didn't know how the *hruss* had survived the
pace the riders had forced on them since leaving the
Conservatory stables. He himself was utterly exhausted, and
he fell more than slid out of the high-cantled saddle. He had
been an itinerant Singer more than half his life, and was a
big-shouldered, saddle-hardened man of six summers, but
this journey had been exceptional. Gram and Jane, who had
neither rested nor eaten since dawn that morning, had to be
almost past endurance as well, but they refused refreshment,
demanding to be taken at once to the Magistrix of Bariken.
Night was hard on their heels as they entered the House.

Bowing to the Magistrix now, in her spacious windowed
apartment, Theo was uncomfortably aware of how sweaty
and disheveled they must all be. Never, in the all too many
Houses he had worked for, had he encountered a woman
more beautiful than this one. Wishing he looked more
presentable, he tried to smooth his blond hair, but it sprang
back immediately into a thick, curling tangle.

Gram and Jane spoke urgently of Maestra Lu's psi
impressions, as Rhia bent her glossy head and listened, and
Theo tried to ignore his trembling legs. He had heard this

story in detail at Conservatory, but he listened again, struggling to comprehend how even a Conservatory-trained Cantrix could pick up thoughts at such a great distance as Lu claimed to have done.

Theo's own training, several generations removed from Conservatory, had never suggested such possibilities. His parents, who had been itinerant Singers like their parents before them, had refused to consider Conservatory as an option. As the rest of the people did, his parents revered the Cantrixes and Cantors who warmed and protected the Houses, but they never aspired to the Cantoris for themselves or for their son. They were proud of the accomplishments of their line, and they were satisfied. They had offered Theo no other choices.

Now the Magistrix herself was speaking.

"Is it really possible?" she said gently, her eyes clear and sympathetic in her smooth face. "Could your Maestra have heard someone's thoughts at such a distance?"

"Maestra Lu can," Gram insisted. Jane nodded, her face lined with worry. Both stood straight, denying fatigue, intense in their purpose. They were thin and weather-worn. Gram's face was angry, and Jane's was worried. "We need your riders to go back up the Pass with us, at the earliest possible hour tomorrow."

"Of course," Magistrix Rhia said. "And of course, we all hope Cantrix Sira is, in fact, alive." Her Housekeeper, long-limbed and dark, sat still as stone behind her, while she leaned forward in her big carved chair, concern in every line of her graceful body.

"We all feel the loss of our young Cantrix very deeply," she went on. "You must have met our messengers on the road."

"We did," Gram said. "They went on to Conservatory."

Rhia turned then to her Housekeeper. "Wil, please arrange for the search party without delay."

He stood immediately and bowed. "At first light, please," Jane begged. "There may be no time to lose."

Theo was impressed by their intensity, their determination to save their young charge. He felt envy again, his old, unwelcome companion. He thrust it aside. It was pointless.

"Our men will be ready to ride with you at dawn," Wil assured them. "Now let me arrange baths and beds for you."

"Yes," said the Magistrix. "You must rest. You will want to be fresh. Singer, you will ride with them tomorrow? We need our Cantrix Magret here. She is all we have now."

Theo bowed with ironic elegance, aware of how grimy he must look. "Of course, Magistrix. Conservatory hired me for this purpose."

The three travelers followed Wil out the door. Theo didn't know which he wanted more, hot food or a bed or a bath, but he meant to make the most of each. He was, however, to be kept from them for some time yet, by urgent questions from an anxious and saddened Magret, a lonely, overworked Cantrix desperately worried about her young colleague.

At dawn the search party gathered in the courtyard, the Conservatory riders having met with Alks and Mike for the first time over a quick breakfast in the great room. Both the Bariken men were taciturn, large and grim-faced. Theo was still tired from the unaccustomed pace of the day before, but was eager to be moving. At least out in the forests of Ogre Pass, he would feel at home again. He shivered inside his *caeru* furs. These northern mountains felt the beginning of the deep cold sooner than the southern timberlands he had traveled through last.

Jane was a shadowy blur in the twilit morning, her breath a shifting cloud before her hood. Gram raised his hand to the two Bariken riders, and the party was off, the *hruss* slogging through deep powder from the snow that had fallen during the night. Alks and Mike led the way, and Theo trailed behind Jane and Gram. With a little chill of apprehension, he noticed that Jane had a long knife strapped to her waist. He was sure it hadn't been there before, and wondered as they rode what intuition had caused her to arm herself so visibly.

As the light grew, Theo saw that all the riders but himself were carrying weapons. Tension flickered under his breastbone. Only once before had he been inadvertently involved in violence between humans; usually the struggle between man and the environment was enough to occupy those who lived on the Continent. As the saying goes, he thought, the drifts are deep in this one. His senses sharpened, and the very air seemed alive with danger.

The powdery snow that hindered the search party's progress also obscured the hoofprints of the *hruss* that had preceded it. Two other riders had risked the dangers of the predawn cold to gain the necessary advantage of a head start, and now they were pushing their mounts up into the Pass as fast as they were able.

At Conservatory, feeling like a *wezel* in a cage, Maestra Lu suffered in her tiny room, wrestling with her fears. She was long past being strong enough to make wild rides into the Mariks. Her physical limitations made her a captive. So despite her longing to be with Gram and Jane, she was obliged to fret and pray and wait, in the age-old manner of mothers.

Sira awoke from her second night alone in Ogre Pass stronger, but very hungry. She had seen a *wezel* the night before as she called up her *quiru*, but the little meatless creature hardly seemed worth the trouble of trying to kill it. This morning she felt she could have eaten even its scruffy hide.

There was a scrap of dried *caeru* meat left, and she chewed it as she broke camp, putting the snow in her mouth for enough moisture to be able to swallow it. She saved the last of the dried fruit for midday, hoping she might come across a living *caeru* today, and be swift enough to bring it down. There was so little wildlife in the mountains, and she had no desire to encounter a *ferrel* by herself, although she supposed if the feathers could be pulled off, there might be some meat on the long bones. She had seen one as a child, swooping down from a mountaintop and picking up a *caeru* pup in its beak as if it were weightless. She could not bring herself even to think of the *tkir*. She only promised herself an early *quiru*, so there would be no risk of being caught by darkness.

She told herself she could make it to Lamdon with no food if she had to. She had walked all day yesterday, although without great speed, and thought that two more days should get her there. She hoped her sense of direction was adequate. A lifetime spent within the walls of her parents' House, Conservatory, and then Bariken had not prepared her for this.

She walked through the day, stopping only to finish off the dried fruit. She scooped snow into her mouth, sucking on it until it was melted, then taking more, feeling almost constantly thirsty. The storm seemed to have passed over. The sky was gray, but the clouds were high over the peaks, and no more snow fell. By evening, Sira felt she had been walking alone through deep powder all her life, as if her memories of Houses and other people were only dreams. She felt entirely alone in a cold white world.

Her muscles ached with the unaccustomed exertion, and

her wounded shoulder was stiff as she sat against a softwood tree at last and dug out her little *filla*. What would she have done if the *filla* had not been left to her? She shuddered to think of it. Darkness slipped over the mountains as she played her little first-mode melody.

The *quiru* grew around her, her fragile little home, all there was between her and the malignant night. She warned herself firmly to stay alert. It was hard, though, so very hard. The emptiness of her belly made her feel euphoric and disconnected.

She settled in under her furs. The *quiru* hung suspended and still in the air, undisturbed by any breeze. Only the creaking of the ironwood trees around her campsite disturbed the silence of the night.

As her eyes grew heavy and her mind drifted, Sira thought in her hunger that she saw the rounded, furry back of a yearling *caeru* pup slipping up to her *quiru*. She imagined she could see the yellow-white blotch on the snow just inside the *quiru*, and that she smelled the acrid odor of its breath. Only her eyes showed out of her own *caeru* furs, and she dreamed that she and the animal looked the same, curled on the snow, two mounds of yellow-white fur in the glow of the *quiru*.

There was a faint cry, distinct and insistent, in her mind, and Sira could not resist its direction.

A half-grown *caeru* pup lay within the circle of light. The *caeru* was as beguiled as she, and lay drowsing in the warmth of the *quiru*, unaware that the other furry mound was not one of its own.

Lost in the strange dream, Sira slowly reached for one of her knives. Slipping it out from beneath the furs, she felt its shape and heft, and measured her target. She tested the action in her mind before she moved; and then she leaped at the animal. Her knife went true, just behind the foreleg and up, straight to the heart of the sleeping *caeru*.

She jumped aside as the *caeru* twisted in its death throes, but not quickly enough. A long yellowed claw caught her forehead, and the hot blood streamed over her cheek. She could not get near enough to cut its throat, but had to wait as it pumped out its lifeblood over the snow.

Plucking a bit of fur from her bedroll, she pressed it over the gash in her forehead. There was no time to worry about this new wound. She carved out the animal's heart and the liver, eating them warm and raw and dripping, standing there in her *quiru* under the lonely stars.

Maestra Lu released the long and fragile tendrils of her thought at last. She could no longer keep her mind extended so far, reaching desperately out into the wilderness. Commanding the *caeru* had taken all her energy. She put down the *filhata* that had been her tool and leaned her head in her hands.

If the *caeru* hunters knew, she thought, they would give me no rest. She smiled wearily and triumphantly to herself. She was sure that Sira was no longer so hungry or so weak. Lu had never reached so far, with such effect, before. There had never been such need. But the effort had taken all her energy, and it had been two days since she had slept a full night or eaten properly.

All at once her reserves of strength were gone. Lu collapsed, unconscious, and her Housewoman found her lying on the cold stone floor the next morning.

By the light of the same morning, Sira stared unbelievingly at the *caeru* carcass inside the fading boundary of her *quiru*. A thousand questions tumbled through her mind. Had she really done this, or had it been a hunger-induced nightmare? She had never killed anything in her life.

She looked down at her hands, shocked and rather queasy to find them crusted with blood, the nail rims dark. Then she nodded to herself, grimly. "At least it is not my blood," she muttered.

Her own blood had dried uncomfortably on her forehead, but fearful that this new wound would bleed again if she cleaned it, she left it as it was, crudely bandaged with a scrap of *caeru* fur.

Before departing the campsite, she clumsily carved out what meat she thought she could carry, wrapping the grisly bits in a section of hide to put in her pack. Soon she was walking again, finding the Pass growing steeper and steeper as she toiled through the snow. The remains of her kill were frozen solid when those who came behind discovered them.

CHAPTER
THIRTEEN

✴ SIRA'S SENSE OF DIRECTION SERVED HER WELL, AND SHE
worked her way through Ogre Pass to the northeast
almost exactly retracing the steps of the trip from Lamdon.
The broad floor of the Pass gave her confidence that she
could not lose her way, and the wind blew the snow flat and
smooth, making it much easier to walk on than the deep
powder under the trees.

She made her camp when darkness began to shade the
mountain peaks around the horizon. Her *quiru* trembled in
the wind, and she felt the vastness of the Continent all
around her. Once she thought she heard a distant roar. It
might have been only the soughing of the wind in the
treetops, but it made her think of the *tkir* and remember
Rollie's warnings. She made her *quiru* even stronger then,
bright and warm, but still she felt very small and vulnerable,
and thinking of Rollie grieved her. The hours of darkness
were noticeably longer now than they had been only a week
before, and for Sira they were an eternity of loneliness.

The night passed without incident. She felt infinitely
stronger for having eaten. In the morning she pressed on,
her pack bouncing lightly against her back, the pain of the
injury there somewhat diminished. She kept her *filla* close
to her body, inside her tunic, the most essential tool of her

survival, and the two long knives were stuck through her belt, near at hand.

At midday she rested and forced down more of the raw *caeru*, refusing to gag at the texture and taste of uncooked meat. She remembered with longing the platter of nursery fruits and the nuts she had barely touched at Lamdon.

She grew hot with the exertion of her climb, but knew better than to remove her furs and feel the bite of the cold. She was grateful for the distant pale sun that illumined the tops of the trees and which occasionally reached past their branches to fall on the road she followed. The snow had stopped, and Sira muttered thanks to the Spirit of Stars for being able to see her path clearly.

The two furtive riders who had discovered her *caeru* kill on their second day out from Bariken were thankful as well that no snow was falling. The tracks created by Sira's passage on the windswept snow of the Pass marked her way as clearly as any signpost, and they also pressed on, tensely aware of how near they were coming to Lamdon. Their *hruss* had been near exhaustion when they rested the night before, but now were well-fed and strong, and paced up through the Pass on their broad hooves at three times the speed of their quarry.

Gram and Jane, with the Singer Theo and the riders Alks and Mike, were fully a half-day behind. Their pleas for more haste had been answered with only slight satisfaction, and their mounts, provided by Bariken, were no match for the rugged *hruss* they had ridden from Conservatory and almost worn out. Theo wondered why Bariken had no strong mounts to offer.

Theo chafed under the strain in his traveling party. Even with the pressing need that had brought them out into the Mariks, he preferred conversation to the grim silence that gripped them all. Alks and Mike were particularly close-mouthed.

The two secret riders were almost upon their quarry, although Sira had walked hard after her midday rest, thinking she might just reach Lamdon before dark.

Topping a rise, she stepped around an outcropping of rock that thrust up through the snowpack. She was about to cross a little gully when she felt the sharp, warning prickle of her psi. It was almost four days since she had any contact with living humans, and her senses were instantly alert, with an almost physical sensation, as if she had heard a loud noise in the silent forest.

The nightmare experiences of the last few days had turned a naive and trusting young woman into a wary, defensive creature. This new Sira wasted no time in wondering about her instincts, but instantly cast about for a hiding place.

The snow was so deep at the sides of the road, and so easily marked, that she could see no way to leave the road without making enormous tracks. There were the irontrees, of course, but their branches began far above her head, affording no cover or escape.

She walked on, hurrying, with her mind open to receive whatever clues might come her way. Someone's mind, obviously, was insufficiently shielded, or she would have received no warning at all. Now, as she concentrated, she could feel little tendrils of uneasy thought leaking from the careless one, like smoke curls from a cooking fire. Someone, she thought, was very agitated. And that someone was not far away.

Sira was out of breath, dripping with perspiration under her furs, and her thigh muscles burned as she traversed the deep drifts. Struggling over the far side of the arroyo, and looking down at the long valley below her, she wasted a

moment in gasping for breath. The day had grown clear, and
the air was so light and empty that she could see the peaked
roofs of Lamdon and the great curve of the nursery gardens
behind them, about four hours away, on the steep slope at
the end of the valley. So near did they seem, she felt she
could reach out and touch them. The danger she sensed
behind her was much closer.

On the near slope of the valley there was a little stand of
softwood trees, young and slender, the branches of several
just an arm's reach above her head. Her shoulder was still
stiff and painful, and she wasn't sure she had the strength to
pull herself up. But she had to try, and as she loosened her
pack enough to free her arms, she thanked the spirit of the
little *caeru* that had given her its life's energy.

She chose the thickest tree. With a little prayer, she
jumped off the snow and grasped a low limb with both
hands. It hurt, but she scrabbled with her feet for extra
purchase and pulled herself up, grunting, bit by painful bit.
Fresh blood leaked from the wound in her back, but she
hardly noticed it, so hot was she from exertion.

She straddled the lowest limb at last. The ones above
were much thinner, but offered more camouflage, and she
climbed until she thought she had gone as high as she dared
without breaking through one of the branches.

She stood with her legs braced on different levels of the
tree, her back pressed against the spongy bark, and she
could look down through the leaves and see the road below.
She felt like a *caeru* at bay with hunters closing in. In a last
attempt to save herself, she concentrated all her psi energy
into one powerful broadcast for help, knowing that the mind
leaking warnings behind her would hear it, too. But she
knew now that she was trapped, and all her instincts for
survival went into a long, silent scream of terror.

*   *   *

Half a day's ride behind her, the Singer Theo's blue eyes went wide as he heard the scream in his mind. He had experienced only the roughest of psi impressions since his childhood; his parents had carefully taught him to close his mind to them. Now this one broke through, with incredible strength and a definite impression of distance. Crude though the cry was, Theo was certain of what he had heard.

"Jane! Gram!" he cried aloud, trying to urge his inadequate *hruss* forward to catch up with the Conservatory riders. "I've heard something . . . something I've never . . . I heard the Cantrix, in my mind! She's up there! She's in danger. Now!" He could hardly believe he had received all of that, but he was absolutely sure he was right.

Jane pierced him with a glance, then nodded to Gram, and the two kicked their weary *hruss* into a gallop, forcing them past Alks and Mike and on up the road at a run. The two Bariken riders looked back at Theo, and then hurried their own *hruss* to catch up.

Theo's instincts were sharp from living all his life on the road. He knew in his gut what they had to fear in that moment. With a hoarse cry, he kicked his *hruss*, hard, brutalizing it into a faster pace.

"Gram!" he shouted. "Watch out! Watch out behind you! They—"

He saw Alks draw his long knife and turn his *hruss* back. Theo had no time even to try to slow his own *hruss* as Alks threw the knife at him with wicked speed. He watched it come for what seemed an interminable time, until suddenly it reached him and the impact knocked him completely off his *hruss*. He fell hard on his back into the snow.

Theo was immobilized with shock, his breath gone, unsure how badly he was wounded, or even if he was still living. He heard the cries of the four other riders as from a distance, knowing a battle ensued, but unable to tell who was victorious. Before it was over, the darkness closed over his head. He tried to resist, but it was as sure and complete as mid-night in the mountains.

Sira waited, the mental spill from one of her pursuers tormenting her until her nerves were on fire with suspense. And now she could hear them with her ears, too. They were making no effort at quiet and every effort at speed. She knew one of them must have heard her silent cry for help; one of them was Gifted. And her call forced them to deal with her as swiftly as possible.

Two strong *hruss* charged over the rise into the valley. With curses, they were reined in. There were a few moments of casting about for her path, but only a few.

Sira recognized their voices before she saw their faces. In a very short time, Wil, the Housekeeper of Bariken, and Trude, the former Cantrix, had found their way to her softwood tree, and were peering up into its branches.

Wil's voice and dark eyes were so familiar and redolent of easier times that when he spoke, Sira could almost have believed his words.

"Cantrix Sira, are you there? You must come down, and let us carry you safe to Lamdon. This political struggle has nothing to do with you."

Sira gritted her teeth. Her breath whistled slightly through her throat, and her legs were trembling with fatigue where they were braced on the branches.

"Cantrix Sira?" This time the words were in the sweet, low-pitched tones of the Conservatory. Trude pressed her *hruss* closer to the tree. Hers was the mind inadequately shielded. Trude's mental discipline had been too long unexericised. Nevertheless, she tried to project sympathy and safety into her voice. She forced her psi; any second-level Conservatory student would have been shamed by the attempt.

"Sira, you poor thing, you must be so frightened. You've been alone up here so long! I'm sure you need hot food and a bath and . . ."

Sira could not help herself. Hot temper flooded her mind. In a fury, and without making a sound, she sent an angry blast of psi to Trude that made the older woman gasp in mid-sentence.

Traitorous bitch, Sira sent. *You are not fit to touch a true Cantrix!*

She heard Trude mutter something to Wil, and then there was a time of ominous and utter silence.

Theo struggled up from the depths of darkness to reach consciousness once again. Something was touching him, pressing tightly against his stomach. With difficulty, he forced his eyes open to see Gram bending over him, tying something around his middle, under his furs.

"Theo," said the rider, his voice tight and harsh. "Can you hear me?"

Theo grunted, trying to say yes. No sound emerged. He caught Gram's eyes and nodded a little. The muscles of his face were still stiff with shock.

"We need to hurry, and that means we have to leave you here for a while." Theo's eyes tried to close again and his head lolled, but he exerted all the will he had to remain conscious. "You'll need a *quiru* in about five hours," Gram went on, "and we'll be back for you, but maybe not till morning."

Theo made a great effort, and forced his rigid tongue to work.

"Cover me," he rasped. "In case . . ."

Gram nodded at him; he had no time for emotions.

"Jane's hurt, too, but she says she can ride, and I need her. I think you ought to try to stay awake. You shouldn't bleed anymore, now." While he was talking, Gram was spreading Theo's bedroll over and under the wounded man, and tucking him tightly into it. Theo could see Alks's knife lying in the snow where Gram had tossed it after removing it from Theo's body.

Both men were aware that Theo would freeze to death when dusk fell if he was unable to call up a *quiru*. Gram did not waste time apologizing, nor did the Singer expect it. There was no question of choice between the life of an itinerant Singer and that of a Conservatory-trained Cantrix.

"Got your *filla*?" Gram asked roughly. Theo felt with his fingers until he had it in his hand. When he nodded, Gram touched his shoulder once and then disappeared from Theo's line of sight.

Theo fixed his eyes on a nearby ironwood tree and listened to the sounds of the two *hruss* departing. He was determined to remain conscious. He had to wait for some strength to seep back into his muscles. He was warm, at least for the moment, but he was too weak now to resist a flood of yearning as he thought of the devotion Gram and Jane felt for the young Cantrix. He did not question their decision to leave him here. There had been no alternative.

Suddenly Theo realized he didn't know what had become of Alks and Mike. He craned his neck to look about him until he saw two furry mounds lying where they had fallen in the snow. There was no movement in them. Three *hruss* stood waiting nearby, shifting their weight uneasily, still saddled and burdened. Only Theo's bedfurs had been removed.

Theo fell back, breathing hard. Dead. Gram and Jane had killed these two. As one of those now dead had tried to kill him. Well, he thought to himself, I don't feel like dying this afternoon. He reached inside his tunic for the bit of metal that had been his mother's, and held it in his hand. He kept his eyes open, but lay very still, gathering his strength. One thing he knew well, and that was how to heal the injuries that inevitably befell those who plied the snowy roads of the Continent. Weakly, he concentrated his psi on the wound in his belly. He had little energy, but he could at least try to slow the bleeding. If only, he thought, he could stay awake.

Sira's softwood tree began to tremble, and she knew someone was coming up. It was so much easier for Wil, because he had his big mountain *hruss* to stand on, and had only to step up a little way to be on the bottommost branch.

Sira looked above her for a way to escape, but the boughs over her head were so thin, already shaking with the impact of the Housekeeper's approach, that she was sure they would never hold her. There was no way out.

Her breathing grew slow and even, and she felt detached from her body, as her mind surrendered to her instinct. She became, in a way, that trapped *caeru*.

She could not remember drawing Shen's long knife out of her belt. Except for having used it with surprising effect on the *caeru* in camp two nights before, she had never used one for so much as slicing bread. Now she held it in her fist, the point down, her long, wiry arm held behind her and away from her body as the tree shivered and swayed under Wil's weight.

It did not take him long to reach her. He wasn't concerned about his own safety, now that they had found her. She was a Singer, after all, and he knew them to be a gentle breed, soft, even effete. Certainly not dangerous. And so he did not hesitate, but climbed higher and higher until he could see her face at last through the quaking branches of the softwood tree.

Sira could see him, too. His eyes were narrowed and his purpose was unmistakable. She breathed deeply, slowly, concentrating.

Keeping the knife behind her, she worked her way around to the opposite side of the tree, and heard with satisfaction Wil's curse as he struggled to follow. He weighed more than she, and the branches had begun to bend and crack under him.

At last he reached the branches she had been standing on, and she saw his brown, lean hand reaching around the trunk. Her breath was steady now. She had not made a sound since they had found her.

Wil reached with a long leg for a limb on Sira's side of the swaying tree. Having found a foothold, he pulled his body around with his hand.

Just as he came around the tree, fully in her sight, Sira switched the knife in her hand so that it pointed out, away from her. The moment Wil pulled himself up beside her, she gathered all her strength and plunged the long blade into him, past the skin and muscle, as far into his body as she could thrust it.

Part of her mind knew that the memory of the act, of the resistance of flesh and tendon and muscle to the knife, would be too ghastly to bear, but at this moment her mind was dissociated from these events. She had stabbed Wil hard, and when he fell crashing through the tree branches, the knife went with him. She had had no chance to pull it out, nor would she have been strong enough. Her hand was shockingly empty when she looked down at it, the air suddenly cold and fresh against her palm.

As if from a great distance, Sira heard Trude screaming and screaming, not mentally but physically, as Wil, already dead, thudded to the packed snow under the softwood tree. Sira heard her, but felt no pity.

Shut up, she sent, in a cold fury.

Trude ignored her, and the waves of shrill sound went on. Sira hissed aloud, "Shut up!" Still Trude screamed.

Sira had never used her psi for ill, not even taking part in the teasing dormitory games at Conservatory, which too often left younger students in tears. But she was more animal than Singer at that moment, all instinct and little reason. She gathered her energy one more time, and sent a tide of psi into Trude's mind, anything to stop her screaming.

Shut up or I will kill you too!

Trude gasped and was silent for a brief moment. Then she screeched at Sira, "You great idiot! Do you know what you've done? I'll see to it you never step foot in a Cantoris again, you whore, you . . ."

Sira did not stop to think. She cut through Trude's mind as brutally as a carver cuts through a chunk of ironwood with his *obis* knife. It was a wordless, formless impact with all the power of her great Gift behind it. Trude fell instantly, and quite permanently, silent.

Sira reached out then with her mind, seeking to see whether Trude still lived. The former Cantrix did, she found, still live and breathe, but she would be incapable of thought ever again. Her mind was completely, irretrievably, broken.

Sira could spare no sympathy at that moment. She pulled out her remaining knife, Rollie's knife, and held herself poised to strike again. Her eyes were cold and hard and the planes of her face were like chiseled stone.

Sira waited. She had no sense of passing time. Her mind and her emotions were frozen as solid as the blue ice of the Great Glacier.

It took four hours for Gram and Jane to reach her. She

only relaxed her muscles and began to move when she heard their voices beneath the tree.

"Cantrix Sira?" called Gram urgently. "Are you there? Sira? It's Gram, and Jane . . . from Conservatory. Maestra Lu sent us when you . . . when she . . ."

Sira's voice was dry and rusty as she answered. "I am here. I will come down."

"Are you hurt?" This from Jane, hurt rather badly herself, and exhausted, but her energy renewed by hearing Sira's voice.

"I was wounded three—no, four—days ago, but it is almost healed. I am well."

Sira appeared on the lowest branch of the swaying softwood tree. "I need a hand down, I think. I have not eaten in some time."

Gram and Jane together reached up to her, and she slipped down into their waiting arms. Trude was a huddle of yellow-white furs on the ground, crouched by Wil's inert body. Only when Gram had satisfied himself that his young charge was all right for the moment did he turn to her.

"Who is this?" he asked Sira.

"It is Trude v'Bariken." Sira spoke without inflection. "She is harmless now. Her mind is gone."

"Are you sure?" Jane had let go of Sira the instant she was safely on the ground, but she stayed so close, Sira could feel the warmth of the rider's breath against her own face.

"Yes," said Sira. "She was a Singer once."

"And this?" Gram prodded Wil's body with his booted toe.

"That was the Housekeeper of Bariken." Sira still spoke flatly. "His name was Wil. I have killed him. Is Maestra Lu all right?"

"She's very worried about you," Jane said.

There was no more talk. Sira's *filla* was brought out.

Gram busied himself bringing the *hruss* close, spreading out bedrolls, and bringing food and cups for melted snow. He rolled the Housekeeper's body away from their campsite, but pushed Trude onto a bed of furs. Her face was blank, and from time to time she moaned softly.

Sira played, and the *quiru* grew. When it glowed warmly around them, they ate, especially Sira. Her young, strong body craved nourishment. But her voice and her face remained distant. Gram and Jane looked at each other with dismay, but said nothing, only fussing over her, coaxing her to eat and drink just a bit more.

"Sleep now, Cantrix Sira," said Jane.

"We'll be at Lamdon by midday tomorrow," Gram added. Sira nodded, and lay down at once on her furs. Jane thrust Trude into her bedroll without gentleness, and then rolled into her own. Gram stoked up the little fire of softwood from his packs, preparing to stand watch.

"I hope Theo's all right," Jane called from her bed.

"So do I," said Gram. "He's good, for an itinerant."

"We'll send him help from Lamdon. We owe him for Sira's life."

"Maestra Lu will see he's repaid." There was a pause, and Gram added softly, "If he lives."

There was no answer from Jane's bedroll but a deep sighing breath as she eased into sleep. Trude seemed to be sleeping as well, but Gram saw that Sira's eyes were open, watching the stars twinkling beyond the *quiru*. Only when she felt his glance on her did she close them.

CHAPTER
FOURTEEN

★ THEO LOOKED UP AT THE PALE REMNANTS OF HIS *QUIRU* IN
the brilliant morning sun. Look at that, he thought,
still holding, and no one to admire it except three lonely
hruss.

It had been a long night, full of nervous wakings and odd
sounds exaggerated by solitude. The wound in his belly
ached, and he felt as weak as a newborn *caeru* pup, but he
was alive, and warm.

He wondered about the young Cantrix. She was ten years
younger than he, and she must have been alone in the
Mariks for at least three nights. Theo thought of Conservatory Singers as delicate and protected, their esoteric Gifts
nurtured and pampered like nursery flowers. His own career
had seasoned and tested him early, but an eighteen-year-old
Cantrix . . . In truth, he didn't expect to meet her alive.

He tried sitting up, but feeling a fresh wash of blood into
his bandages, decided against it. It seemed he would have to
lie here helplessly until someone came for him. His *filla* was
close at hand, and there was some food in his pack. There
was nothing for him to do but keep still and wait.

From time to time through the day and then through the
second night, Theo managed to play his *filla* just enough to
keep the *quiru* strong and warm around him. Breathing
deeply enough to play was painful, and so he kept his *quiru*

just big enough for himself and the *hruss*, who crowded close to be near the only living human in the camp, and to feel safe in the light. The legs of a corpse lying just inside the edge of the *quiru*, with the upper body abandoned to the darkness, made a surreal and chilling sight. As there was nothing Theo could do about it, he tried to remember not to look in that direction.

To pass the time, he tried to listen with his mind, to stimulate whatever reflex it was that had responded to Cantrix Sira's mental scream, that had come alive in that moment of great stress. But his efforts were wasted; he heard nothing but the wind stirring the branches of the ironwood trees. He could think of no other way to pass the long, empty hours.

On the second morning, he drifted out of a light doze to see *hruss* and riders coming in to the clearing where he lay. When he was sure he was really awake, and not dreaming, he grinned crookedly at the welcome sight of Gram, who dismounted quickly and bent over him.

"Hello, again," Theo said, his voice creaking with disuse. "Back so soon?"

Gram smiled down at him, tremendously relieved. It had gone against all his upbringing to leave a wounded man alone in the snow. "Thank the Spirit," he said. "No more lives lost."

Cantor Rico of Lamdon now knelt by Theo to examine his wound.

"This could have been fatal all by itself, Singer," he said gruffly. The Singers at Lamdon had been horrified at the offenses against two Gifted ones in this intrigue, notwithstanding that one was only an itinerant. Rico swallowed his anger before continuing. "You'll have to ride in a *pukuru*, so we can get you to safety."

"Just so I don't have to stay here another day, Cantor,"

said Theo with a painful attempt at a chuckle. "I'm tired of the view."

Rico lightly touched Theo's arm through his furs. "Good work, Singer." His voice was unsteady. "You will want to know that Cantrix Sira reached Lamdon safely. She and Jane will meet us on the way."

"Good news," said Theo, and then wearily closed his eyes. No more deaths, that was good. And now perhaps he could rest, at least for a while. He wondered where they would take him to heal, and allowed himself to hope that it might be Conservatory.

Cantor Rico cared for his wound, redoing the bandage before playing a healing *Doryu* melody on his *filla*. Theo could feel his flesh responding to Rico's psi, the warm, prickly sensation that left the wounded area tingling when it was over. Theo had often healed such wounds in others; it was a strange feeling to be the recipient rather than the giver. Rico finished his treatment by playing another melody, in the first mode this time, and Theo promptly fell into a sound, renewing sleep.

He slept a good deal that day, gently drawn along in a small *pukuru* behind one of the big *hruss*. The sound of the bone runners gliding over the snow beneath him was soporific, and the draught for pain that Rico had brought from Lamdon gave him a good deal of relief. He felt considerably stronger when the party stopped for the night.

As soon as he realized a campsite had been chosen, Theo automatically reached for his *filla* to call up the *quiru*. He paused abruptly with his hand on it, forestalled by the sound of one already playing nearby. The perfection of the tone, the intonation and liquid phrasing, overwhelmed him with emotion. In his weakness, hot tears formed behind his eyelids and he fought to resist them.

The *quiru* not of his making swelled around him with

incredible swiftness, and the warmth caressed the exposed skin of his face as he tried to twist his head to see who the Singer was.

Gram, watching over him, saw his efforts, and turned the *pukuru* so that the wounded man could look directly into the circle of people around the tiny campfire that was already crackling gently.

Theo saw the girl with the *filla* at her lips, a very tall, lean young woman with a bandage above one eye. He had no need of an introduction. When she stopped playing, the *quiru* complete, he regretted the cessation of that mesmerizing, silvery tone. She felt his gaze, and looked over at him.

"I owe you thanks, Singer," she said. Her voice was deep, and tired, too old a sound to be coming from such a young person.

"No thanks are necessary, Cantrix Sira," Theo said, his voice still weak and thready. "I am glad to see you . . . well." He had been going to say "alive," but felt it was perhaps not tactful.

"Yes, I am quite well," she said dryly. Their eyes met, and Theo knew she was quite aware of what he had almost said. He grinned at her, and although she did not smile, she nodded acknowledgment.

There was a flash of psi around the circle by the fire, and Theo looked at Cantor Rico, whose face was grim. Theo caught the feeling of the psi but did not know how to interpret it. That it had come from Rico was made clear by the look of him. Theo gritted his teeth in frustration.

He looked again at the Cantrix, and thought he could guess Cantor Rico's feelings. Sira's face was impassive, the lips set firmly together. The yellow light of the *quiru* made her bandage gleam dully, and her face looked sallow. Deep lines were etched in the youthful skin.

I am not the only one who needs to heal, Theo thought,

but my wound is only of the body. He was surprised to find his old friend envy supplanted by a wave of pity. He stirred restlessly, trying to ease the pull of his healing belly wound.

"May I help you sleep, Singer?" asked Rico, pulling his own bed of furs closer to the sled. Theo hesitated, hating his weakness, but then acquiesced. He felt weary and helpless. He closed his eyes and relaxed his mind as Rico began, in his deep voice, a short *cantrip* for sleep. It was easy, he found, to let the psi of the *cantrip* into his mind, to drop down into sleep. For Theo, who had been a Singer on his own for three summers, it was an experience that made him feel more a child than the independent man he had been for so long.

Hours later, with the *quiru* still strong in the utter blackness of the night, Theo woke again. He looked about the circle of sleeping forms. Only Sira was sitting up, her bedfurs pulled up around her shoulders, gazing into the graying embers of the fire.

Sensing Theo's gaze, she looked across at him. He raised one eyebrow in silent question, not wanting to disturb the other sleepers. Sira gave the slightest shake of her head and turned her eyes back to the fire.

Something fine has been destroyed in this misadventure, Theo thought. He closed his eyes again. What a pity, he mused as he fell asleep. What a waste.

CHAPTER
FIFTEEN

★ THEO HAD NEVER TRAVELED WITH SO LARGE A GROUP, nor had he often traveled in a group with another Singer since he was less than four summers old. Between the Conservatory and Lamdon, a party of twelve had been mounted, and Cantor Rico and Cantrix Sira were handling all the *quirus*.

Not, Theo admitted to himself, that he was up to participating. His belly was healing, but the enervating loss of blood he had suffered kept him drowsy. He spent the long hours of travel mostly in sleep.

By the second night of their journey to Conservatory, Theo had decided that Cantrix Sira was the most silent person he had ever met. She spoke only when spoken to, and then in the briefest of sentences. Her face was closed and unreadable, and he could see Rico and Jane exchanging worried glances over the young Singer's head. Theo wondered what exactly had happened up in Ogre Pass. No one offered to tell him.

Cantrix Sira insisted, in her silent way, on being the one to bring Theo his tea and *keftet* in the evenings. Tonight, as the others were helping themselves from the cooking pot over the fire, she knelt beside his furs and held out his bowl and cup.

148

"Cantrix, you shouldn't wait on me," he said, embarrassed.

"You must allow me to," she said in her odd deep voice, and then helped him to a sitting position, propping his saddlepack under his bedroll so he could lean against it. She did it so naturally that he forgot to be surprised at the touch of a full Cantrix. He took a deep sip of the tea.

"Join me, then," he said, his mouth quirking into his crooked grin. She looked at him somberly, the firelight glinting on the angles of her lean face. He thought she was going to refuse, but then she nodded, and he knew it was to indulge him. It was reason enough, he thought. She went to the fire and bent over it.

When she returned, her bowl held only a scant few mouthfuls of food. He looked into it and laughed without thinking, then gasped with pain when his belly wound reminded him it was still there.

It took him a moment to recover while Sira watched him, her bandaged eyebrow raised in question. "That little bit of food was hardly worth a trip to the fire, Cantrix," he said finally. She looked into the bowl and shook her head.

"Just not hungry?" he asked. She didn't answer. Theo said gently, "I know you've had a bad experience. You need to eat, though. When you're traveling, you need to eat and drink when you can."

She turned her angular face to him. "Thank you, Singer. I will." She took a spoonful of *keftet* and put it in her mouth.

"Cantrix." Theo cocked his head at her. "You should probably chew it, too." He wanted to make her smile. Obediently but solemn, Sira began to chew her food. Theo sighed and leaned back, carefully adjusting his bandages.

"If I were healthy, Cantrix," he said softly, "I'd sing you the song about the *ferrel* that picked up a *wezel* and then dropped it because it was too thin to bother with. Dropped it right into the courtyard of the House of Filus and they turned it into a pet. It got so fat it needed a room all its own, and when the *ferrel* came back for it, it was too heavy to carry." Theo's eyes twinkled at Sira, and despite herself she smiled a little at the silly image of a fat *wezel*.

"Is that the kind of song you like, Singer?" she asked.

"So it is," he said. "Also the only kind of song I know." This earned him another little smile. Theo quickly grew tired from the effort of talking, but he tried to conceal it. She saw his fatigue immediately.

"You must rest now, Singer," she said, and reached for his bowl and cup.

"Tomorrow," he said sleepily. "Tomorrow you must teach me a new song, Cantrix. One I don't know."

"Yes," she said. She helped him to lie down, moving his saddlepack to just within reach. "Now sleep," she told him, as if he were a boy instead of a man at least two summers older than she.

"Good night," he murmured. He felt warm and lazy, as if he were floating in a warm bath. A tickle in his mind, almost not there, said *Thank you* once again, but he was almost asleep, and not really sure he had heard it. If it had really been there, it would have marked the second time in his adult life he had truly heard someone's voice in his mind . . . both times the voice of this surprising young Cantrix.

Sira, from her saddle, was the first to see the roofs of Conservatory above the trees as the travelers made their slow way up the snowy ride. The pace of the journey had been leisurely, adjusted for the *pukuru* carrying Theo, and restricted by the shortening hours of daylight. It had taken six full days.

Sira looked at the fur-bundled figure of the itinerant and saw that he was sleeping again.

Turning back, she felt Cantor Rico's gaze on her, but pretended otherwise. She had carefully ignored the looks passing between Gram and Jane during the trip, and Gram's little worried frowns. There is nothing I can do to ease their fears, she thought with great sadness; anything I do or say to reassure them would be deception. She wanted only to see Maestra Lu, rest in her comforting presence, and unburden herself of the awful things she had done. The weight of memory was unbearable. Over and over again she remembered the slice of her psi through the fabric of Trude's mind, and the rush of triumph she had felt as the weaker mind broke under her attack. Only Maestra Lu could tell her how to live with the guilt of that moment.

The shaggy *hruss* filled the Conservatory courtyard with their noises and bulk, and a somber group appeared out of the great doors, assembling quickly on the steps. The day was brutally clear, the sun glancing off the snow and the rippled glass windows of the House. The Magister himself stepped forward to greet the travelers.

"Conservatory welcomes you," he said, and Sira saw that Theo was awake, trying to twist his head to see who was speaking. "We are very grateful to you for bringing Cantrix Sira home."

Home, Sira thought. Perhaps I will never be at home again. She willed away the tightness in her throat, and stared over Magister Mkel's gray and venerable head. Maestra Lu was not in the gathering on the steps, although Isbel was, and all her old classmates except Arn.

Her healing wound stiff from the long ride, Sira slid off her mount, and made a painful small bow to Mkel. The big *hruss*'s hooves clacked and slid on the clean-swept paving stones, and the others in the party were dismounting as well, stretching and smiling with relief. Mkel, however, watched only Sira, the patterns of wrinkles in his face deepening as he observed her closely.

"Are you well, Cantrix?" he asked. Sira nodded, holding herself rigidly upright. She was self-consciously aware of her bandaged forehead.

Jane quickly dismounted, and came to stand beside Sira. "The Cantrix is tired, Magister," she said in a low tone. "We have been riding for hours."

"Of course," said Mkel. "All of you must come in and bathe and eat." He nodded to several Housemen who were waiting to take the *hruss*. The students and House members gathered on the steps opened the great doors wide and led the party inside, while two burly Housemen moved to the *pukuru* and unhitched it from the *hruss*, each taking an end to carry Theo up the steps. He waved them off.

"I can walk," he told them. "Just lend me an arm." With help from one of the Housemen, he struggled up from the *pukuru*. He had to wait one dizzy moment for his sense of balance to return. Then he straightened as best he could, and grinning crookedly at the welcoming party, staggered up the steps and into Conservatory almost under his own power.

Sira's old classmates stood apart, watching her as she entered the House. They bowed as formally as strangers. She knew they were curious, trying not to stare. They were waiting for her lead, of course. A few short months ago they would have immediately plunged into a lively, silent conversation with her, full of questions and jibes. She was one of them no longer. She was Cantrix Sira, and she could not go back.

Mkel made his way through the group. "Cantrix Sira, we will talk after you have refreshed yourself."

Sira nodded again. "Thank you, Magister." Her voice sounded harsh in her own ears. "I will not be long."

"Please, Cantrix, take as much time as you need. I will speak with Gram and Jane first. And Cantor Rico."

Rico bowed to the Magister, and they stepped indoors. Sira looked uncertainly at Isbel.

Isbel, her rosy face solemn, bowed politely and carefully. *Cantrix Sira, a bath first? Or are you hungry?* she sent, presuming on their old friendship.

"A bath, please," Sira said aloud. Isbel took a sharp breath, hurt, but said nothing more. Sira looked straight ahead. "And something to drink."

Kevn bowed to Sira. "I will get tea," he said aloud, as respectful as he would be with any Cantor or Cantrix. Sira almost wished they would tease and taunt her as they used to. She wished Isbel would take her hand, or put her arm about her waist, but she could not initiate the contact.

She started down the corridor, toward the *ubanyix*. Isbel followed. When they had left the others behind, Sira turned to her old friend. "Where is Maestra Lu?" she asked.

Isbel was pale and tense. "I will bathe with you, Cantrix," she said quietly, "and I will tell you about Maestra Lu."

Sira saw the small widening of Isbel's eyes that meant she was opening her mind, but she shook her head, a small gesture of helplessness. "I cannot do it right now," Sira whispered through suddenly trembling lips. "Please tell me."

They had arrived at the door of the *ubanyix*, and Isbel opened the door. "Spirit of Stars," she said lightly, "it is empty."

She closed the door and turned again to Sira. Immediately she said, "I am so very sorry to tell you, Cantrix Sira, that our old teacher died ten days ago."

There was a charged silence. Sira counted back over the last days, and then wordlessly slipped her furs off her shoulders. Isbel helped her with her soiled tunic and trousers, dropping them on the yellow-white mound of discarded furs.

Sira slid quickly into the warm water, and began to wash crusted blood from her wounds. Isbel frowned at Sira's extreme thinness. All her bones seemed exposed, her stomach concave, and her babyish breasts shrunken almost to nothing. Her forehead and a nasty gash beneath her collarbone was discolored, and would certainly scar. Only her dark hair was as abundant as it had been.

Can we talk now, Cantrix? Sira? sent Isbel gently.

Sira's pupils were wide with shock, and her lips white. She shook her head. "I cannot," she said again, tightly. "Not yet."

The warm water lapped around her shoulders and the ends of her hair floated out in front of her. She remembered being in this same bath with Lu, and she ached to see that dear face again.

"Mkel told us Maestra Lu knew you were safe before she died," Isbel went on. She leaned forward in the scented water. "You were her favorite student, Sira."

Sira turned to her friend, her face a mask of suffering. "I caused her death," she blurted.

Isbel sucked in her breath in dismay. "No, Sira, no. Of course you did not! How can you think that? Whatever Maestra Lu did, she did because she had to. You cannot take responsibility for it."

There was a silence.

"Sira?"

Sira closed her eyes and leaned her head against the carved ironwood tub. Isbel watched her helplessly.

"Sira, this . . . this thing that happened . . . you have no blame in it. You were just their Cantrix. . . ."

"Just their Cantrix . . . that is it, is it not?" Sira said distantly, her eyes still closed. "All the years of study, of struggle for perfection . . . and they own us, like well-trained *hruss*." She was quiet for a moment before going on. "It is the way we speak of the itinerants . . . Oh, he's just an itinerant, we say. . . ." Isbel knew no way to answer that.

When Sira opened her eyes again, they were hot with unshed tears.

"Shall I warm the water, Cantrix?" Isbel whispered, not knowing what else to do.

Sira nodded, allowing her old friend to do something for her. She wondered to herself why she had struggled so to survive. What had it been for? And there is no one left to answer that question, she thought. She longed for the sound of Maestra Lu's voice, answering her questions, guiding her. Maestra Lu's reach had been long, but no one could reach from beyond the stars.

Isbel's *filla* trilled sweetly as the water temperature rose and the scent from the floating herbs intensified. The familiar walls of the *ubanyix*, the robes hung on hooks on one side, the towels stacked as usual, were all painful for Sira to see. She splashed water on her face, on her eyes, wishing the tears would spill as freely down her cheeks.

Isbel slipped back into the water, her cheery countenance grave in a way Sira had never seen. "Open your mind to me, Sira," she whispered.

Sira looked grim. "I like you too much to do that to you, Isbel," she said flatly. "You do not want these memories."

Tears appeared in Isbel's eyes. "I wish I could help. What a terrible ending for your first assignment . . . We were all so proud of you, so glad for you. . . ." She paused. "You are the best of us."

"The worst of it is," said Sira slowly, "that I worked deliberately to be the best . . . I thought that was what mattered . . . and in the end, it did not count for anything."

"Your next assignment will be better," Isbel said. Sira did not answer.

In silence, the two girls washed and dried themselves, dressing in clean clothes, and binding their hair. The tea had been left outside the door. Other bathers came in while Sira drank her tea. Isbel touched her hand once, then left her, with a brief bow, outside the door, and Sira turned in the direction of Magister Mkel's apartment. Her memories dragged at her, slowing her steps as she walked down the long corridor.

"Cantrix Sira, come in," Cathrin greeted her gently. For as long as Sira could remember, Cathrin had been part of Conservatory, motherly and bustling, busy with her own brood, or fussing over one of the little Gifted ones. Cathrin was unGifted, generous, and comfortable.

Now she led the young Cantrix to a chair and brought a tray of nursery fruits and nuts, with tea and a cup of water. Sira drank some water to please her. Her appetite had disappeared completely along the road to Conservatory.

"Cantrix Sira," said Mkel, coming into the room suddenly, "I am sorry to have made you wait." Cantor Rico was just behind him.

Sira rose, and bowed to her two seniors. The faces of the two men were set in angry lines. Cathrin withdrew, her own face sad and resigned.

"Please, sit, both of you," the Magister went on. "And eat, Cantrix Sira, or Cathrin will be after me."

"Forgive me, Magister, but I do not believe I can eat anything just now. My apologies to Cathrin." Sira sat again and picked up the cup of water.

Mkel and Rico were both watching her closely, and their

psi fairly sparkled in the room. Sira's own mind remained shielded, instinctively. It was the way she had controlled herself as a child, before her Gift was molded and disciplined by stringent training. Mkel sensed her need for privacy, and continued to speak aloud.

"Cantrix, now that your danger is past, I hope you will recover quickly from your experience." He smiled sympathetically at Sira, and she nodded slightly. The poultice Maestro Nikei had pressed over her eyebrow pulled at her skin, reminding her.

"I am fine, Magister, thank you," she said.

Cantor Rico spoke. "We want you to understand the events around the assassination of Magister Shen."

Sira looked at him out of eyes too wise for her eighteen years. "I know Alks and Mike were working with . . ." Her voice caught. She cleared her throat and her jaw muscles flickered. "They were working with Wil. And Trude," she added as an afterthought, and Rico and Mkel looked at each other sharply, hearing the inflection as she spoke the former Cantrix's name. "I do not know who actually shot Shen, or Rollie . . . or me. It does not matter."

"You are quite right, Sira," Mkel agreed in a low voice. She had never seen him so grim. "It does not matter who did it. What matters is who caused them to do it."

Sira waited, very still.

"Perhaps you were aware that there were tensions at Bariken," Mkel went on. "Rhia was actually ruling the House in all but name. Evidently that was not enough for her."

"Cantrix Sharn was very concerned," Rico put in, "but there was little she could do. The tradition of inheritance makes it difficult to deal with an incompetent Magister or Magistrix. And nothing serious enough had happened before now to bring Bariken before the Magistral Committee."

Mkel spoke again. "There is no doubt that Rhia arranged the assassination. Apparently she had expected to be Magistrix at Tarus, but the birth of a younger brother stood in her way."

"Rhia." Sira thought of the glossy-haired, elegant woman who had offered her the opportunity to go to Lamdon, which she had been so thrilled to accept. Now she felt a great weariness. "I met her. I spoke with her, but I felt no danger."

"I should think you would be very angry, Cantrix," said Rico. Sira could think of nothing to say. Maestra Lu's lined, white face glowed in her memory. I should have known, she thought. My arrogance stopped me from knowing.

"You may rest assured that Rhia has been removed as Magistrix of Bariken, and will be placed under the jurisdiction of the Magistral Committee. Their judgment will be harsh, I am sure. It may be that there will be a regent at Bariken until Trude's son by Shen is old enough to rule the House." Mkel paused. "Magret has gone back to working with Cantor Grigr for the time being, and can use your help when you feel ready to go back."

Sira looked straight at Magister Mkel. "I am sorry about Cantrix Magret, and I hope you will tell her so, but I cannot go back."

Mkel and Rico glanced at one another. "All right, Cantrix," Mkel said calmly. Evidently the two men had discussed this possibility. "Perhaps you will rest here at Conservatory until you feel ready for another assignment."

Sira shook her head, and her eyes were bleak. "Forgive me, Magister," she said in her deep voice. "Rollie, who was my friend, died in the Pass, and I almost did, and Maestra Lu died trying to save my life, and right now I cannot imagine what it was all for. I spent my youth trying to be the best at what I do, and Rhia, and"—the back of Sira's throat was suddenly dry, and she swallowed with a small clicking sound—"Wil, and Trude were content to destroy me for their own ends. What am I . . . what are all of us about, if we mean no more than that to the people we serve? I was trapped by my duty as much as by my ambition . . . I am ashamed and I am sad and I cannot be what they want me to be anymore."

It was a long speech, and the two men were silent for a long time after Sira was finished. She had turned her eyes down to her lap, to her long-fingered hand holding the empty water cup. At length, Rico spoke.

"Cantrix Sira, we are all as deeply shocked as you by what happened. The Conservatory Singers have always been cherished and protected. An isolated incident . . ."

"Excuse me, Cantor Rico," Sira broke in, and her eyes and voice hardened. She looked up again, seeming ten years older than she was. "Isolated or not, this incident is part of my life. I will try to understand it, but until I do, I will not be anyone's Cantrix . . . I will be my own person."

Rico looked helplessly at Mkel. The Magister was watching Sira. "Sira," he said. "We need Cantrixes. We need them desperately. Give yourself some time to recover. We will wait for you." His voice carried strong and skillful psi-inflections of empathy, and Sira closed her eyes briefly. Her lips trembled, and for a moment she looked eighteen again. Then her mouth grew firm, and her eyes opened.

"Thank you," she said calmly, "but I will not change my mind." She rose, as if perfectly composed, and bowed to her seniors with deep respect. Then, alone, she left the apartment.

CHAPTER
SIXTEEN

✶ THEO RECOVERED QUICKLY UNDER THE CARE OF CONSERvatory. Maestro Nikei treated his wound daily, giving him precedence during Cantoris hours. It was not customary, but no one objected; everyone at Conservatory regarded the itinerant Singer as something of a hero. Theo, leaning back in one of the carved chairs to submit to Nikei's ministrations, felt the tingle of his body as the *filla* played and Nikei's psi coaxed torn flesh and muscle to come together. Afterwards, he sat on one of the benches and watched as Nikei dealt with other ailments.

One day, as they left the Cantoris together, Theo questioned the Cantor, "Don't you ever use the first mode for healing wounds?"

Nikei frowned. "I use the third, to prevent infections that slow the healing. Why would I use the first?"

Carefully, Theo said, "I often use it to help the injured person relax. The healing seems to go faster. The fear that comes with a wound slows the mending, don't you think?"

Nikei looked at him sharply. "I did not know that itinerants practiced much healing."

Theo chuckled. "We must, or we lose too many travelers!" They were entering the great room, and Maestro Nikei signaled to a waiting Housewoman to bring them tea. "Perhaps fear is not an issue here at Conservatory," Theo said mildly, indicating the House with a wave of his hand. "Outside, I have seen travelers so frightened by being hurt that they have to be restrained from doing themselves further injury."

"But what happens to hurt them, outside?" Nikei asked.

Theo's smile was lopsided and wry. "Everything happens, Maestro Nikei! They fall off the *hruss*, they cut themselves with their knives, they run into the branches of softwood trees, they get blacktoe."

"Blacktoe?" Nikei frowned again. If this was his usual expression, Theo thought, it must cause some anxiety among his students.

"Blacktoe," he told the Cantor. "When the feet get too cold, the ends of the toes start to get dark, and then they must be warmed immediately, and slowly, or the traveler can lose them. The same for fingers. Blacktoe can kill a person if it's not caught early."

Nikei's frown smoothed away at last. "Ah, yes, I have seen this, but had not heard that name for it. I am very interested in what you say, Singer." Their tea arrived and they sipped at it. "Healing is the most difficult part of the Gift to develop. I had assumed, therefore"—he hesitated, and went on delicately—"that . . . ahem . . . those Singers who do not become . . . hmm, who do not come to Conservatory, that is . . ." Nikei fell awkwardly silent.

Theo grinned. "Rather the opposite," he said cheerfully, unoffended. "Some of the best healers are itinerants. We learn it very early, out of need."

Nikei shook his head. "The first mode. For injuries. It is a new thought."

Theo savored a momentary sense of belonging. As he watched the House members come in and bow deeply to Nikei, however, he realized there was still a great chasm between them. At least Nikei conversed with him. He did not speak to any of the Housemen or women, only nodded acknowledgment to one or two. The Cantor was as aloof with his own House members as if the Glacier itself lay between them.

In a few days Theo was moving restlessly about the House and the nursery gardens. Still swathed in bandages under his tunic, he was stiff and sore, but his energy had returned in full, and he needed something to do. Only after the evening meal, when he sometimes lingered with the students in the great room, telling stories of outside, did he feel fully occupied.

Those evenings were lovely and long. Theo's position as one of the group that had rescued Sira gave him special privileges. The students stayed in the great room an hour and more past their usual time to hear him talk. He told them of the Southern Timberlands, and the Houses on the Frozen Sea, where tiny ships like floating *pukuru* dared the ice-clogged waters for fish that tasted fresh as sweet snow.

Once he told them the fable of the Ship, and the little ones watched wide-eyed, not knowing what was truth and what was invention.

"The Spirit of Stars," Theo recited in a low tone that he knew made his youngest listeners shiver, "sent the Ship, like the greatest *pukuru* you can imagine, drawn by the six strongest and biggest *hruss* It had. Spirit knew the people would need plants and animals that did not grow on the Continent, and so the giant *pukuru* was packed full of fruit seeds and grain seeds and people seeds, and when it landed on the Continent, it overturned, and they all spilled out and began to grow! The upside-down *pukuru* became First House, and First Singer warmed it so the seeds would grow big and strong."

"But, Singer," a little boy asked, "what happened to the six big *hruss*?"

Theo nodded gravely to him. "Do you know, that's a very good question." He pointed to the thick windows of the great room, where the darkness of the long night lay beyond the glow of the *quiru*. "Have you ever seen the stars?"

The boy nodded. "On my way here, with my father," he said in a sad childish tone. He and his class were not yet adjusted. Theo saw one of the older students touch the little boy's shoulder.

"Did anyone show you the Six Stars?" Theo asked. The boy shook his head. "The Six Stars shine above the eastern horizon when you're outside at night. Those were the *hruss* that drew Spirit's big *pukuru*. When it overturned, to spill the seeds and to become First House, the *hruss* were freed, and they raced up into the sky. They still run there, across the sky each night, trying to get back to the Spirit of Stars."

The Housewomen came to fetch the little ones then, and Theo said good night to them. The older students smiled and nodded to him, several speaking aloud as they said good night. Isbel, who Theo knew had been Sira's closest friend, was the last to leave the great room, making sure he had everything he might want before she retired.

The next morning, she teased him. "Tell me another story," she said as they walked from the great room after the morning meal. He grinned down at her.

"Do you want to hear about the Singer from Trevi who had to sleep in the stables because he wouldn't go near the *ubanyor*? Or the girl at Conservatory that Magister Mkel had to shut up in a room because she asked too many questions?"

Isbel giggled and he smiled to see the twinkle of dimples in her cheeks. "I do not ask too many questions! I am a serious student trying to learn more about the Continent!" She tossed her auburn head and looked up at him.

"A serious student?" Laughing, he bowed to her. "Then

sing for me. Here I am at Conservatory and all the music I've heard has been the *quirunha*."

"I will, if you like, tomorrow. It will cost you a story, though. Now I see Cantor Nikei looking at us. He will scold me for keeping you too long."

"Wait a moment, Isbel!" Theo held up his hand to stop her from leaving so quickly. "I want to ask you about Cantrix Sira," he said. "I haven't heard any news. Is she all right?"

Isbel's green eyes grew dark, and her smile faded. "I do not know, Singer. She has had a bad experience, and she will not open her mind to me."

"Open . . . ?"

Isbel sighed. "She only speaks aloud. With all of us. She is far away from us, somehow, because of what happened to her in Ogre Pass."

Theo swore softly. "By the Ship, that was a bad business!"

Isbel looked at him quizzically. "I have never heard that expression, Singer."

"By the Ship?" Theo grinned and shrugged. "They say it in the southern Houses. What do you say when you want to swear?"

Isbel blushed and laughed, her sad mood dispersing like snow clouds on a mountain peak. "It is hard to swear when you do not speak aloud. But I know 'By the Six Stars,' and"—she lowered her voice carefully—"and *ubanyit!*"

Theo laughed loud and long. "Is that the worst you can do, Isbel? It's a good thing you don't travel with itinerants!"

Isbel blushed again. She saw Maestro Nikei approaching, and covered her mouth with her hand, but her eyes still sparkled with laughter as Nikei reached them.

Theo and Isbel bowed to the Cantor. Theo had to follow

the healer out for his daily session in the Cantoris, and he left Isbel smiling after him.

It was in the nursery gardens that Theo at last met Sira one morning, walking slowly among the flats of plants and seedlings where they lay cosseted in yellow *quiru* light. She was alone, bending over a tray of herbs to breathe in their fragrance, and she turned with a flash of irritation when she heard someone behind her.

He could see her check her reaction when she recognized him. She bowed slightly.

"Hello, Singer. I am glad to see you recovering," she said gravely.

Theo flashed his lopsided grin. "I'm fine, thanks. Enjoying my convalescence." He was not quite as tall as she, but he thought she could not weigh half what he did. "And you, Cantrix Sira?" he asked. "Have you recovered?"

Her answer avoided his real question. "My wounds were not so serious as yours. They are almost healed." Absently, she traced her scarred eyebrow, recently bandaged, with a long forefinger. Its darkness would be forever marked by a slash of white.

"You know, Cantrix," Theo went on in a light tone, "I've been an itinerant for more than ten years, and I've never had an experience like that one! Even when I accidentally came too close to the Watchers, they didn't try to kill me." He chuckled. "Although they did shoot at me. But it takes time to heal . . . in many ways."

Sira stopped and turned, her back straight and the angles of her face hard. "Singer," she said harshly, "it is over. I do not think of it anymore."

Theo's eyebrows lifted. "Good for you, Cantrix," he said mildly. He hooked a little ironwood bench forward with his foot and settled heavily onto it, adjusting his bandages and resting his big shoulders on the back. It occurred to him that perhaps he should leave her alone, but an impulse, an intuition, drove him on. "So that means you're ready to go back?"

"No!" Sira said sharply, and then stopped, visibly controlling herself. Theo watched her tense face a moment before he went on.

"Another Cantoris, then? Probably a good idea. After all, as the saying goes, the *ferrel* builds more than one nest."

"My plans are not yet made, Singer." Sira bowed again, clearly meaning to end their conversation. "I am sorry you were injured helping me, and if I may help you in turn, please ask." She turned away with an air of finality.

"It seems to me, now that I think of it," Theo went on comfortably, as if she had not tried to dismiss him, "that I heard a rumor that you have refused another Cantoris."

Sira thumped a fist down on a nearby table, making the seed flats jump. "I swear, a Singer cannot take a breath but what the whole Continent knows it!" Her flash of anger made the air around her glitter.

"Oh, I think your term is too general," Theo said. "It's just Cantors and Cantrixes whose every breath is of interest to Nevya."

Sira turned and looked at him. "I do not understand," she said.

Theo shook his head. "Sorry, Cantrix. Forget that."

Sira stood very still for a moment, looking out into the humid air of the nursery gardens, and then, as if she had forgotten all about Theo, she strode away, leaving him alone.

Sira was healing, although not in the way Mkel hoped she would. She had spent many hours in the nursery gardens, breathing in the damp earthy air and thinking, with the gardeners watching her surreptitiously. She tried not to notice, but she was aware that her story had spread throughout the Conservatory, and everywhere she went the House members looked at her with interest and sympathy. She wondered if they would feel such sympathy if they knew the whole story. In her dreams she felt that flash of psi over and over, and the crumpling of Trude's mind beneath it. Often she woke, shaking, wishing hopelessly in the dark that Maestra Lu were there. Only Maestra Lu could understand.

She had avoided the Cantoris altogether since her return. In her mind she went over and over all that had happened, and her resolve hardened like a pond at the end of summer as it gradually freezes from the top down.

Isbel sought her out one afternoon in her room. *Cantrix Sira? Would you like to talk?*

Sira shook her head. "Isbel, there is nothing to talk about," she said aloud.

Open to me, my friend.

"I cannot," Sira said. "I am no longer the same person I was when I lived here."

"You are to me," Isbel said stoutly. She did not like speaking aloud when it could be avoided, but she wanted to please Sira. "I want to help you find yourself again."

"That person is gone," Sira said. "We can never walk back in the same footsteps."

"That sounds like something the Singer Theo would say."

"Theo? Have you been talking to him?" Sira leaned wearily against the wall. "I think I have never met anyone with so much conversation."

Isbel smiled. "Yes. He is so funny, and such blue eyes, like a summer sky. We all like him."

"Isbel, can you come and bathe?" Sira asked abruptly. Isbel nodded, hoping her friend would open to her when they were in the privacy of the *ubanyix*.

"And do you have a sharp knife in your room?"

Isbel frowned. "I have the knife I use for cutting *filhata* strings. It was sharpened last week in the abattoir. But why?"

"Bring it, please," Sira said with a flash of the authority she had already tested at Bariken.

Isbel turned obediently and went to her room to fetch the knife, carrying it back carefully wrapped in a bit of leather, and then she followed Sira to the *ubanyix*. Sira knew she wanted to send to her, but she kept her mind carefully shielded from her friend. They walked down the long corridor, looking much as they had when they were students together, the pretty plump girl and her tall, solemn friend.

In the *ubanyix*, the girls shed their tunics and trousers and immersed themselves in the warm water. Sira unbound her long hair and ducked her head below the surface of the water for a moment. When the thick mass of her hair was soaked, she knelt on the bottom of the tub with her back to Isbel and said, "Please cut it for me."

Isbel sucked in her breath in dismay. "But Sira, why? Why cut your beautiful hair?" She held the knife awkwardly in her hand, as if it embarrassed her.

"Where I am going I do not want it," Sira said, and leaned back slightly so that her hair hung directly in front of Isbel.

"But, Sira . . . Cantrix, I mean . . . where are you going?"

"Away. And I am not a Cantrix anymore, Isbel. I am just a Singer."

The odd little tableau held for a long moment, and then Isbel, helpless before the force of Sira's determination, took the heavy wet hair in her hand and began to cut. Sira reached over her shoulder and caught the long pieces in her hand as they fell, so that they would not foul the bath. When it was finished, Sira put her hand to her head and marveled at the lightness of it. Her fingers slipped easily through the cropped locks, and she felt free.

Theo was almost disappointed one morning to realize that there was no longer any pain or stiffness in his wound. He stretched his shoulders and arms, feeling soft and lazy from the weeks of easy living. He had enjoyed every day of his recuperation, hearing the *quirunha* daily in the best Cantoris on the Continent, and watching the intensity and single-minded discipline of the Conservatory students. The students had treated him as familiarly as one of their own House members, and he would look back on this time as one of the best of his life, a shining interval of community with these chosen ones.

He had not seen the Cantrix Sira at the *quirunhas*, although he attended them all. In fact, she had been conspicuously absent from all House functions, and he assumed she was having her meals in her room. Since their encounter in the nursery gardens, he had had no news of her at all. She startled him, then, by showing up at his door one morning.

He bowed courteously, trying to hide his surprise at her cropped hair.

"May I speak with you, Singer?" she asked politely.

"At any time, Cantrix. Could you call me Theo, do you think?"

"Will you call me Sira, then?"

Theo grinned at her. "Probably not. You're a Cantrix, after all."

"Perhaps I shall go on calling you Singer," Sira said, with a flash of her dark eyes. She stepped past him into his room.

Chuckling, Theo pulled forward the single chair for her to sit on, and seated himself on his cot. He waited for Sira to speak.

"I have questions for you," she said slowly, and her

young face was intent. The short hair, brushed away from her cheekbones, relieved the sharp angles of her face, and Theo liked the way it looked.

"I prefer that no one know I have asked these questions," she said.

"Go ahead." Theo grinned at her. "I'm as quiet as a *caeru* in a snowstorm."

Unsmiling, Sira said, "I want to know everything about being an itinerant Singer."

Theo was silent for once, only searching her face for meaning. Sira quickly looked away, down at her hands linked in her lap.

"Please, Singer. Theo. You are the only one I can ask."

Theo sighed. "Cantrix Sira. The life of an itinerant is not easy. Constant exposure, loneliness, hard work . . . I don't want to brag"—his ready grin came up again—"but we're a tough bunch."

"I will not be a Cantrix anymore. I want to choose my own way." Sira's mouth was stubbornly set. Theo sighed again.

"There is nothing I would like better than to give you whatever you need, Cantrix . . . I mean to say, Sira," he amended gently. "But I know this business, and it would waste your Gift.

"You have something others would give a great deal to have, your Conservatory education. You have a place where you belong, people who care about everything you do."

"People who wish to control everything I do," Sira said bitterly.

"Sira, believe me," Theo insisted. "You must not throw away the advantages your life has given you. I'm sorry, but I can't teach you an itinerant's trade. In any case, it would require practical lessons, not just talk."

"Take me with you, then, when you leave. I will be your apprentice."

"You belong here, not out there in the mountains and forests. I can't be the means of taking you away from those who need you. I can't bear that responsibility."

Sira sat still for a moment. Then she nodded to Theo, but avoided his eyes. "Thank you just the same," she said. "I will consider further." She stood and bowed. "I would appreciate your not discussing our conversation with anyone."

Theo stood, too, opening the door for his visitor. "Let me help you in some other way, Sira."

She shook her head. "I do not know what that would be, Singer." He held up an admonishing finger, and the smallest smile turned up Sira's lips. "Theo."

He bowed. "Sira . . . give yourself time."

She did not answer, but moved away in silence. He shook his head, watching her narrow frame moving down the corridor. Such intensity, he thought. Perhaps that is what my Gift lacks.

Sira found it was not easy to prepare alone. She had no metal, as Cantors and Cantrixes never had need of it, but she had to obtain provisions and equipment, which were as essential as information. She had never cooked for herself. She had never saddled a *hruss*. But, determined on her course, she visited the kitchens and the stables and the storehouses, begging supplies.

The Housemen and women knew her, of course, and the dramatic tale of her survival in Ogre Pass had preceded her. The people in charge of the things she wanted were inclined to be indulgent with her. They looked curiously at her closely cropped head, but she was a full Cantrix, and they asked no questions. Slowly her small room began to fill with the things she needed—a knife, a cooking pot, a bowl and cup, some grain and dried meat, a small cache of softwood. She started to worry that they would not fit into a saddlepack.

The problems of *hruss* and saddle plagued her the most. As inexperienced as she was in matters of trade, she knew these were valuable, and that such metal as there was often was spent on them. All she had of great value was her *filhata*, given to her by the Conservatory itself before her first *quirunha*. It had been sent back to her from Bariken, and now she offered it to the man in charge of the Conservatory stables.

Erc was a paternal man, and he regarded her with sympathy.

"Cantrix Sira, you don't need to part with your *filhata*. Magister Mkel would be glad to give you a *hruss* and tack if you need to ride somewhere."

"No. I cannot ask him. And I do not wish you to ask him, please, Erc. I am not going on Conservatory business."

"What other business does a Cantrix have?"

"I do not think I need to explain," Sira said as sternly as she knew how.

Erc was abashed, and Sira regretted the necessity of being brusque. "Of course, Cantrix. But we can lend you the *hruss* and saddle, and you will return it when you can."

"Thank you, Erc, but no. I much prefer to pay for it."

Erc's genial face creased with worry, but he pressed her no further. Awkwardly, he accepted her *filhata*, encased in its fine wrapping, and after showing her a saddle and saddlepack, took her to the stalls to choose a *hruss*. Sira did her best to look knowledgeable, but the *hruss* all looked the same to her, and she accepted the first one Erc recommended, a comparatively small animal with shaggy chin and fetlocks.

"When will you want it ready, Cantrix?" he asked.

When she opened her mouth to answer, Sira realized that this was an important moment, the final step of her going. Her voice trembled ever so slightly.

"Tomorrow morning, please," she said. Erc bowed deeply in acknowledgment.

"It will be saddled and fed," he said.

Sira bowed and set off for her room, empty saddlepack thrown over her shoulder. I will be ready, too, she thought. Ready to live my own life.

CHAPTER
SEVENTEEN

THEO APPROACHED MAGISTER MKEL AT THE MORNING meal. Cathrin was at Mkel's left, overseeing the meal from their table in the center of the great room. Most of the students, teachers, and visitors in residence were also present, crowding the room with more than two hundred people. Theo waited as a messenger spoke in a low tone to the Magister, who nodded heavily and looked very grave. When the messenger departed, Theo bowed to Cathrin first, and then Mkel.

"Good morning, Cathrin. Magister, I'm afraid that I've enjoyed the hospitality of your House long enough."

"Oh, please don't speak of leaving so soon, Singer," said Cathrin warmly. "I've enjoyed your stories so much."

"You're a patient listener, Cathrin," Theo said with a grin. "But I can't work up enough pain in my wound to justify this holiday any longer."

"Are you quite sure, Singer?" asked Magister Mkel. He was courteous as always, but distracted. Involuntarily, Theo looked after the messenger, curious about the news he had carried. Cathrin was reaching out her plump hand to touch her mate's.

"Please be sure that Nikei agrees the Singer is healed, Mkel."

"I will miss seeing your face at the center of these tables

every day," Theo said to her. He turned back to Mkel. "But if you have a party ready to travel, I will be glad of the work, Magister."

"You will always be welcome here, Singer," said the Magister. "You have our deepest gratitude for your service to Cantrix Sira."

"Thank you," said Theo. He grinned again. "But if I don't get back to work soon, I'll have no new stories for Cathrin next time I see her!"

Cathrin laughed, and Mkel nodded. "Just let Maestro Nikei examine your wound, if you will, Singer, to set Cathrin's mind at ease. Traveling parties are frequent here, as you have seen, and I will recommend you to one."

"Thank you, Magister."

"You may wish to know," Mkel went on, "that the Magistral Committee has ruled and acted on the disposition of those involved in the attack on the Cantrix and the Magister of Bariken."

Theo raised his eyebrows and waited. Mkel looked at his mate, and then back to Theo. His face was dark and grim, and incredibly weary.

"Trude and Rhia," he said, "were exposed in Forgotten Pass, a day's ride north of Lamdon. It was done three days ago. It must be over now."

Theo sighed. Life on the Continent required fierce and swift justice. It was a brutal punishment, one that had been used as long as Nevyans could remember. In this case, Theo thought, being left to the elements, deliberately abandoned to the cold, was no less cruel than the fate the two women had meant for Sira.

"Has Cantrix Sira been told?" he asked.

"No," Mkel replied. "That will be my next task."

Bowing again, Theo left them and made his way through the long tables to a seat. He looked around at the now-familiar faces of the House members and wished he didn't have to strike out into the mountains with strangers once again. Isbel was across the room from him, and she waved when she caught his eye. He winked at her, enjoying her dimples as she giggled. Her classmates were clustered around her, except for Sira. The young Cantrix was absent.

Theo finished his breakfast of yeast bread and nursery fruit, and then hurried to catch up with Isbel as she left the great room. She saw him following, and slowed her pace. Her auburn head just reached his shoulder as they walked on together.

"I hear you will be leaving us," she said, with a little pout of regret.

"By the Six Stars, word travels around here as fast as a *wezel* can run!"

Isbel laughed, a merry chime that fell sweetly on the ear. Theo could hardly resist an urge to stroke her head, as if she were a little girl. How he would miss the beautiful voices of these young Singers!

They walked on to where their paths diverged, while Theo wondered how to ask Isbel about Cantrix Sira. They stopped at the turning of the hall, and Isbel looked up at him.

"I do not know where she is," she said, and Theo was startled. "I was not prying," Isbel said quickly, "but you are sending rather clearly."

Theo shook his head helplessly, wishing he had Isbel's control, then immediately wondered if she heard that, too. If she did, she didn't show it. She put her hand lightly on his arm.

"None of us knows where she is," Isbel told him. "I think it is kind of you to be concerned for her."

"Someone must know!" Theo exclaimed in frustration.

"Magister Mkel asked me," Isbel said, "and I assume he

has asked others. If one of the students knew, we would all know. I fear she has found a way to leave."

"Isbel . . . you can't mean she's left Conservatory?"

She dropped her hand and sighed. "Yes. And she cut her hair."

"Yes, I saw her, but . . . surely she didn't go alone!"

"Go where?"

The hall had cleared of people as they talked, and he and Isbel stood alone for a moment. Theo looked grim. He ran his hand over his own hair, cut short again by a House-woman in the kitchens only the evening before.

"When I get ready to travel, I always cut my hair," Theo said. "The itinerants I know who are women all wear their hair short. Long hair is too hard to care for."

Isbel's green eyes were wide. "Would she . . . could she do that?"

"Would she? I think so!" He shook his head. "Could she? I don't know. She's strong. And you, all of you here, are remarkably Gifted. Unfortunately, there's much more to an itinerant's work than singing up *quirus*."

"She said I was not to call her Cantrix." Isbel's rosy face grew sad. "She has always been independent. But she is as dear to me as anyone I know."

"It's my fault," Theo said bitterly. "She asked for my help, and I refused it. I thought that would stop her." He struck a fist hard into the palm of the other hand. "I never thought she would go alone!"

"Singer, we must tell Magister Mkel," said Isbel.

"But what can he do?"

"He can find out who has left the House. I cannot believe she would want to be out in the mountains by herself again."

Back they went to the great room, but they found it almost cleared of people. Isbel led the way to the Magister's apartment, where they were admitted immediately by Cathrin. The Magister looked grave as Theo explained his last conversation with Sira.

Isbel broke in. "We must stop her, Magister!"

"I do not know how we can do that," Mkel said heavily. "We cannot force her into a Cantoris."

"But she is in danger!" Isbel's eyes filled with tears and her voice rose like a child's.

Theo lifted his hand. "Isbel, I'll go after her. I promise." Isbel fell silent, but her lips were trembling, and she put a hand to her mouth.

"Do you know of anyone who has left the House in the last day, Magister?" Theo asked. Half of his mind hurried ahead, already dealing with the details of a hasty departure.

"I will ask the stableman," the Magister said. He looked suddenly aged, with lines of care etched ever more deeply into his face. Cathrin hovered behind him. "This has been a bad business from beginning to end. I wish I had listened to Maestra Lu. She was against Sira's assignment to Bariken."

Theo stood abruptly. "I must take the blame for this, Magister." Mkel looked up at him, shaking his head, but Theo said, "She asked me to tell her all about an itinerant's work, and I refused. I should have come to you."

"We could only have argued with her. She has a right to her own decisions."

Theo had to smile ruefully. "She's as stubborn as last winter's icicles, that's certain. But I will find her, Magister."

Cathrin broke her silence. "We must hire the Singer to go after her, Mkel. She can't know what it is she's doing." She looked pleadingly at Theo. "At least bring her back so we can talk to her."

"I will try," he said. Privately he thought, it's a big Continent on which to find one girl, Gifted or not. The task ahead looked enormous.

*   *   *

It took one thirty-hour day to prepare to leave, which, Theo estimated, put Sira two days ahead of him. Erc, the stableman, had dispatched two *hruss* from the stables the previous day, one for Sira and one for an itinerant without a traveling party, an old Singer named Lorn who had told no one his destination. Theo could only guess at the direction they had taken.

On the day of his departure, Magister Mkel, Maestro Nikei, and Isbel gathered to bid him farewell. It made him grin to see them grouped on the steps, as if he were a Cantor, to receive full ceremonies whenever he made a move. He stopped smiling when he saw the evident concern on all their faces. He knew they were deeply fearful about Sira.

"Good luck, Singer," Magister Mkel said formally. "We thank you."

"Stay well," Maestro Nikei added.

"I hope you can find her," Isbel added softly.

Theo bowed to Isbel. "I hope so, too," he said. "And you must try not to worry. You have your Cantoris to think of."

She inclined her head, and the sun gleamed red on her hair. "So I do," she said. She would be Cantrix at Amric in a few short weeks.

There was nothing more to say. Theo lifted his hand in farewell, and turned his *hruss*. Isbel watched him with her hands clasped under her chin. He looked back once and winked at her. Only the smallest smile appeared in answer. If he had hoped to see the dimples, he was disappointed.

He had said to them: "If she has decided to become an itinerant, her first step will be to register at Lamdon. I don't know this Lorn, but if he has no traveling party, he may also need to go to the capital."

Magister Mkel had agreed, and had given him a written message for Cantrix Sharn, which Theo carefully stowed in his saddlepack. Theo had seen the message; it begged Sharn to persuade Sira to return to the Conservatory, to think further before abandoning her duty and her destiny. Theo doubted it would make a difference to Sira, but it would certainly affect his own reception at Lamdon.

He rode away from the Conservatory alone, into the silence of the snowy mountains. Not much like a Cantor now, he told himself. No Cantor or Cantrix rides alone on the Continent . . . although he could not know what company Sira might have. Suppose she was alone? No, surely not. She would have this itinerant, whoever he was, with her. Theo wished he could be sure where they had gone.

Lamdon was eight days' ride away. They would be lonely days, cold and worrisome days. Theo was not afraid of traveling alone; he only hoped Sira would not have already gone when he arrived.

He rounded the curve of the courtyard, and the walls of Conservatory disappeared behind the irontrees, leaving only its great roof visible. He looked back once, regretfully. In his head he heard the faintest echo of Isbel sending, *Goodbye, Singer.*

Theo shook his head ruefully. He liked Isbel too well to be envious. But I would sing up a thousand *quirus*, he thought, to learn that skill.

CHAPTER
EIGHTEEN

SIRA SAT CROSS-LEGGED ACROSS THE CAMPFIRE FROM Lorn, and wondered how old he was. He seemed ancient to her, especially to be living the strenuous life of an itinerant. He had insisted on doing the *quiru* himself, and it wavered and faltered distressingly around them and their *hruss*. Last night she had wakened to find it almost dissipated, and had refreshed it with her own *filla* while Lorn slept on, unaware.

Sira sighed. There had been no choice of traveling company. Lorn had been the only itinerant she could find who was not consulting with Magister Mkel or the House-keeper about his departure; she was afraid she now understood why. Who would hire such a person?

It would be only a few days' ride to Lamdon, she told herself, and then she would declare herself an itinerant, and try to find an apprenticeship with someone else. It should not be hard to avoid Cantrix Sharn, if she came in to Lamdon through its stables and attracted no attention to herself. In the meantime, she had hoped to learn something about the work beyond *quiru* duties, but two days with the old itinerant Singer had made her doubt his ability to teach her.

Lorn reached forward with his gnarled hand and stirred up the remnants of the fire. "Not so easy, starting a fire with flint and stone, is it?" he said. Even his voice seemed old and frail to her, and she wondered if he could sing anymore.

"I will try it again tomorrow," she said. "I need to learn."

"You'll get it," he said, and laughed wheezily. "You'll learn to cook, too, or be awfully hungry. Hot food is important in the mountains."

Sira said nothing. Lorn's cooking had not been an inspiration, although she knew he was right about the importance of hot meals. Stars winked through the shaky *quiru*, and she decided to get into her bedroll early, since she would certainly be up redoing the *quiru* before the long night had passed. She thought that Cantors must not be the only ones in short supply if this man was able to eke out a living as an itinerant Singer.

A long, wailing cry sounded through the hills, making Sira sit bolt upright. Lorn laughed again.

"Don't worry," he told her. "Just a *ferrel* hunting in the dark. The fire keeps them away from us. We'll build it up a little." He dropped some softwood on it, and it flared and grew.

Sira lay back down, but her skin prickled uneasily. The comforts of her room at Conservatory seemed very far off. She tried not to remember what Theo had said. I am free, she thought. At least I choose my own way. She was glad she had not heard the *ferrel* cry when she had been alone in Ogre Pass.

She did not sleep until long after Lorn was snoring softly in his own bedfurs. She renewed the *quiru* once he was asleep, and felt better seeing it strong and glowing above their campsite. The *ferrel* screamed again, and she shivered, but the fire was still glowing, and she fell asleep at last under her warm furs, grateful not to be alone, even if Lorn was not an ideal companion.

The next day snow began to fall as the road led higher

into the Mariks. Lorn had said they would take the upper mountain route, going through Windy Pass to Lamdon and saving several days, rather than traveling east to pick up the wider and more clement Ogre Pass. The softwood trees were thinning out, leaving only the huge ironwood trees and their network of thick, shallow suckers that reached across the trail. Lorn assured Sira they would be at the top of the pass before dark.

When night fell and the trail they followed had not yet opened into the narrow fissure that was Windy Pass, Sira reluctantly began to suspect that Lorn had made a mistake. He was silent, and she did not ask, but she felt tension all around her.

She still could not start the fire by herself, try as she might. When it died out a third time, Lorn did it for her once again, but with none of the teasing there had been the night before.

The next morning, Sira saddled her *hruss* without help. It groaned as if in pain as she drew up the cinch, and Sira loosened it, thinking it must be too tight. Lorn looked over and shook his head.

"You'd better tighten that up. Pay no attention to the *hruss*; it thinks it wants the cinch loose. But it won't like that saddle ending up under its belly." He snickered. "And you'll have a mouthful of snow!"

Sira turned back to the saddle and saw that now the cinch was indeed hanging loosely from the beast's rib cage. As soon as she put her hand to it, the *hruss* took a deep breath and swelled out its ribs, and the cinch looked tight again. Sira laughed, and poked the *hruss* gently in the belly. When it relaxed, the cinch swung free. This time Sira pulled it firmly, and then waited until the *hruss* had taken several breaths, to make sure the cinch was snug. She patted the animal and went to get her saddlepack.

Sira had tried to cook breakfast, too, and, as a reward, had to eat scorched grain. Lorn took a taste and frowned, eating cold dried meat with his tea instead. Sira ate every bite of her concoction, defiantly, and now she could feel its weight in her stomach as she pulled herself up into her saddle.

When Lorn led the way out of their campsite, and turned into what seemed to be a road, Sira's sense of direction was offended. It didn't feel right to her, but she had made so many mistakes in their two days together that she hesitated to challenge the old man's choice.

They rode for several hours in an increasingly heavy snowfall that obscured the trees and obliterated the outlines of the road.

"Doesn't usually snow so much about now," Lorn muttered, half to himself. "Usually get clear skies when the deep cold is starting."

Sira looked about uneasily. It had not been so many weeks since she had traversed Ogre Pass, and these surroundings looked nothing like it. Could one pass be so different from another? The snow fell in curtains about them and the trees still loomed close over the road.

"Singer," she said as courteously as she could, "I think perhaps our direction is wrong."

He pulled up his *hruss*. "I don't understand it," he said. "We should have been in the Pass by now."

The *hruss*'s fetlocks were heavy with the wet, unseasonal snow which Sira knew would freeze unpleasantly when dark fell. Their path, which looked less and less like a road, had grown steep and treacherously slippery.

"We must go back," Sira said firmly. "Retrace our steps until we strike familiar ground. We have missed the entrance to the Pass."

Lorn shrugged, and then nodded. "Might as well," he said. "Snow's getting thick."

The path they were following had grown narrow, and turning was difficult. Sira could not see the downslope to her right through the blinding snow, and it worried her. She had an impression of space, emptiness there, that might mean a cliff or a talus slope under the snow.

"Be careful!" she called over her shoulder to Lorn, as her own *hruss* turned with difficulty in the close space between heavy rocks and trees on the uphill side and white blankets on the other.

Sira had heard the expression "white weather" many times, but had never experienced it. Sky, ground, rocks, and trees disappeared into pallid curtains of snow. She felt dizzy. She was losing her perspective and only barely retained her sense of up and down by watching her *hruss*'s withers and head. The animal was feeling its way gingerly down the trail, and Sira felt every bunch and quiver of its muscles in her own legs and arms. A sudden squeal from the other *hruss* chilled her spine as if a handful of wet snow had been dropped inside her furs. She heard Lorn make one short sound like a grunt or a curse.

"Lorn, are you all right?" she called. She pulled up the *hruss* and listened hard. She heard only the hiss of snow and the huffing of her mount. For a moment, panic tugged at her, a familiar feeling of being utterly alone in the wilderness. Then she heard Lorn's voice, shaky but audible.

"Sira! Wait!"

She looked back, but could not see him or his *hruss*. Laboriously, she turned her own *hruss* once again, and urged it gently back up the steep path. "Lorn!" she called again. Suddenly the *hruss* stopped sharply, and Sira realized the other animal was down, lying in the snow at her own *hruss*'s feet.

The enveloping whiteness made it difficult to see anything, but sliding down from her saddle, Sira could make out Lorn on the snow by his fallen mount. Snow reached in under her hood and made her neck and hair wet, and she kept a hand firmly on her *hruss*'s neck to orient herself in the blank whiteness of the weather.

"Can you get up?" she asked fearfully.

Lorn's figure moved a little, and then Sira heard, "It's my leg. Afraid it's broken."

"And your *hruss*?"

"He fell on a boulder. Severed his hamstring." There was a painful pause. "I cut his throat."

Sira's stomach turned over, but she nodded with respect for Lorn's quick and merciful action. "I will make a *quiru*." She made her way carefully back to her saddlepack, clutching at the *hruss* and the saddle as she went. They would have to stay here until the snow let up enough to see properly. Her mouth was dry. She had no experience with broken bones, and no confidence in her ability to deal with them. And how would they get down from here?

She pulled her *filla* out of her pack and fought her way back. Taking some snow into her mouth, she waited for it to melt, squatting by the dead *hruss*'s body across from Lorn. When her mouth was moist enough, she put the *filla* to her lips and played until a strong, warm *quiru* was established around them. In its light, and the blessed relief from the white weather effect, she could see Lorn clearly.

She was not encouraged. His face was gray with pain, although he made no sound, and he looked close to fainting. He lay against the still-warm body of his *hruss*. Her own *hruss* sniffed the dead one, stamping and shifting nervously as it smelled the blood that had pooled under the poor beast's head.

Sira untied Lorn's bedroll from the back of his saddle and spread it out with difficulty, working it under him. Snow still fell into the *quiru* and dampened her face as she tried to work. Everything would be wet with melted snow in an hour. The *quiru* would have to be kept very warm, and Lorn's leg would require whatever help she could muster. She wondered briefly how they could be found, so far from the traveled road, but thrust that worry aside. More immediate matters needed all her concentration.

"Lorn, I will try to ease your pain. I do not know if I can do anything about the leg. Please lie as still as possible and let your mind be open."

The old Singer nodded, his teeth gritted. Sira's earlier impatience with him dissolved in admiration for the unflinching way he accepted the accident and its consequences.

She began to sing, wordlessly, a simple melody in the first mode. She was rewarded by seeing his face smooth and relax almost at once, and his body release its tension. Then she took up her *filla* and played in the second mode, with her eyes closed, trying to see the injured leg.

The weakness in her Gift appalled her. Her psi encountered the chaos of broken bone and torn flesh, and could go no farther. She had almost no idea of what to do.

The mountain *hruss* were heavy, muscular creatures. Lorn's had fallen with its full weight on his leg. Sira put her *filla* down. After some thought, she dug through Lorn's saddlepack until she found a large piece of softwood. She took a deep breath, put her hands on the crushed leg, and straightened it with one swift, strong movement. Lorn gave a long, deep groan, but did not open his eyes. Sira bound the leg to the piece of wood with strips of leather cut from the injured man's saddle.

"I am sorry," she muttered aloud. "All I can think to do is to try to get you down to the traveled road."

She sat back on her heels, wet and exhausted and afraid. Around her *quiru* the whiteness was as blank and forbidding as a solid cliff of ice. Lorn lay still and quiet against his dead *hruss*, and her own *hruss* nudged at her anxiously. Sira felt as if she had been in this spot forever.

Thirst and hunger finally moved her to action. It was easier this time to get to her saddlepack, and she untied it and laid it out on her bedroll. The *hruss* whickered at her, and she patted its big shoulder. "Be easy," she said to the animal. "We will not be going anywhere today."

She cleared a spot of the wet snow and set out softwood twigs and a little tinder, and began to try again with the flint and stone.

For the first time, she was successful, and she breathed a prayer of thanks as a curl of smoke, no less white than their surroundings, rose into the *quiru*. There was a chuckle from Lorn. "Finally got it?" he said through pale lips.

"Finally," she said. She was inordinately proud of her little fire as it crackled gently.

"Can't fix my leg, can you, Cantrix?"

Sira looked sharply at the old man. She had told him nothing of her background. "I am just a Singer," she said lamely. "Like you."

Lorn ignored that. His voice was weak as he went on. "Conservatory doesn't teach that, I guess. It's bad, though."

"I am afraid it is bad," Sira said. "But I am not a very good judge. Without a *pukuru*, it will be difficult to carry you back to the main road."

Lorn's eyes fluttered weakly, and Sira hung her head, feeling helpless. What would she do now? Food, she decided, was the first thing, and then she would think, long and hard.

As she busied herself with *keftet* in her little cooking pot, Lorn roused again. "You'll have to go back without me."

Sira shook her head. "You could die here alone, and without my singing the pain would be terrible."

"I may die in any case."

There was a long silence. Sira made tea, and handed Lorn a cup. She stirred the grain and dried *caeru* meat over the fire, trying not to burn it this time, adding snow when it looked dry. At last she said, "I will make a sled and pull it behind the mare."

Lorn managed a dry chuckle. "You can't even saddle your own *hruss*!"

"I can and I did," Sira reminded him. "When the weather clears, we will go down. Together." It sounded simple enough, except that Sira had no idea where they were, or if she would recognize the road if she found it. But she could bear no more deaths on her conscience.

Lorn nodded and closed his eyes. They both knew he would die if she left him. He said weakly, "Thanks, Cantrix."

"Just Singer," she said, but very quietly.

CHAPTER
NINETEEN

✳ THE SNOW CONTINUED ALL NIGHT AND MOST OF THE NEXT
day. When finally it began to taper off, it was
already too late for them to make a start. Sira had sung for
Lorn several times, when the pain began to rise again, and
he accepted her help gratefully. She had cooked for him,
too, inexpertly, but they ate everything regardless of its
quality. Between their two saddlepacks, they estimated they
had food for about five days; but it was not food that
worried Sira.

She fashioned a makeshift *pukuru* from Lorn's bedfurs,
using the cinch, flank strap, and ties from his saddle as a
harness. She remembered the cushioned, bone-runnered
pukuru that had carried the injured Singer to Conservatory;
hers would not be so comfortable. The deep snow would
have to cushion Lorn until they found the main road, she
thought, where perhaps there would be softwood trees to rig
as runners.

The second morning in their precarious campsite dawned
without snow. Now Sira saw a steep, treeless slope falling
away to the east, as if they were on some winding mountain
trail, certainly not one of the roads they had been seeking.
Lorn's face looked as gray as his hair, his eyes sunken and
glazed. The bowl of *keftet* she gave him he barely touched.

Sira ate, and fed the *hruss*, and then carefully turned it

190

around on the narrow path. She began to try to fasten the clumsy runnerless sled to the back of her own saddle. She knew little of knots and had never tied anything but her hair when it was long, and the leather was thick and unwieldy in her fingers. She fashioned an awkward sort of tether to attach to Lorn's bedfurs, splitting the other end to tie to either side of her saddle.

Mounting her *hruss*, and urging it into a gentle walk, Sira turned sideways to watch the improvised *pukuru* as it slid over the snow. She was afraid it would slide right under the *hruss*'s hooves, or that it would come undone. They left the body of Lorn's *hruss* behind without a glance, and traveled for what seemed an impossibly long time, with Sira constantly looking backward.

The path was treacherous, but the *hruss* was surefooted and careful, and more than once Sira patted it gratefully on the withers. Once she had to stop and tighten the cinch, doing her best to make it comfortable for the animal but still safe. Lorn appeared to be asleep, so she mounted again and they resumed their slow progress down the mountainside.

Softwood trees began to appear again, and the sky cleared. Sira could see why Lorn had thought this was a road. Their path widened and smoothed, little by little. She wondered how she could learn all the roads and trails of the Continent, the way an itinerant must. Certainly not alone; she would need to apprentice herself to someone. The thought made her grit her teeth; the independence she longed for seemed further away than ever.

At midday, Sira reined in her *hruss*, and got down to check the injured man. Lorn's color was no better, and he didn't rouse when she spoke to him. Rather than do battle with the flint and stone, she ate some cold dried meat and fed the *hruss* with a bit of grain from her hand.

Climbing back in the saddle, she set off again, stopping

once in a while to adjust the sled or retie a strap. Through
the long day they rode, until Sira's neck and back ached
from the strain of guarding the *pukuru*, and her legs
trembled with fatigue from bracing herself in the saddle.

At last the trail came out into a broad, more level stretch
of packed snow that looked as if it might be a road. Sira
stopped the *hruss*, shakily dismounting and leaning against
the stirrup for a moment to let her muscles recover. She
thought Lorn might recognize the road in the morning.
Tonight they would camp here, and eat, and tomorrow they
could decide their route.

Lorn still slept, even as she untied the sled and smoothed
his bedroll around him. She spoke to him, and touched his
shoulder, but he did not respond. She even extended a gentle
tendril of her thought into his mind, but he was not
dreaming and the waves of his thought were blank and
unreadable.

A glowing *quiru* was firmly established around the little
party when dark fell. Sira struggled with the fire, almost
giving up until she heard a *ferrel* scream in the distance.
Then she tried one more time. The muscles of her wrists
ached with the effort, but she was rewarded by the smoke
that rose at last from her little pile of tinder and softwood.
She cooked *keftet* again, and ate all of it quickly, although
it was cold in the middle and burned underneath. The *hruss*
nuzzled her shoulder and she realized she had forgotten to
feed it.

"Sorry," she murmured, rising quickly to dig grain out of
her saddlepack. The *hruss* dipped its muzzle into the grain,
and Sira spared a moment to worry about how flat the
saddlepack was getting. The softwood was in shortest
supply. It had never occurred to her to bring an axe, and she
had no idea whether there would be deadfall to burn.

She bent over Lorn, but he lay ominously still and quiet

as he had all day. Sira did not know what else she could do for him. She turned back to the *hruss* and snuggled close to the animal's warmth for a moment before unsaddling it.

Finally she rolled into her own furs, first checking to see Lorn was well-covered, and that the *quiru* would last the night. She slept fitfully, with dreams of great roads that led endlessly nowhere.

When the weak light of early morning woke Sira, a glance told her that Lorn was no better. She knelt by him, noting his poor color and his irregular, shallow breathing, and knew as surely as she had ever known anything that he would wake no more.

She knelt where she was a long time, thinking about this man who had spent his life as a Singer in these mountains and had yet made a fatal error, bringing it to an end. She would be better than that, she thought, when she had learned this new craft. She would be the best at it, or not bother at all.

Sira could not leave Lorn while he still lived. They had no real relationship other than that created by their traveling together, but she could not abandon him to die alone. She would do what could be done for the old Singer. She tried not to think about what would happen next. Even a man at the point of death was some company; when his spirit left his body, she would be alone in the mountains once again.

In the late afternoon of that day, the old Singer took one last rattling breath, and then was still. Sira, watching him, knew he was dead. She prayed briefly for his passage beyond the stars. Then with a pan from her saddlepack, she began to dig into the crusted snow beneath a nearby ironwood tree. It took some time, and she was wet with perspiration when she had scooped out a hole big enough.

She rolled Lorn, wrapped in his furs, into his makeshift grave. There was little else she could do.

It was growing dark, and she needed to renew her *quiru* for another night in this place. First she looked around to try to judge her location. She knew the east and west of it, but she had no way of knowing where she was in relation to any House except Conservatory, or even to a main road. Her education had been painstaking and intensive, but it had omitted the geography of the Continent; that was not something a Cantrix needed to know.

She knew that west was the direction of Conservatory, Magister Mkel, and Isbel, and more arguments to persuade her from her decision. At Conservatory she would have to confront her memories, and that seemed pointless; nothing could make them go away. She shook her head even as she thought of it.

To the east lay mystery . . . other Houses, possibly the Watchers, certainly Lamdon, somewhere. Could she find them? There was risk in turning east, but the choice was hers. If she could find Ogre Pass . . . She reached for her *filla*. She had come so far, and fearful as she might be, she had no wish to turn back. In the morning, she would ride east.

CHAPTER
TWENTY

★ THEO WAS NOT FOND OF TRAVELING ALONE, BUT HE WAS
no stranger to lonely campsites. He was careful to
make a *quiru* early and to build a substantial fire. Mainly he
regretted leaving the warm atmosphere of Conservatory,
and his first night in the mountains seemed long and empty.
He tried to pass the time before sleeping by whistling a tune
he had heard one of the students play, putting it to his *filla*,
thinking up words for it. It was when he lay down in his
bedfurs under the starred splendor of the mountain night
that he felt his loneliness the most, and wished for the
thousandth time that he was not destined to be always an
outsider.

The season was just beginning its shift into the deep cold
of the year, when less snow would fall and the bite of the
cold would grow deeper and deeper. Theo carried extra furs
with him, purchased from the Conservatory abattoir with
the last bits of metal he owned. He would need more work
soon, he knew, to keep himself supplied. He smiled to
himself, remembering a fable Isbel had told, in which metal
bits flew from the feet of the Six *Hruss*. Unfortunately,
itinerant Singers had to work hard for those bits!

In the morning, he pulled on an extra layer of *caeru* furs
to protect himself against the sharpening cold. He made an
early start rather than have to renew the *quiru* just before

leaving it, and he rode throughout the day in the immense quiet of the mountains, his furs pulled closely around him, not whistling now.

At midday his progress was interrupted. An inexplicable impulse came over him to leave the road, to turn up a lightly wooded slope to his left. He stopped the *hruss* and thought for a while, trying without success to identify his feeling. It was no more than a hunch, an intuition. At length, telling himself never to ignore the Gift, he turned the *hruss* up the hill.

At the top he found a clear, flat place that had been a campsite fairly recently. There were the snowy ashes of a softwood fire and the rounded depression typically made by a bedroll. There was also an ominously shaped mound under an ironwood tree. Theo dismounted with a sinking feeling in his belly, and dropped to his knees beside the mound.

Although covered with snow, the furs and leathers on the body were still visible, despite the evident care that had been taken to protect it.

Gingerly, Theo brushed away the snow, unfastened and pulled back the hood which had been painstakingly tied over the body's face. It was not a face he recognized. An elderly man, creased and weathered, with wispy graying hair, had been laid to his final rest here in the snow. Theo had no wish to disturb the body, but he knew he should learn as much as possible about anyone who had died out here in the mountains.

Gently, he explored the furs and clothing, shaking his head sadly as he discovered a *filla* still wrapped in soft leather, tied to the old man's pack. He also found that one of the legs had been inexpertly splinted. Crouching there, Theo wondered who this old Singer had been, and how he came to this isolated and inadequate grave. And where was the person who had laid him here? If the Singer had had a traveler with him, there might well be another body in the vicinity.

Theo scanned the area carefully. Snow had filled in any footprints, but a second body should not be hard to see. He forced himself to search hard for that which he devoutly hoped not to find. At last, having made no more sad discoveries after a reasonable amount of time, Theo mounted and rode away from the campsite, whispering a quick prayer for the dead. He hoped he wouldn't need to say another one soon. Surely, he thought, this was Sira's traveling companion, and now she's alone for the second time in the Marik Mountains.

Sira hadn't realized the season was changing until she felt the sting of the deeper cold through her furred gloves. The wet snowfall high in the mountains had confused her. She had ridden alone for one full day, heading due east, dreading the end of the day, the early dark, and the long night alone.

The emptiness of the mountains was a tangible presence to her, with every sound magnified into a thrill across her nerves. She made her camp at the first sign of dusk, raising a strong yellow *quiru* into the evening light that shaded swiftly from violet to purple as she worked. Her *filla* sounded small and desolate under the looming peaks.

She struggled with the flint, but could get no spark to leap on to her little pile of softwood. The thought of a fireless campsite and cold food for the days ahead was disheartening, and she slumped onto her bedroll in despair. How have I reached this state once again? she asked herself. Why do I insist on having things exactly my way, and at such cost?

She looked around at her little campsite. Only her *quiru* looked right. She longed for hot tea and its faint comfort.

Probably, she told herself, she was not stacking the

softwood properly. Sighing, she took out the flint once again.

Before she struck it, a sound fell upon her sensitive ears, and she lifted her head, listening hard. A slow chill ran across her scalp as she listened and grew certain that something or someone was approaching. It was not yet dark enough for a *tkir* to be hunting, surely. Apprehensive, she stood and faced the direction of the sound. She could see nothing, but she heard hoofbeats . . . a *hruss*'s hoofbeats, softened by the snowpack. She closed her eyes and reached out with her mind, seeking the identity of the approaching rider.

Theo had pushed the *hruss* hard all day, but the canopy of cloudless sky was tinged with violet now, and if he didn't stop soon he would be risking the cold. Alone with his thoughts for many hours, his fears for Sira intensified. He was trying to hurry, although he knew the chances of actually finding her were slender. After all, he fretted to himself, how would she know in what direction to travel, much less where the road was that led into the Pass? He had been afraid of finding her body somewhere along the way, and he had watched carefully to see if there were recent tracks that showed anyone turning away from the road into the surrounding mountains. But he had seen nothing, and half-relieved, half-fearful, he pressed on.

The glow of a *quiru* up ahead, a slender finger of light glowing like a beacon about a half hour's ride away, came as a surprise in the empty landscape. Theo hurried his *hruss* again, hope making his heart beat faster under his thick furs. The beast obediently stretched its long stride, its wide hooves making soft thuds on the snowpack, and Theo patted its shaggy neck in appreciation.

Her campsite was tucked between two shallow folds of

the snowy ground. Theo could see her clearly outlined in the *quiru* as he came closer, and he grinned broadly, hardly believing his good fortune.

He rode into her camp beaming with smiles, and was surprised and alarmed to see Sira, always so self-possessed and aloof, standing in a fireless *quiru* with tears running down her face, looking out into the dark, waiting for him.

"Cantrix Sira!" he exclaimed, and swung one leg over the horn of his saddle to jump down. "It's me. It's Theo!"

"I know," she said, and she began to sob aloud, her face crumpling like a child's. "I could hear you," meaning of course his mind. He strode forward and stood inches away from her. Every instinct in him wanted to hold out his arms, to comfort her, but of course one did not touch a full Cantrix unnecessarily.

"Then what is it?" he asked helplessly.

She shook her head, unable to speak. All at once he understood, with a flash of intuition almost as clear in his mind as her call for help many weeks before. She had braced herself for this journey, had rebelled against everything she knew, and had watched a man die and then buried him; and she was alone out here in the dark for the second time in her short life. His arrival had released her iron control at last, and as the long weeks of struggle demanded their price, she had broken down completely.

He looked at the sobbing girl, so young to have seen so much, now lost and alone. With a shake of his head, he offered to bridge the distance between them by holding out his arms. Sira took the one long step that was needed, moving into his strong embrace and weeping helplessly against his shoulder for a very long time.

When she had finally cried herself out, all of her fear and loneliness and disillusionment streaming out in waves of sobs, Sira was embarrassed and shy at having displayed her feelings in such a way. But Theo, drying her face, sitting her down on her furs, and beginning preparations for a meal with pragmatic efficiency, commenced his usual flow of talk as if comforting crying girls was an everyday occurrence with him. Indeed, she thought, perhaps it was. She watched him start her fire with an easy flick of his wrist over the flint, and scoop snow into the pot for tea.

"I'm glad to have company out here," he said. "Two days alone is enough to think all your thoughts and be ready to talk about them. Now, some conversation, some *keftet*, some tea . . . that's the civilized way to spend an evening."

He looked up at her swollen eyes, the scarred eyebrow, and her thin tear-marked cheeks. "You're a wonderful sight for a lonely traveler," he said without irony, and winked at her.

Sira watched him where he squatted easily by the fire, slicing *caeru* strips into a second pot. Despite his size, he was light and quick in the cramped space of the campsite. She was afraid to try to speak with lips that felt puffy and shaky, and so she sent to him, *Theo, I am glad to see you, too.*

His head snapped up and he stared at her. "I heard that!" he said. He paused for a moment, and then said, "Can you teach me to do it?"

"Perhaps," she finally said aloud, her voice still thick with the aftermath of weeping. "If you receive easily"—she had to clear her throat before continuing—"you can probably send as well." She took the cup of tea he passed her, pressing her hands around its warmth. She shuddered slightly with the last spasm left from her tears, and then sat quietly, waiting for her composure to return.

"You know, Theo, we all heard minds spontaneously as

children," she told him. "I will try to think how to teach you."

Theo stirred the *keftet*, looking into it, and concentrated, his forehead gathering in deep lines as he tried to send her his thought.

"Do not force it," Sira said, seeing his effort. "It simply feels like sending your thought out away from you."

Theo tried again, more calmly. He sent, *The meal is ready.*

Sira smiled at him. "Ready? I heard 'ready.'"

Theo's lopsided grin was rueful. "It's a beginning, I guess! I was trying to tell you our meal is ready."

Good, she sent. *I am hungry.*

He winked at her, delighted. "Me, too," he said.

CHAPTER
TWENTY-ONE

✳ SIRA AND THEO RODE TOGETHER DOWN INTO OGRE PASS
under a clearing sky, and made their next camp on
the broad floor of the Pass between steep slopes. They
camped facing northeast, toward where Lamdon lay, now at
a distance of five days' ride. During the day they had
experimented, with Theo sending to Sira, and she mind-
listening and reporting to him what she heard. Frequently
Theo laughed aloud at the result, Sira smiling in return,
while the *hruss*'s pointed ears flicked back and forth
between them, listening to their voices.

Sitting by the fire in the evening, Theo asked Sira to bring
out her food supplies so they could measure what they had
together. It looked a meager pile to her, little cloth sacks of
grain and dried meat, but Theo said it would be enough. "If
we don't take side trips, we should be able to eat three times
a day until Lamdon." He stowed all the food supplies in
Sira's saddlepack. "Take care of that," he admonished,
grinning. "Empty bellies make cold company."

He did not try to persuade her to go back to Conservatory.
He told her of the concern of Magister Mkel and her friend
Isbel, and she nodded acknowledgment but did not answer.
He let the matter rest. He would send word from Lamdon,
he decided. He had been hired to find her, not to force her

to return. If Magister Mkel felt otherwise, Theo would simply return the bits of metal he had been paid.

They went to sleep early, wrapped snugly in their furs. The sounds of the wilderness around them, noises that had been threatening and fearful when Sira was alone, now seemed friendly and companionable. The night was windless and clear, and the smoke from the embers of their softwood fire drifted in a narrow spiral high into the empty purple sky above the Pass.

They slept long, and Theo woke with the sun bright in his eyes. The morning was quiet, but the *hruss* held their heads high, ears turned forward, staring at something beyond the sun-faded *quiru*.

Theo rolled over quickly and looked up from his bedfurs into a semicircle of men, furred and conspicuously armed with bows and knives, sitting their *hruss* around the campsite. The glitter of the early sun on the snow made them luminous ghosts, and he had to squint through the brilliance to try to identify them. His belly clenched in the sure recognition of trouble.

Sira lay in her bedroll, still sleeping, with her face toward him. Without stopping to think, he sent to her, *Wake up now, but move very slowly when you do. Sira! Wake up now. Slowly.*

Sira opened her eyes at once and looked directly at him. She said nothing and her face was unreadable, but clearly she had understood enough to respond. She slowly pushed back her furs and sat up to face the riders ranged around their camp.

The scene held a moment in complete silence, until one of the *hruss* outside the *quiru* stamped impatiently.

"Sorry to disturb you, Singer," came a raspy voice, directed at Theo. His accent was strange, thick and guttural. His furs were heavy and well-worn. "You will break camp now, please," he went on. "One of us will give you a hand."

Theo slid barefoot out of his bedfurs and reached for his boots, while Sira watched in tense silence. He felt for his long knife where he had left it in one boot. He and Sira were only two against six, but he put his hand on the knife just the same, and measured the distance between himself and the leader.

"Chad will take your knife," the man rasped, indicating one of the riders.

Theo straightened with the knife in his hand. The man closest to Sira drew his own knife and pointed it, almost casually, at her throat.

Theo sighed. He reversed the knife and held it out to the man called Chad, hilt first, who tucked it inside his own boot. Sira's knife, Theo remembered with regret, was in her saddlepack with the cooking things. Her *filla*, though, like his own, was tucked safely inside her tunic.

She sent to Theo, *Who are they?*

And he responded, *Watchers.* Even in the stress of the moment, he took pleasure in his growing ability to hear and send.

What next?

Careful, he sent back. He couldn't tell if she actually understood him, but surely she could guess. He was standing now, fully dressed and grim-faced.

"What do you want with us?" he asked the newcomers gruffly.

The raspy-voiced one nodded at Chad. "Saddle the *hruss*," he said, and then replied to Theo. "We need you at Observatory, Singer. Your traveler can stay or come, as she wishes."

Chad dismounted and busied himself with the *hruss* and their tack, and Sira set about dressing herself to ride, looking to Theo for guidance. He nodded at her and then turned back to the leader.

"By what right," Theo said through gritted teeth, "do you abduct us?"

The Watcher was unmoved by Theo's anger. "By right of need," the raspy voice came back, and then he turned his back on them, giving instructions to one of the others.

"We don't enjoy this, Singer, but we have no choice." This was Chad, who was handing the reins to one of his own group, and taking Sira's and Theo's bedrolls to tie onto their *hruss*.

"You would leave me alone here without my *hruss*?" called Sira to the leader. Her deep, resonant voice rang across the campsite, and Theo caught his breath, suddenly realizing the Watchers had no idea what they had found. They had assumed he was the Singer and Sira the traveler. He held his breath, hoping Sira would understand and keep silent.

The leader turned back to look at Sira more closely. He was short and squat of build, with hard, intelligent eyes.

"We need *hruss* almost as much as we need Singers," he said. "But we need people at Observatory, too. Come with us; you would likely die out here in any case."

"Mount up, traveler," said Chad. "You too, Singer. We don't waste sunlight."

Slowly and deliberately, Theo moved toward his *hruss*. He caught Sira's eye and tried to send to her, *Don't*. She raised her scarred eyebrow at him in question, but kept silent as she moved to her own *hruss*. They mounted warily, without sudden motions. Two of the strangers kept their *hruss*'s reins. Chad picked up all the remaining equipment from the campsite and stowed it on his own saddle.

Once again Theo tried. *Cantrix. Not tell.*

Sira's face was a frozen mask. To Theo she sent, *Do not tell them I am a Cantrix?*

Yes. Yes! he responded, and the briefest nod from her told him she had the message.

I will not. She leaned back on the cantle of her saddle and folded her arms across her chest. Theo could see she was more angry than afraid. "I can guide my own *hruss*," she snapped at the man who held her reins.

"Soon enough," said the raspy-voiced one. "When we are out of the Pass."

Theo rode silently, stony-faced.

What will they do with us? Sira asked.

He tried to respond, *They want me to work. To sing.* He was fairly certain she could not get much of that thought. The group around them traveled in heavy silence. As they rode down through the Pass in a southerly direction, away from Lamdon, Theo inspected them as closely as he could. That they were a determined, even desperate group was clear. Theo held little hope for an escape.

The group traveled southeast across the Pass, apparently directly for a mountainside. After two hours of riding, with the Watchers still holding Sira's and Theo's reins, they left the Pass by a path that led through a litter of snow-capped boulders and up a narrow snowy canyon. The path had been invisible from the Pass itself. For another hour they climbed steeply twisting, treacherous slopes where the firn, growing deeper in the cold season, seemed almost to hang over their heads. Their way was so steep that Sira had to hold on to her saddle horn at times to keep from sliding off. Theo watched their path closely, but could not see how he would ever remember it. It was almost featureless, an unmarked route through a tangled, precipitous landscape.

"Now you can have your reins," said the leader, whose name they had learned was Pol. "You could never find your way back alone from here." He looked directly at Theo. "Believe me, Singer. Too many men have died trying."

Theo mustered his most cheerful grin. "Must be some House," he said jovially, "if men die trying to get away."

Unexpectedly, Pol gave a short bark of a laugh. His men were silent, their faces set and expressionless. Sira turned unreadable dark eyes on him, and then away.

When the party rode out onto a narrow, terrifying path that circled an immense cliff, Theo looked over his shoulder and gazed in wonder at the vista below. The broad reaches of the Pass they had left hours before swept from the southwest to the northeast, seemingly almost beneath the *hruss*'s feet, and beyond the Pass the Mariks rose in majestic, forbidding splendor. He understood how their abductors had found them; the smoke from their fire and the light of the *quiru* must have been clear and inviting beacons. But as hard as Theo looked, he was unable even now to trace how they had climbed to this spot. Their route was lost in a jumble of rocky cliffs and canyons, invisible from this steep perspective.

He took the reins that Chad handed back to him and glanced ahead, where the *hruss* were strung out along the cliff path. He was sure the path ended in a cul-de-sac, but even as he watched, the lead *hruss* suddenly turned right, as if straight into the bare rock of the cliff, and disappeared. Theo's heart sank; how would they get away from this place?

When he arrived at the turning, he and his *hruss* had to squeeze through a narrow opening, the rock walls scraping his legs as he passed. Ahead was another steep path, winding further and further into a wilderness of rock and snow. At last the leader turned downhill into a broader and easier road across a mountain valley. Theo's shoulders tingled from the tension of the climb, and he rubbed them to restore the circulation as his *hruss* found easy footing on the descent.

It was almost dark when they approached the House. The

leader of the Watchers nodded toward it and grated, "Observatory. Home."

Theo was astonished that the Watchers had made the trip out and back in one day, thinking they must have started very early, risking the dark of the morning hours. Riding without a Singer, they must be desperate indeed. Had anything gone wrong, their whole party would have been lost to the cold.

The House clung stubbornly to the southeastern slope of a narrow peak that towered over those around it. Observatory looked smaller than most of the Houses Theo knew, with an odd, circular addition high on its roof, like a knob or a bowl dropped upside down. He regarded it curiously, but asked no questions. The *quiru* glow around the stone walls was faint and pale.

We will not sing, Sira sent to Theo. He heard her quite clearly. His only response was a shrug. He suspected these men would be ready and willing to let them both die.

I will not, in any case, she sent further. *They cannot force me.* He looked at her face, its narrow mouth set firm, and he had to smile. She would not be an easy one to subdue, he thought with rueful pride. Cantrix Sira would surprise the Watchers.

They rode up to the House in gathering dusk. No welcoming party waited on the rough, slanting steps to receive them. Sira looked down at the steps curiously as she walked up to the door, and realized that they had originally been straight but had shifted and broken as the ground moved below them, and had not been repaired.

The House was cold, colder than any House Sira had ever been in. The corners were dank and moldy, and the floors were icy to the feet. Without ceremony, Sira and Theo were led to narrow, dark rooms furnished only with the simplest of cots and chairs. They were not treated roughly, only matter-of-factly, as their saddlepacks and bedrolls were dropped off with them. Sira's knife was gone from her saddlepack, and every bit of their food had been taken. She was glad she kept her *filla* inside her tunic, close to her body; no one had threatened to search her.

In Nevyan fashion, the "guests" were taken to bathe next. Sira found the water dark and tepid, with two or three other women also in the wooden tub. They looked at her with silent curiosity, and she turned her face away, avoiding contact. She carefully hid her *filla* in a fold of her tunic when she undressed, and endured a cold and unpleasant bath rather than reveal herself by warming it. She wondered how long it had been since the water had been changed, and she took a perverse satisfaction in knowing that the other women must also be cold. She shivered in angry misery as she dressed again in the same clothes she had been wearing.

The dismal cubicle she had been given was at the end of a dark corridor, with empty rooms around it, for which she was grateful. In her own room, at least, she thought, she would have light and warmth. She brought out her *filla* and used it, softly, to brighten the air around her. The room grew warmer, but hardly more cheerful, as the increased light revealed the creeping fungus in the corners of the ceiling, and beads of condensing moisture here and there on the walls. Sira sighed as she tucked her *filla* away.

They had apparently missed the evening meal, and no food was offered. There was nothing to do but go to bed. Sira piled her furs over the ragged blanket on her cot and slid under the mound, the chill from the wall making the bed frigid. She could not sleep until her body's warmth had heated the space she curled herself in. What this House needed, of course, was a *quiru*, a strong one. A healthy, warm House *quiru*, established by a full Cantor or Cantrix, and maintained for some weeks with a daily *quirunha*. That would put an end to the growing molds and fungus.

But I will not do it, Sira insisted into the darkness. Not for them.

In the great room, Sira sat silently next to Theo at the morning meal. The community of Observatory was assembled, but there was little talk around the tables, and the indifferent food, consisting almost entirely of meat, was eaten quickly and without ceremony.

These people look ill, Sira sent to Theo.

His answer was jumbled a bit, but she understood *Cold*, and *Damp*. She nodded, and then caught Pol's eyes on her.

Careful. Pol watches us, she sent.

He is not stupid, Theo responded with surprising clarity.

Sira admired the quickness with which Theo's mind-listening and sending were improving. What a talent, she thought to herself, to have been wasted by not properly training it. She remembered young Zakri, and the ball rolling quickly away from him, and she felt a sharp pang of sympathy. Then she looked around the gloomy room, seeing the reddened cheeks and noses of the House members here, and she grew angry again.

I would like to teach you more, she sent to Theo. *But they will find me out. And we must not sing for them or we will never get away.*

A hard cough from a child at one of the tables distracted her and she turned toward it. She found Pol's short, powerful figure in her line of vision as he rose from his place and came toward them.

"If you have finished your meal, Singer," he said, standing before Theo with his arms folded, waiting.

Sira rose with Theo, feeling curious eyes on them from the House members as they left the great room. Pol led them down a corridor and opened a heavy door.

"Our Cantoris," he said in his grating voice, with a wave of his hand into its shadows. Sira could just make out the dais in its center. "Here you will sing."

Theo put his head to one side and looked down at Pol, an amused expression on his face. "You must think you've captured a *ferrel*, Pol, when all you've got is a poor little *wezel* in your trap."

Pol's eyes narrowed in his craggy face as he looked up at his two captives. "I'm not so sure about that."

"I'm just an old mountain Singer," Theo went on, his face bland and his tone light. "I can't warm a whole House. You need to send to Conservatory for a real Cantor."

"I think perhaps Conservatory has already sent us someone," Pol rasped, staring hard at Sira.

Sira's neck prickled and she felt her face grow warm. There was a long moment of tension, and Pol began to smile. Sira wondered how he had guessed, and supposed he had understood that she and Theo were communicating without words. Or perhaps her voice had given her away. Indeed, thought Sira, he is not stupid. Only cruel. She stood very tall.

"You will have nothing from me," she said.

"Oh, I think we will," Pol said with offhanded triumph. "By the Ship, I think we will! Sooner or later." He closed the door of the Cantoris with a solid thud.

In the great room the next morning, Sira and Theo met Jon v'Arren, an itinerant Singer who had been struggling to keep Observatory warm by himself with only his *filla* and his small, traveler's *quiru*. He was muffled in furs, a middle-aged man who looked exhausted.

"Will you not try to help?" he asked Theo. "I've been here two weeks, and I can't get the place warm. I'm no Cantor, unfortunately."

"I'll try," said Theo, ignoring the look Sira gave him. "But where is their Cantor?"

"Their last one died. He had no Gifted one to train, apparently, and so they got me."

"How did they find you?" Sira asked.

"I was with a party in Ogre Pass, and they attacked us. I think they killed someone. The man who hired me was a hunter, looking for *tkir*, and he shot at them. They shot back."

Sira saw Pol in a corner of the great room, and no one else close enough to overhear their conversation. "What about your travelers?" she asked in a low tone. "Did they just leave them there to die?"

"We were only three hours out from Bariken," Jon said, "and they should have made it back. I hope." He shook his head. "They're crazy. Do you know what they do here?"

Theo and Sira both shook their heads.

"They watch the sky," Jon said.

"They truly do that? Still?" Theo asked incredulously.

"Every night. Two of them go to the top of the House and look through a limeglass roof at the sky."

"A pair," Sira said, "like Cantors."

"Well, maybe. And even if I were able to establish a real House *quiru*, it would have to fade enough by dark so they could see the stars."

Sira had heard the old fables of Observatory and the apocryphal stories of the Ship, and so had everyone else she knew. They were regarded as children's stories. She could hardly believe that these people really waited here to be saved. The idea was preposterous.

"This is not sane," she murmured.

Jon gestured carelessly around the room. "I don't understand any of them. They don't even complain about the cold. Half of them are sick, and their babies die."

"Is there even a *filhata* in the House?" Sira asked. "A House *quiru* takes more than a *filla* to establish."

Jon looked at her with dawning hope. "Can you play a

filhata? I've never even had one in my hands." He turned to Theo. "You? Are you a Cantor?"

Theo gave his lopsided grin. "I'm only an itinerant like yourself, my friend. I wouldn't know which end of a *filhata* to blow into!"

Sira smiled a little in spite of herself. But Jon was looking at her intently. "You, then?" he asked. "Are you a Cantrix?"

Sira grew somber. "I was once," she said. "No more."

"Can you stop being a Cantrix once you have become one?"

"I did. And I will not sing."

"But you'll never get away, you know. You're stuck here, as I am. We may as well be comfortable, don't you think?" he pleaded.

"I am sorry," Sira said firmly. "I will not sing for them. And I will not stay. Pol has guessed at what I am, but it makes no difference to me."

Jon sighed, his weathered face gloomy. "We're going to be cold, then. And you can't get away. They'll never let us go."

Sira was silent. *I will not be used again*, she thought. *They cannot control me. There is no reason for me to sing here.*

At midday, swallowing *keftet* that was too short on grain, Sira looked around the great room for Jon. "He's in the Cantoris," Theo murmured.

She nodded.

"He sings several times each day," Theo added. "And he's exhausted."

Are you going to sing?

Yes, Theo responded. His eyes met hers. *They're cold.*

Sira did not object, and he did not try to persuade her to sing. *Each of us has to deal with these Watchers in our own way*, she thought. She felt someone's eyes on her and looked up to see Pol's face, at the center table, turned intently toward her. The child with the cough hacked and hacked from one side of the room. Sira closed her mind to the sound, and looked steadily back at Pol until at last he turned his eyes away. It was a small and bitter victory. Sira finished her tea and rose from her seat.

The House was slightly warmer and brighter as she walked back to her room, hearing at a distance the faint sound of Jon's and Theo's *filla* from the Cantoris. She was surprised, going into her room, to find a carefully wrapped object lying on her cot. Its shape was unmistakable, and she shook her head sadly as she folded back the stiff and moldy wrapping to disclose an old, cracked, discolored *filhata*.

It must belong to the House, she thought, and now there is no one left to play it. Its carvings were scratched and dented, and its gut strings hung untuned and out of condition from the pegs. She took it up, thinking the instrument felt tragic, abandoned, as if it had a life of its own that she sensed through her fingers. She wondered about those who had played it in times past, and whether anyone would ever play it again. At least, she thought, she could polish the body and restring it without giving in to Pol. She could hardly resist it. Its cracked wood called to her, its silent voice more persuasive than any human's.

Theo found her tracing the carvings of the old *filhata* over and over again with her long fingers. When she saw him, she held it out.

"Someone left this on my bed."

He took it from her, shaking his head. "It's not in very good shape."

"I can repair it, if you will find some cloths and oil for polishing and *caeru* gut for new strings." She paused. *But they will know I am working on it.*

He nodded.

Do you understand why I will not sing?

Theo smiled gently at her. *I do.* He added something else that she didn't catch, and when she looked at him, waiting, he tried again. *Your own decision,* he finally managed. "They are ill, though," he said aloud. "I have to do what I can."

Sira took the old *filhata* into her lap. "That is their choice," she said firmly. "They could rejoin the rest of the Houses, and have Cantors and Cantrixes, and be healthy. I will not sing for fanatics."

Theo's crooked grin reassured her. "I'm not trying to persuade you, Cantrix."

"You must not call me that," she said. She indicated the battered *filhata* on her knees. "But I could teach you on this," she offered.

Theo reached out and touched the instrument. "This was a long way to travel to find a teacher," he said, "but you have a willing student! I'll go dig up what you need. Can't wait to start."

He left Sira's room, and she sat still, holding the ancient *filhata* and searching for its past with her fingers, like trying to recall a forgotten tune. She sat there some time, thinking how sad a place this was, this lonely and isolated House, cut off from the whole of its people by some wild and fabulous idea. The greatest tragedy of all, to her, was that the traditions of its Singers should have been allowed to die out. She remembered the child coughing and coughing in the great room, but she hardened her resolve. If they wanted to be well, there were things they could do. They had no right to disrupt other people's lives, to imprison and use them. If she sang for them, she would only be supporting their insanity. She would not do it.

Never, she promised herself, I will never sing for these rebellious people.

CHAPTER
TWENTY-TWO

✱ THEO HAD SOME TROUBLE GETTING WHAT SIRA NEEDED to restring the *filhata*. Observatory apparently had no Housekeeper, and its various functions seemed only loosely organized. He found his way alone to the abattoir, a cold place at the back of the House that was so dark he could hardly see inside. Three Housemen labored there, doing their best to supply the House with meat and to cure the hides of the *caeru* brought to them by the hunters. They were using an odd smoky lamp, a device Theo had never seen in his life, to slightly dispel the gloom. It reeked of rancid *caeru* fat and its shaky flame guttered around a wick of rag.

Theo stepped just inside the door. "Hello. Want some help?"

They looked up in surprise. The oldest, a wrinkled skinny man of about eight summers, left his work and came forward.

"You're the Singer, aren't you?" he asked with evident bewilderment.

"So I am," Theo said with a smile. He entered the room and shivered at the chilly damp. In all Houses, the abattoir was the least pleasant place, close to the outside for convenience, with blood and refuse littering its floor. This was the worst Theo had seen; he doubted these Housemen could see enough in the dim light to clean it properly between hunts. "Would you like the place a bit warmer, Houseman?" he asked.

The man squinted at him silently. A younger Houseman came up behind him and spoke to Theo. "This place is never warm," he said.

"Colder than a *wezel's* nose in here," Theo agreed. He withdrew his *filla* from his tunic and showed it to them. They stepped back respectfully, and one of them pulled a stool forward for him. Theo sat on it, hoping it wasn't sticky with gore. It was too dark to tell.

The abattoir was an oppressive place to raise a *quiru*. The very air seemed greasy and its dankness was heavy and resistant to Theo's psi. He felt as if he were pushing against it, like trying to force his way out of a snowbank. Finally he closed his eyes and pictured himself in the mountains, imagining a campsite among the irontrees with the pale violet of twilight falling around it. He played a lively *Iridu* tune, and the dark air began to lighten around him. Abruptly and rather unmusically he switched to *Aiodu*, the second mode, which he sometimes used when he wanted his *quiru* to last a long time. When he was finished, he opened his eyes and saw the abattoir clearly for the first time.

It was small, but otherwise much like those of other Houses. Skinned *caeru* carcasses hung against one wall, and a pile of hides lay on a workbench. Others were pegged to dry, and the Housemen had been scraping these, their efforts considerably hindered by the cold. There was only one soaking vat that Theo could see, surrounded by piles of the ironwood bark that was used for tanning. Now the light of Theo's camp-style *quiru*, and the warmth that made the Housemen smile, revealed the work needing to be done.

"That's a nice bit of work, Singer," said the older man.

Theo stood, feeling something sticky on the stool catching at his trousers, disciplining himself not to look just now. He made an ironic bow. "Thanks."

The younger man was shedding his filthy tunic, reveling in the warmth. "You should do that in every room of Observatory," he said.

Theo shook his head ruefully. "That would not be possible," he replied. "This one will diminish by evening, you know. I, or any other Singer, could spend every waking moment playing up *quiru*, and still not be able to warm the House. Probably collapse in the end, besides."

"You are welcome to play here at any time, Singer," the older one said. "What can we do to bring you back?"

Theo's ready grin made them smile back at him. "Well," he said with a wink, "there just might be something." He went to the workbench, where coiled, split *caeru* gut was ranged in untidy rows. "I could certainly use some of this."

The Houseman followed him and lifted the largest coil from the bench. "It's yours, Singer." He took a wood-handled *tkir* tooth from a peg on the wall, cut a long length of the gut cord with its sharp serrated edge, and handed it to Theo.

Theo took it and bowed again, although very little bowing seemed to be done here. He was on his way out of the abbatoir, now a considerably less dismal place than it had been, when the younger man called to him. "Singer?" Theo turned back at the door. "Could you warm my family's apartment, just once? My mate's never well, can't seem to get warm, ever."

Theo hesitated a long moment. "I'm sorry, Houseman," he said at last. "I wish that I could. It would be unfair to warm one apartment and no others. I promise you, though, that I'm doing all I can." The man nodded in resignation, and Theo went out slowly, weighed down by the need of these people. It was too much to hope that he could really make any difference in this House. He simply didn't know how.

The kitchens were neither so dark nor so cold as the abattoir had been. Theo found several Housemen and women working there, cutting chunks of *caeru* meat and dicing a tiny harvest of vegetables to fill a pot of *keftet*. Neither fruit nor nuts were in evidence, and the wooden tubs of grain were distressingly small. Even here, with the softwood burning hot in the ovens, mold crept down the walls from the high ceiling.

Theo bowed to the woman who appeared to be in charge. "Housewoman," he said, "can you spare some clean rags and oil?"

She looked at him, her hands on her hips. Her gray hair was tied back neatly, although the tunic she wore looked as if her best efforts could never get it clean. She eyed Theo as if he were a small boy begging sweets.

"What are they for, Singer?" she asked crisply. "We have little to spare."

Theo tried to smile on her. "Someone left me an old *filhata*," he said. "I had in mind to try to repair it."

"Can you play a *filhata*?" she asked, a glimmer of hope in her face. When he shook his head, she sighed deeply. "Then what point is there, Singer?"

There was a moment of silence, and Theo ventured another grin. "Now what would have happened, Housewoman," he said, "if the people had said that to First Singer? First Singer had to start somewhere, didn't he? Don't you know that story?"

The Housewoman looked suspicious, folding her arms tightly across her bosom. "What story?"

"Well," Theo began, and looked around him for someplace to sit. The other Housemen and women came closer, curious. Theo, despairing of a chair, leaned his hip against a table and addressed his little audience.

"Well," he said again. "You know that when the Spirit sent the great *pukuru* to the Continent . . ."

"You mean the Ship," put in the Housewoman firmly. "Spirit of Stars sent the Ship, with all the people and plant seeds."

Theo's grin grew wide. "The Ship, then. When the Spirit sent the Ship, and it overturned and made First House, it started to get cold right away." There were nods around him. They apparently knew this story, but they were happy to suspend their work and listen to it once again, told in a new voice.

"It started to get cold, and the people began to shiver. What were they going to do? They looked around them, outside the . . . the Ship, and they saw only irontrees. They got colder and colder, and First House got very dark when First Night came.

"It was during First Night that the wonder happened. First Singer began to sing to a little baby, who was cold and crying. First Singer hated to hear children cry, and he tried to make his lullaby a warm, sweet one to comfort this child.

"Now if the mother of that child had told First Singer to be quiet, not to disturb her child, what might have happened? First Singer might never have seen that first glow that came from his warm lullaby. The people might have perished during First Night.

"But the mother didn't tell First Singer to leave them alone, and First Singer sang the warmest lullaby he could think of. First House grew warm and light, and the people survived."

The Housewoman made an abrupt noise with her tongue. "Singer, do you think you're going to work a wonder?"

Theo's smile faded, and he stood up. "I do not know," he

said, sounding like Sira for a moment. "But if something great does not happen here, this House is going to perish."

The other workers moved uneasily, the mood broken. A young Housewoman sniffled and turned away. The Housewoman in charge moved to a drawer and took out a handful of cloths. "We're not going to perish," she said firmly. "But you might as well try to fix that old *filhata*. Mrie, fetch a bit of cooking oil for the Singer." As the girl went to do as she was told, the Housewoman turned back to Theo. "No need to frighten the young ones," she said, "but it was a good story. You're no First Singer, I suppose, but we could do with a wonder."

"So we could." Theo took the oil and the cloths, and bowed to the Housewoman. She surprised him with a stiff bow of her own, something at which she had evidently had little practice.

"Good luck," she said.

"Thank you, Housewoman," Theo said. She turned back immediately to her work. Theo was thoughtful as he carried the things back to Sira's room. If he learned to play that *filhata*, he thought, it would be wonder enough.

Sira and Theo worked on the *filhata* for three days before it was ready to play. Theo sharpened his own well-kept knife for Sira to use, and she cut the strings carefully from the *caeru* gut, saving the leftovers in a scrap of oiled cloth. She stretched the strings delicately from the body of the *filhata* to the pegs, and then removed them to cut and cut again until they were just the right thickness. While she was cutting strings, Theo polished the marred surface of the *filhata* with oil, and tried to converse with Sira silently.

These cracks . . . carvings, he sent. Then something else that was a blur she could not understand.

She looked over at his work. *The body is intact?* she asked, and he nodded yes. *Good*, she sent.

It is hard to send without . . . His sending blurred again, and Sira shook her head, smiling a little. Theo sighed. Aloud he said, "It's like digging through a snowdrift. Why is my best sending only when I'm in trouble?"

Sira chuckled, but still she answered silently. *Emotion provides energy,* she sent. *The first sendings are always spontaneous. Receivings, too.*

"Doesn't frustration count as an emotion?" Theo asked aloud. He slapped his knee. "I have plenty of that!"

Send me a description of the filhata *now. Show me how it looks, what you are doing. It will come.*

Theo ran his fingers over the whorls and ridges of the carving. *The cracks are in the carved sections,* he sent as clearly as he could. *The wood has dried and split. But the body of the* filhata *is whole, and should resonate all right.*

If Sira did not understand all that he sent, she hid it from him. She only nodded with satisfaction, and took the instrument back into her own lap. Now she strung the strings more tightly, twisting the pegs till they drew taut. She began to tune them, patiently adjusting and readjusting them at both ends, sometimes using the knife to trim a bit more, sparingly.

At the end of three days she wrapped the instrument and placed it carefully on the single shelf in her room. Theo smiled with satisfaction.

Tomorrow? he asked her.

Yes. Your first lesson tomorrow. They were in perfect accord, and they walked down the gloomy hallway to the great room for the evening meal, one dark head and one fair, one tall and thin and one powerfully built. They were friends now, Sira thought, truly friends. The Spirit of Stars had sent her an unexpected blessing, and she was grateful for it. It was the only light in the darkness of her imprisonment in this place.

The next day Theo worked with Jon in the Cantoris for an hour or more, and then came to Sira's room, looking tired and drawn.

Rest first, she sent to him.

He nodded and sat on the cot, leaning his big shoulders against the wall. *This must be the driest wall in the whole House,* he sent, and Sira laughed a little. He did not laugh with her. Sira grew quiet, and she caught a flash of Theo's feeling. It was troubling, and she tried to shield her mind, but their rapport was growing stronger each day. The people of Observatory were cold and ill. She knew it. She would not sing, just the same. She wondered if Theo thought she was being selfish, or perhaps cruel. As she thought that, he looked up at her quickly.

No, he sent. *I do not.*

Sira looked down at her hands, suddenly shy. She had not kept her thoughts low, forgetting his growing abilities.

I think you are doing what you need to do, he went on. *And I am doing the same.*

She wished she could touch his hand. It seemed a summer since she had felt the touch of another human being. This thought she did keep low, however; she would not want the Singer to misunderstand her. He had held her as she cried in Ogre Pass, but there was no need now. She was neither sad nor frightened.

For the first time in her life she wondered how the Cantors and Cantrixes bore the isolation and loneliness that was their lot. Many worked in the Houses for six summers or more before being called home to Conservatory. All those years without a touch of a human hand seemed suddenly an enormous burden to Sira. She thought of Isbel, on her way to Amric now, and sighed.

What is it? Theo sent to her, his blue eyes dark with concern. She shook off the mood.

It is nothing. Are you ready?

Ready.

As Sira reached for the newly repaired *filhata* and placed it in Theo's hands, he sent carefully, *I am grateful to you for teaching me.*

I am glad to have something to do, she sent to him. *I am not used to such inactivity.*

Theo grinned at her. *You could sing, Singer.*

Sira made a face at him. *Do not make me regret that I taught you to send!* He laughed.

It was a new experience for Sira to be easy in the company of anyone but Isbel and perhaps Maestra Lu, but she and Theo had spent days together, practicing mind-listening, talking, sharing all their meals. In a way she felt as if he were filling the void created in her life by the loss of Maestra Lu. She took pleasure now in showing how to hold the *filhata*. With the briefest of touches she placed his left hand so, and showed him how to poise his right above the strings. She tried to look at him critically, as her teachers had done with her. He was her student now, she thought, her responsibility, though she was truly too young and inexperienced to teach. The unknowable Spirit had put them together in this way, and they could only try to do Its will in the best way they knew.

A prickle of tears surprised Sira as Theo bent his blond head and tried the strings of the ancient *filhata*. It seemed many summers ago that she had held a *filhata* for the very first time; it was hardly credible that it had been no more than two. As she adjusted Theo's hand position, Sira reflected that in fact she was barely nineteen years old, four summers. She felt as old as the very stones of Observatory.

CHAPTER
TWENTY-THREE

✳ SIRA SAT ALONE AT THE MORNING MEAL AND LISTENED TO
Jon and Theo working in the Cantoris, the sounds
of their *filla* coming faintly through the stone walls. They
did their work early so that what *quiru* they were able to
create would begin to fade by night, in accordance with the
requirements of the House. It was an unnecessary precau-
tion; the *quiru* light was never bright enough to fade the
light of the stars.

Pol sat at the central table, and Sira felt his cold gaze
upon her. He was waiting, she knew, for her to acquiesce,
and follow her colleagues into the Cantoris. She tried not to
think of the repaired *filhata* lying useless in her room.
Stubbornly, she took a long time over her tea, letting him
watch her sit idly and pointlessly at the long table.

The meals here left her hungry, and she sometimes
dreamed of the nursery fruit that was so abundant at
Conservatory. She was certain that fruit would not grow in
the inadequate *quiru* of Observatory. Grain, yeast bread, and
meat, with a paltry sprinkling of vegetables, were all there
had been from Observatory's kitchens.

At length, Theo and Jon joined her. Jon looked tired and
reproachful, but Theo sat down beside her, smiling, as
cheerful as ever.

I am hungry, he sent. Sira reached for a bowl of the greasy *keftet*, grown cold by then.

This is all there is, she sent back. Jon had a bowl also, and was eating listlessly. Theo tried some, and made a face.

You should eat anyway, Sira sent to him.

If I eat my keftet, *will you teach me the* filhata?

Sira's mouth curved in a smile, and Jon looked at her curiously.

"What's funny?" he asked.

"Nothing," she said, and stopped smiling. She pushed her bowl away. It was really not polite to be sending when Jon could not hear them. The practice was so good for Theo, though. She watched Jon as he slumped over his bowl of *keftet*. What exactly was the difference between Jon and Theo? Was Theo more Gifted, and Jon less, or was it a matter of circumstance? Jon did not interest her at all as a student, while Theo seemed rich with untrained talent and special abilities.

She rose from the table, compunction making her careful to keep her face impassive as she sent to Theo, *Meet me after your meal*.

He, too, showed nothing on his face when he sent, *I will be there very soon*. As she left the great room, she heard him telling Jon some joke, trying to bring a smile to the dour face, and her own smile returned. Theo, she thought, was an unusual man, and worthy of any instruction she could give him. She looked forward to seeing him learn.

The first lesson on the *filhata* was of course tuning. Sira showed Theo the middle, deepest string and sang the C pitch for him, to which it must always be tuned. To be sure he understood, she spoke aloud. "You must memorize the C," she said. "Begin and end each day by singing the C until it is as automatic to you as your breath." She sang it again, and he sang it also.

"I believe I have already memorized it," he said.

"Have you, Theo?" she asked. "Do itinerants memorize it also?"

He shook his head, and then he grinned happily. "I can't speak for all itinerants," he said, "but since I was little I have always remembered all the pitches." He showed her by singing *Iridu*, the first mode, that began on the C pitch.

Wonderful, Theo, she sent to him now. *Your Gift includes perfect pitch. You will be an easy student to teach.*

Thank you, Maestra, he sent with a little bow. Sira's smile faded.

You must not call me that, she sent. *I have not earned it.*

He raised his eyebrows, but made no further comment. He watched her long fingers as they deftly turned the pegs in the neck of the *filhata*, and soon tried it himself. C was the middle string; from the top to the bottom, they were E, B, F, down to the low C, up to G, D, A. Sira showed him the little exercise by which she had learned to check the tuning: C-G, D-A, E-B, F-C. Theo plucked it slowly, carefully, grinning like a small boy with a new toy. He did it again, and again, and then Sira gave him a new exercise and he played that one too, slowly at first and then more deftly.

After some time, they both sat back, satisfied. Sira had not noticed until that moment that her hands had been on Theo's, guiding them, adjusting their position, and his curling hair had brushed her cheek as she leaned close enough to demonstrate the exercises. She had been too absorbed to notice. It had been exactly as if she were back at Conservatory, with all the Gifted ones with whom she had grown up. Now she felt shy again, realizing, but Theo's enthusiasm covered any embarrassment.

Will you play something for me? he asked. *Something hard!*

Sira smiled. *Something hard? I am somewhat out of practice, remember.*

But as she took the *filhata* in her hands, automatically checking the tuning once again, the feel of the carved wood and the strings under her fingers recalled a melody she had played long ago. She had not held a *filhata* since Maestra Lu's death, and she found herself moved by an emotion she had not yet expressed.

As she began the melody, she forgot where she was, the cold and dark and her frustration and anger, and she poured her soul into the music as she used to do before her experiences had changed the course of her life. The air in the little room grew warm and bright, and Theo's own psi floated with Sira's in an ecstatic moment of forgetfulness. She could feel his mind there with hers, his strength and calm, and the closeness was a great comfort.

When it ended, they were quiet together for some moments. Sira drew a deep breath, and Theo closed his eyes wearily. An odd sound from just outside the room made him open them, and they looked at each other in surprise. It came again, a small, mewling cry like that of an infant. Sira laid down the *filhata* and went to the door.

The corridor outside her room had grown bright and warm with the overflow of heat from Sira's playing. Two young women were seated on the floor, leaning against the outside wall of Sira's room, basking in the warmth. Each had a heavily wrapped baby in her arms, infants with running noses and cheeks reddened with cold or fever— Sira was not sure she could tell the difference. The younger of the women, painfully thin and with wispy yellow hair, had her eyes closed, her head lolling. The other one was trying to shush her child, the one who had cried. She turned her face up to Sira when she opened the door. She looked dull and ill, but her voice was defiant.

"Sorry to disturb you, traveler," said the woman, "but it's warmer here. My baby's sick."

The woman let her head fall back against the warm wall again. It was clear even to Sira that she was more ill than her child. Sira shuddered slightly as if in pain, and folded her arms around herself.

"It is all right," she said at length. "You have not disturbed me." As she returned to her room and closed the door, she reflected that she had not been truthful. The sight of them, sick and cold and hopeless, was deeply disturbing to her. Sira felt helpless and trapped.

What is it? Theo sent to her.

There are two women out there, with their babies. They are sick, all of them. Sira lifted her shoulders in a hopeless gesture.

Theo went to the door himself, and looked out. After a moment he stepped into the corridor, softly closing the door behind him. Sira could hear the murmurs as he spoke to the women, and then the shuffling sounds as they got up from the stone floor and moved away. When she went to the door and opened it again, they were gone, and Theo with them.

Not knowing where else to work, Theo led the sick women to the Cantoris. At least in the Cantoris, where he and Jon had labored with their *filla* that morning, there was some warmth and light. He did not bother with the dais, however, but asked the women to make themselves as comfortable as they could on the wooden benches.

The younger woman, with the blond hair, was very ill indeed, Theo discovered. He took his *filla* from inside his tunic and played in *Doryu*, the third mode, and as he attuned his mind to hers, his own body began to ache with her fever. He experienced with her the effort it took for her to hold her baby, her arms trembling with weakness, and he felt her great fear that she would die and leave her baby behind. It was very painful for him, but he could not shield himself and still heal her.

He continued in the third mode, searching with his psi for the hottest spot in her body, the source of the illness. It was in her throat, he thought, and probably the same for her baby. He played until he was exhausted, trying to cool her, switching to *Iridu* to try to soothe the pain of her throat and her muscles. He did the same for her child, and it was somewhat easier, as there was no wall of emotion to be breached.

The other woman was not seriously ill, but terribly worn and tired from caring for her friend and for her own baby. Theo did what he could for her, and at length both women stretched out on the benches, drowsing with their infants beside them. Theo frowned down at them both as he stood and stretched his stiff muscles.

"You're good at healing, Singer," came Pol's rough voice from the back of the Cantoris. Theo looked up at him and shrugged.

"I can only do so much," he said.

"Why is that?" Pol challenged. Theo walked to the back of the room so that his voice would not disturb the resting women.

He spoke softly, but looked directly down into Pol's eyes. "Your House is in bad condition," he said bluntly. "It's cold, the food is bad, the walls are damp. Your people are sick."

It was Pol's turn to shrug. "What can I do about that?" he said. "We brought you, and Singer Jon. Summers are better here. It's our destiny to suffer until the Ship comes."

Theo made a disgusted sound. Pol turned his small fierce eyes back to the women resting on the benches. "They understand that," he said. "They have always lived this way." He looked again at Theo. "We have a song, you know," he said, "that used to say we will wait a hundred summers for the Ship. Now we sing that we will wait a thousand summers for the Ship."

"I have been to every House on the Continent, Pol," Theo

said, shaking his head. "No other House believes as you do. You're sacrificing your people for a foolish fable."

Pol set his mouth. "It's no fable, and all Observatory knows it." He went to the doors of the Cantoris and stood there, looking out into the shadowy hall. "Shall I send someone to fetch those women?"

Theo nodded slowly at him. "Yes. I'll wait."

"Others will want your help when they hear."

"I'll do what I can, but I am only one Singer."

Pol disappeared abruptly through the doors, and Theo went back to watch over the sleeping women. The older one was breathing easily, her baby resting quietly beside her. The younger woman, her wisps of yellow hair awry, was sleeping, but her breath rattled nastily in her chest, and her infant whimpered in its sleep. Theo picked up the baby, careful not to disturb its mother, and held it close to his chest. It was hot, its skin dry and marked with rashes.

"Poor little one," he murmured to it, putting his cheek to its soft fringe of hair. "I'm sorry, baby. Fables are not much good to you, are they?" As he waited for someone to come, he sang bits of a lullaby he had heard long ago, he could not remember where. In another lifetime, perhaps.

> Little one, lost one,
> Sweet one, sleepy one,
> The Ship will carry you home.

He held the baby until a Housewoman came and, smiling gently at him, took the infant into her own arms. Then Theo went slowly and wearily down the dark, cold corridors to his own room, and collapsed on his cot. He closed his eyes against the feeble light, and saw in his mind Pol's fiery gaze. Sira is right, he thought. These people are insane.

CHAPTER
TWENTY-FOUR

★ IT BECAME A CEREMONY AT THE MORNING MEAL FOR SIRA to sit long over her tea while Pol leaned his arms on the table in the center of the great room and watched her. She was careful not to look at him, but she felt the intensity of his gaze as he waited and watched, willing her to give in. Sira had the advantage in this strange conflict, because she had nothing whatever to do, and Pol had more responsibilities than one man could carry. And so each morning she sat, stubbornly, staring at the carved wood of the table or looking out through the thick windows at the surrounding treeless peaks, until Pol was forced to leave the great room to resume his duties.

As Sira waited, she endured the inadequate efforts of Jon and Theo in the Cantoris across the hall. The air in Observatory brightened slowly as they worked. Her own inactivity stifled and irritated her, and she used it to fuel her resentment and strengthen her resolve.

Sira? We are finished, she heard clearly one morning as she sat alone in the great room. Guilt assailed her as she looked up at Theo in the doorway. He had grown thinner, and his shock of blond hair seemed less vigorous. Her own hair she had kept short, but she knew her skin was suffering from the poor food. Her hands felt dry and there were blotchy patches on her arms and legs.

Coming, she sent quickly to Theo, and got up hurriedly. Only one or two Housewomen and men were still moving about the great room, clearing things from the long tables.

"Singer?" said a Housewoman, coming up to Theo. "Can I get you some tea? Some food?"

"Thank you, Netta," he said, smiling at her. "I could take some tea to my room."

"I'll bring it right away," she said, and bustled off.

Do you know all their names? Sira sent curiously.

I am learning them. Theo leaned wearily against the doorjamb.

I know hardly any.

He smiled at her, too. *Well, I am not a Cantor,* he sent. *Only an old itinerant.*

I do not understand.

Theo's smile faded. *I know you do not. But itinerants live among the people, not separated.*

Do Cantors and Cantrixes not live among the people?

Theo shook his head. The Housewoman brought his tea, and he carried it in his hand as he and Sira moved down the corridor.

"I must speak aloud, Sira," Theo said. "I'm tired this morning; it's hard to send."

She nodded, and he went on to answer her question. "Everything in a Cantor's life separates him from the unGifted. He is taken from his family . . ."

"Not taken!" Sira exclaimed.

Theo shrugged and his smile was tired. "All right, given up by his family. He grows up at Conservatory, and then goes to a Cantoris where he is never touched by a single person, where he is spoken to only by his title, where he never mates or has children. . . ."

Sira drew breath to interrupt again, but thought better of

it. It occurred to her that Theo was saying something important, and she pressed her lips together and listened.

"Tell me, Cantrix," Theo said, grinning now as she flashed him a look. "What friends did you have at Bariken?"

Sira lifted her head. "My senior was my friend."

"No others?"

"Well, there was . . ." A painful pause ensued. "There was Rollie," Sira finished bitterly. "She was killed."

"Did you spend time with Rollie? Have tea together?"

"Only outside. She was a rider."

Theo nodded in sympathy. "This is the way with Cantors and Cantrixes. They have only themselves for company. They neither know nor understand the people they work with."

"Serve," said Sira flatly.

Theo ventured to touch her shoulder. "Yes, of course. Serve." He reached into his tunic and pulled out a bit of shining metal on a thong around his neck. "This belonged to my mother, and her father before that, and generations of Singers past remembering. They also served, and served well."

Sira did not know how to answer him. They had reached her room, and she went in ahead of him. Tiredly, Theo slumped on her cot. *Itinerants*, he sent to her now, *live with the people. Among them. And* . . .

Sira did not catch the last thought he sent, and raised her eyebrows. He went on aloud. "And know them, what's important to them, what they care about."

Theo closed his eyes for a moment, and Sira watched him. His skin, too, suffered from the bad food and the constant cold of this place. Sira had not thought about how much she liked his appearance until this moment, as she saw that his brown cheeks were less smooth, the lines around his eyes and mouth deeper, and perhaps not so much from laughter now as they had been.

She put her hand delicately on his, although he did not have the *filhata* in his hands. She liked touching him, feeling the hardness of his hands and arms, the warmth of his skin. She had not thought about that, either, until now. *Rest*, she sent to him gently. *Rest, my friend. I will teach you afterward.*

Theo smiled just a little without opening his eyes, and Sira drew a fur over his lap. Quietly, she left the room, closing the door as softly as possible as she went out.

She had seen very little of Observatory. Suddenly, she felt constrained to see it all, to understand why Theo would allow himself to be used this way. Seized with purpose, she strode down the corridor. She would start, she thought, in the place that had been her favorite, both at Conservatory and at Bariken: the nursery gardens. She did not even know for sure where they were, but the release from inactivity felt good to her, and she walked quickly.

This House, she discovered, was laid out much as Bariken had been. The gardens were in the back, protected between the two long wings of apartments and workrooms. Sira marveled at the phenomenon of a House, built untold centuries ago far above the other Houses of the Continent. She wondered if even the Watchers themselves understood its mysteries.

She peered into the nursery, but the gardens of Observatory were not inviting. Sunshine filtered through the glass roof, but it was weak, diluted. There were shadows in the corners, and the plants languished in the cold. The miracle, Sira thought, was that Observatory had any vegetables at all. There was a faint scent of offal, and Sira suspected the waste drop was too close to the House; perhaps they had no choice.

A gardener saw her and came toward the door. Sira did not even recognize his face, and she withdrew quickly, feeling that she had no place here.

She had no desire to visit the abattoir, and as far as she knew, there was no manufactory at Observatory. There were only the kitchens and the family apartments to see, then. More slowly, thoughtfully, Sira walked through the corridors, listening for the sounds of family life. The halls were quieter than at Bariken, but of course, Observatory housed considerably fewer people. She heard one or two children laughing, and at least one crying, before she reached the kitchens.

Several Housewomen were there, huddled together at a small table. It was still warm from the preparation of the morning meal, but Sira saw that even the radiant heat from the ovens could not banish the ubiquitous mold that crept across the walls. She stopped in the doorway, struck by the attitude of the women.

One of them Sira recognized as the older woman who had been outside her apartment on the day of Theo's first lesson. She was weeping, silently and steadily. Two other Housewomen held her hands and leaned close to her, nodding rhythmically to the silent sobs, in the manner of an often-observed ritual. Helplessly, Sira stood and watched them. A sense of foreboding came over her. Suddenly she had to know.

"Excuse me," she said, her voice rough in her own ears.

A woman she had not noticed, gray-haired and wearing an apron, came from behind some large wooden tubs full of grain. "Yes," she said. Her hands were on her hips, and she had the definite air of being in charge.

"What has happened?" Sira asked, dreading to know and yet needing the answer. "Why is this woman crying?"

The woman eyed her as if wondering whether she

deserved an answer. At last she said, "Her friend has died, her friend Liva. And her baby with her."

Sira's heart sank like a stone cast into the Frozen Sea. She did not know the name, but she knew with a terrible certainty who Liva must have been. She remembered the two women sitting weakly on the floor outside her apartment to take in the lavish excess of her *quiru*. Oh, Spirit, she thought. I am so sorry.

The woman's weeping went on, silent, inexorable. The gray-haired Housewoman said without expression, "Do you want something?" Sira looked at her in surprise. No title, no recognition. It was a strange feeling, and not a pleasant one.

"I . . . I had wanted to see . . ." She faltered. She had no business here. She had neither child nor friend to weep for. Theo was absolutely right, as he so often was. She did not know these people, not their names, not their cares.

"I am sorry," she said at last. She bowed to the House-women, who stood stiff and unmoving before her. "Perhaps another time," Sira said, and stepped backwards through the doorway, away from the sight of routine, hopeless grief.

Sira did not tell Theo of what she had seen, but she was moody and quiet during their lesson together. Theo was working in *Aiodu*, the second mode, striving to master the fingering pattern. Sometimes Sira was impatient with him, seizing the *filhata* to demonstrate, her long fingers secure and precise on the gut strings. Today, though, she was methodical and tolerant.

You must release the wrist, she sent. *Tight muscles inhibit other muscles.*

Theo nodded. He put the *filhata* in his lap for a moment, and rubbed the back of his right hand. *Tired,* he sent.

Sira took his hand in hers and massaged the wrist. *You must stop when you feel this tension, here,* she sent, pointing to the tendon in the back of his hand, *and begin again with your wrist in a better position.* Theo turned his hand over and captured Sira's gently.

There is something bothering you? he asked.

It was almost automatic for Sira to pull her hand away, but his own felt strong and comforting to her, and she let the contact go on.

Did you know that the young woman died? The one you treated last week?

He looked into Sira's face, the blue of his eyes dark, almost violet at this moment. *I did. She and her baby were very ill.*

Do you think I could have saved them? If I had warmed the House?

Theo lifted one shoulder, expressively. Sira sighed and took her hand away, wrapping her arms around herself. So many deaths, she thought, to weigh on my conscience. She felt old and tired. *If I begin to sing here,* she sent slowly, *I fear I will be trapped forever.*

Theo watched her, but kept his own counsel. When she looked into his face, she saw only patience and acceptance. *Do you not resent me?* she asked.

His crooked grin flashed at her. *Only because you can already play in* Aiodu *and I cannot. Now help me!*

Sira smiled a little, too, as he picked up the *filhata* and began again. But the feeling of ancient weariness did not leave her. How long could she go on like this? How many more deaths could she bear before she broke?

CHAPTER
TWENTY-FIVE

✦ "THEO HAS BEEN A GREAT HELP TO US," RASPED POL, standing above Sira in the great room.

She stood to look down at him. For weeks she had sat deliberately idle every morning until he left the great room, and in all this time he had never before stopped to speak to her.

"Theo has more sympathy for fanatics than I," Sira answered coldly.

Pol chuckled. "You are a stubborn woman. Do they teach you that at Conservatory?"

"At Conservatory, Gifted people are taught to serve the people of Nevya," Sira said, and was surprised by the flicker of doubt she felt in herself even as she said the words.

"You don't think Observatory is part of Nevya?"

Sira folded her arms in front of her, knowing as she did so that it was to bolster her courage in the face of strange emotions, not because Pol himself disturbed her. "Observatory chooses to be separate. You attack innocent Nevyans and kidnap Singers. How could I think you are part of Nevya?"

"We have a great duty," Pol said somberly. He was very serious. "We must Watch. There is no one else to do it."

Sira felt the rise of indignant anger, and the air about her sparkled as her breath came quickly and her eyes narrowed.

"And so," she said softly, "you add to your many offenses the sacrifice of your people to a foolish belief of many ages ago."

Pol's small eyes glittered in the light created by Sira's temper. He smiled thinly. "Will you come with me, Cantrix? I have something to show you." Sira pressed her lips together, about to refuse, but Pol held up a propitiating hand. "Indulge me this one time, please," he said. "There is reason why we believe. Proof."

"I will come," Sira said. "But you must not call me by a false title."

"As you wish," Pol said. He led the way out of the great room, his thickset figure purposeful.

Sira had not been to the wing of apartments where most of the House members lived. She followed Pol now down a long, dark corridor and up a staircase only dimly illuminated by a grimy window. The unkempt state of the House made her shake her head once again. She heard voices, children crying, the sounds of family life, muted as if the very life of the House were ebbing away. Finally Pol opened the door of a large apartment at the very back of the House.

They went through what were evidently Pol's own rooms. If he had a mate, or children, Sira was not aware of them. The apartment was filled with oddments, stacks of ledgers, what looked like a grain barrel, a stack of bows and fur-flighted arrows, even a saddle complete with saddlepack. Even here mold stained the walls, and the floors were frigid. At one end of the room, Pol opened a door and stood aside for Sira to precede him.

This room was different. A long, polished table filled it, and the window was clean, so that the weak mountain sunshine made the room light enough to read by. Pol held one of several chairs for Sira, and she sat, her anger replaced now by curiosity.

From a cupboard that lined one wall, Pol slowly and carefully withdrew a fur-wrapped object that he laid gently on the table's surface.

"This," he said with reverence, "is why we Watch."

He looked at her intently for a moment, making sure he had her full attention. Then, without taking his eyes from her face, he carefully untied the thongs that held the wrapping in place. When they were loose, he laid them aside. Slowly and dramatically, he slid the fur covering from the object that lay on the table between them.

Sira gazed at it without understanding. At first she thought it might be a slab of stone, although knife-thin and polished, with marks carved into it. It was about the size of her *filhata*, and almost as dark as an *obis* knife. She realized after a moment that it reflected the *quiru* light exactly the way bits of metal did, flashing and glinting as they were passed from hand to hand. Still it took some time to sort out her visual impressions. When at last she understood, she felt breathless with surprise.

"Is that . . . can that be metal? All of it?"

"It is," Pol said, and ran his thick hand reverently across its face. Sira followed his gesture and saw that the marks were not carved into its surface but somehow set below, covered and yet not hidden by the surface, set in by some mysterious technique she could not guess at. It was a beautiful, a mystifying thing, and for a moment she was speechless.

"So much metal," she whispered at last. "More than I have seen in my whole life put together. What is it?"

"It's a picture of the stars from which we all come." Pol carefully lifted the object so she could see the whorls and streams of light-points spilling across the darkly shining surface. His voice was low as he said, "This . . . is from the Ship."

Sira stared at him in amazement. "But those are fables!" she finally cried, utterly unable to accept the idea.

"No, Cantrix, they are not. Look here, these six stars. They will come from there."

"Who? Who will come? Why will they come?"

"If we knew once who they were, we no longer remember. But they will come for us. To take us to a better, an easier world. To take us home."

Sira rested her arms on the table across from Pol, and looked at him with sadness. "You believe this? This is why you all live here in isolation and suffering?" She shrugged her thin shoulders, but her face was sympathetic. "It is an illusion, Pol."

He pulled the artifact back to him and covered its shining surface again. His face settled back into its hard and remote expression. "It is no illusion, and even the Magistral Committee knows it, although they pretend they do not."

"Pol, I do not think the Magistral Committee indulges in pretense. It is more likely they understand what this great piece of metal is, and know better than to be slaves to a myth," Sira said. She stood, stiff with anger and frustration. "Allow us to leave Observatory, Pol," she said through a tight throat. "Nothing you have shown me justifies our being held here like prisoners."

Pol's voice was raspier than ever as he spoke. "Leave, then. Try it."

"You know perfectly well it would be impossible without a guide. We would starve before we found our way out of these mountains. You forced us to come here. We are as much in your control as if we were locked away."

He looked up at her with his arms folded. "We do what we have to do in this world," he grated. "We need to Watch, and we need Singers. Watching is our destiny, just as yours is to sing."

Sira was silent. The harsh truth of his words squeezed her soul. He was right, she thought. No matter where she went, her destiny pursued her. Perhaps freedom was an illusion for more than just Singers. But this . . . this sacrifice of generation after generation . . . this was fanaticism.

Pol tied the wrappings over the artifact and stowed it with great reverence in its cupboard. As he closed the cupboard again, his thick hand rested on the wooden door for a moment before he turned away. It is a devotion with him, she thought. A belief. He truly awaits this mythical Ship.

Sira was shaking her head sadly as she followed Pol out of his cluttered apartment. She saw no hope, no hope at all, for the people of Observatory.

CHAPTER
TWENTY-SIX

★ JON V'ARREN TOOK A MATE FROM OBSERVATORY A FEW
months after Theo's *filhata* studies began. She was
a thin, tired-looking woman with two children whose father
had gone too far away from the House on a hunting trip and
had been caught by the cold. Sira and Theo attended their
brief mating ceremony in the great room, and Sira watched
from a distance as Theo helped Jon move his few possessions to the family's shabby apartment. At Theo's next
filhata lesson, Sira was particularly silent, her lips pressed
tightly together in her narrow face.

I am better in Aiodu, *am I not?* Theo sent, trying to stir
Sira from her dark mood.

She nodded absently, adding, *And in* Doryu *too.* She
reached out automatically to adjust the position of his
middle finger, so that it rested securely on the C string. He
played the scale in *Aiodu* again, and then modulated to
Doryu almost as smoothly as Sira herself. It was a passage
he had practiced in private, to surprise her, but she only
nodded again, and was silent.

Finally Theo put the *filhata* aside. *Something is wrong,* he
sent.

He felt her shield her mind at once. He raised his
eyebrows and watched her, waiting. Her face was thinner
than ever, the white slash of her eyebrow like a flash of

lightning above the thunderclouds of her expression. Finally she turned her eyes, dark and troubled, on him.

She opened her mind once again. *Theo,* she sent, *we should talk about your future.*

He grinned at her. She was as formal in their relationship as if they sat in a Conservatory practice room and not in a cramped space at Observatory far from the mannered society of the rest of Nevya. *I am listening, Maestra,* he sent to her.

You must not call me that, I have told you, she responded, and no smile lightened her features.

Theo touched her hand. It seemed to him that bit by bit she allowed more contact. He tried not to hurry her. To him she seemed fragile and vulnerable, young and old at the same time, and weighed down by the burden of a great and overwhelming Gift.

At this moment she let his hand rest on hers, but she turned her eyes away.

Since Jon has seen fit to take a mate, she began—and Theo sensed very clearly her underlying distaste—*I fear you will also wish to . . .* She actually shuddered a little, and Theo held her hand more tightly.

Sira, I will not do so, he assured her, and as he sent the thought, he knew it was no less than the truth. In his turn, he swiftly shielded his mind, as he realized in a blinding flash why he would never take a mate from Observatory, or from any other House. He had not allowed himself to understand his feelings until this very moment.

Sira's eyes came back to his. *What is it, Theo?*

He let go of her hand. Keeping the private thought low, hidden as she had taught him, he sent to her again. *It is nothing, Sira. Do not worry.*

He rose from Sira's cot where he had been sitting, and wrapped the old *filhata* carefully, placing it on the shelf over the bed. *Thank you for the lesson,* he sent formally, and bowed to her as he always did. Sira rose too, standing only a few inches, but so very far, away from him. The sharp angles of her face glowed in the bright light their practice had created, and Theo felt his pulse quicken.

Suddenly he needed to be away from her, and quickly. He bowed again and left her looking after him as he hurried out. He would bathe, he thought. The *ubanyor* was not his favorite place, but today it seemed just what he needed.

Theo warmed the *ubanyor* with a swift *Doryu* melody on his *filla*, glad that the tub was empty and he was alone. He was gratified, even in his black mood, to see steam rise almost at once from the water. Certainly, he thought, I am a better Singer than I was. That thought led him back to Sira, though, when his intention had been to stop thinking of her.

He sighed as he stepped down into the carved tub. His thick hair touched the water when he had immersed himself up to his shoulders, and he was surprised by its length. How long had they been here? He had not kept track, but it must be almost a year by now. Sira cut her hair often, keeping it cropped very short, as if she were ready to leave at a moment's notice. Theo had let his grow, usually tying it back with a bit of thong. Not since his childhood had it been so long.

He was resigned to a long stay at Observatory, and he knew he was less grieved by their imprisonment than Sira was. His studies gave him great satisfaction, and his *filhata* skills were growing quickly in the hours he spent alone with her, practicing, listening, working. He had not been out-doors in all that time.

What I need now, he thought, is a trip through the mountains, a few nights under the stars to regain my balance. Perhaps the hunters could take me, just for a few days. He took up a rough, unscented bar of soap from a niche in the tub and soaped his hair savagely, knowing perfectly well Pol would never allow him to leave Jon alone in the Cantoris once again.

"I must be the greatest fool on the Continent," he muttered softly to himself, "to fall in love with a Conservatory Cantrix!" The soap slipped from his hand, and he swore. "By the Six Stars," he exclaimed as he searched for it under the water, "I hardly know what I am anymore!"

Left alone in her narrow room, Sira sat on the edge of her cot, her long-fingered hands lying idle and empty in her lap. In her mind she allowed the image she had been suppressing to float to the surface.

It was Theo that she saw, Theo with a mate, family, children, a Theo who did not play the *filhata*, but only made small, camp-style *quirus* despite all their work together. This, Sira told herself, was what she feared.

The greatest sacrifice, for some Cantors and Cantrixes if not for Sira, was the complete and absolute abstention from sex. Theo, who had grown up without the discipline of Conservatory, might not understand the necessity for chastity. As his teacher, she must explain it to him. At Conservatory, one of the men would have undertaken this lesson, just as one of the women took that responsibility for Sira and Isbel and the other girls. But here, at Observatory, Theo had only Sira for a teacher.

Sira sighed, and her stomach fluttered uneasily. There was no point in postponing what needed to be done, however. Delay would not make this discussion any easier. She closed her eyes and sent, *Theo, where are you? I need to speak with you.*

The answer was clear and immediate. *I am just leaving the* ubanyor. *I will be right there.*

Sira paced her little room. If only she could get out of this cursed House, she thought, see the stars and breathe the fresh, free air of the mountains. The thought of her captivity made the air around her gleam and flash as her temper flared. I will never get used to being a prisoner, she thought angrily. Never!

When Theo stood in her doorway, the sparks of her anger still glimmered around her.

How can you bear this eternal confinement? she burst at him, not at all what she had meant to send.

He smiled a little, his usual crooked smile, and sent back, *Is this what you needed to say to me?*

Sira took a deep breath and shook her head. *No,* she sent more calmly. *It is not. I just . . .*

Her thoughts were confused. What had she really meant to say? Sex, yes—She needed to tell Theo about her fears and concerns, and he would never understand. He stood before her, his blond hair still damp and curling from the *ubanyor,* his familiar blue eyes ready as always to laugh at something. Sira sat down abruptly on her cot.

I thought . . . I needed to tell you why Cantors and Cantrixes abstain, she began awkwardly.

Theo came and sat beside her, and lightly picked up her hand in his own. *But I know that, Sira,* he sent gently.

Her brown eyes came up to his. *But then I just realized,* she sent ingenuously, *that I have another reason for wanting you to abstain.*

He was still smiling, and he brushed her hair back from her cheek with the barest of touches. She did not pull back. Her eyes were wide and troubled. *Tell me, Sira,* he prompted.

I do not want you to mate, she sent, as flat and clear a thought as a child's. *I want you to myself.*

Theo's grin broadened. *And so it will be,* he sent, his eyes sparkling as brightly blue as the sky in summer.

Sira shook her head, and the tears he had only seen in her

eyes once before welled up. *No, you do not understand,* she sent, *I cannot mate, or* . . .

Theo laughed aloud. Now he held her hand in both of his. *Do you think I do not know that?* he sent.

Mating weakens the Gift, Sira sent. *A Cantrix or a Cantor must never mate while they have the responsibility of a Cantoris, must never put their House in danger because of personal weakness.*

"But, Sira," Theo whispered aloud, "you have no House. No Cantoris." He brought her long fingers to his cheek and held them there.

She shook her head. "It does not matter," she said very softly. "I could never put my Gift at risk." She dropped her eyes. "Even though I have misused it in the worst possible way. It is what I am."

"What do you mean, you have misused it?" Theo asked gently.

Sira turned her head aside. "I cannot speak of it."

"Not even to me?" Theo lightly kissed the fingers he held. "I love you, Sira."

Sira's tears slipped down her cheeks, one at a time. "Theo, you must not love me. I . . . I used my psi as a weapon. I harmed someone . . . Trude, it was. I ruined her mind. I might as well have killed her."

"But Sira, she was dead in any case."

Sira turned her wet dark eyes on Theo again, and the white slash of her scarred eyebrow arched upward. "What do you mean, dead in any case? She was alive, but I broke her mind with mine. I killed the Housekeeper Wil v'Bariken with a knife, but I forced Trude into madness."

Theo's face was grim as he remembered the events in Ogre Pass. "The Magistral Committee exposed them, both Rhia and Trude, in Forgotten Pass," he said with bitter satisfaction, "and they were right to do so. You should have no guilt where Trude is concerned. The decision to dispose of them was inevitable."

Sira was still for a long time. She could hardly comprehend what the news might mean to her. For so long she had carried the weight of the memory, of Trude's mind breaking before her own strong and angry psi, that she hardly knew now how to put it down. Perhaps she could. Perhaps she could release the memory. She was not yet sure, but hope dawned on her tearful face, and years seemed to drop away from her.

"Theo, I have nothing to offer you for your love."

Theo laughed again. "You have everything to offer me, everything I have ever wanted!" he cried. "The training I was denied, the knowledge I craved . . . and your company."

But I cannot stay with you, Sira sent to him. *I love you as well, but I cannot stay here.*

Theo slowly, tentatively, drew Sira into his arms and rested her head against his shoulder. *On the coast of the Frozen Sea they have a saying,* he sent. *"We cannot eat tomorrow's fish today."* Sira wiped her cheeks with her hand, but she did not pull away. Theo held her a little more tightly, smiling over her head as he put his cheek against her short dark hair.

That means we must deal with each day's challenges as they come, he sent. *And so you and I will do together, Sira.* She nodded against his shoulder, and he hugged her thin body close against his own. *We will be more than friends, then,* he sent, *but we will never compromise the Gift.*

At that, she sat up and looked into his eyes. Her cheeks had grown pink with her tears and her hair was ruffled. "How," she asked, "can you be so wise?"

Chuckling, Theo shook his head. "This isn't wisdom,

Sira. I'm just a hard-headed old itinerant. We have to be practical in my business."

"But you are more than an itinerant now, Theo," Sira said to him gravely. "You are much more."

He released her reluctantly. "If I am, it is due to your teaching." He stood and reached for the *filhata* on its shelf above the cot. "So perhaps we had better get back to work." He unwrapped the instrument and checked its tuning.

Sira smiled and smoothed her hair with her fingers. *Play that modulation for me once again, please,* she instructed, adjusting Theo's middle finger on the C string. *From* Aiodu *to* Doryu. *It was quite good.*

Theo bent his head and began to play once more. Around him the air glowed and vibrated with his emotion, and when he looked up at Sira for her approval, she thought perhaps his eyes, like her own, were a bit too bright. If only, Sira thought, he did not look so thin. For the first time, she allowed her doubts to surface, and she turned away from Theo.

Again, he laid aside the *filhata*.

I am sorry, she sent. *I cannot concentrate.*

We will work later, he answered.

Sira nodded. Then she stood swiftly and held out her hand to him. "Theo," she said aloud, smiling down at him. "Show me Observatory. Observatory as you see it."

He grinned up at her. "Now that's a fine idea," he said. "And I will."

CHAPTER
TWENTY-SEVEN

✳   THEO LED SIRA THROUGH THE DARK HALLS OF OBSERvatory to the nursery gardens. They stepped through the door into the gloomy great space, smelling of soil and the tang of growing things. A short gray-haired man hurried forward, wiping his hands on his trousers as he came, and greeted Theo with enthusiasm.

"Singer, I'm glad to see you," he said. "We're happy to have one of your *quirus* anytime you can manage."

Theo turned to Sira. "This is Ober, the gardenkeeper. Ober, meet Sira."

The man nodded briefly to Sira, but his attention was for Theo. "Let me bring you a bench, Singer," he said, and bustled to one corner, coming back with a small bench which he carried to the very center of the space.

Theo followed him, taking his seat on the bench and pulling out his *filla*. "Sorry I couldn't be here before, Ober," he said. "So many people have been sick."

Ober nodded sadly. "Always are," he said. "But we're glad to have you here now. Every little bit helps."

Sira saw that three or four other gardeners were coming forward to listen. Theo was still for a moment, concentrating, and the men were respectfully silent. Theo brought his *filla* to his lips and began a sprightly tune in *Iridu*, and the air around him began to glow almost immediately. Sira

closed her eyes and let her mind float with Theo's, following his musical thought and supporting his psi with her own.
She nodded to herself as she listened, thinking that his
technique was quite satisfactory, and that there was a
swiftness, an economy, to his *quiru* that her greater finesse
precluded.

She was thinking that she might now explore *Lidya* and
Mu-Lidya with Theo, and was planning just which exercises
might be best for him, when she began to be aware of the
feeling in the group around her.

Sira was not used to being open to random emotions.
Being linked with Theo's psi left her without the refuge of
her usual shielding, and had this been her own *quiru*, she
would never have allowed it.

The men in the nursery were fully concentrated on Theo,
his melody, and the warmth and brightness of his *quiru*.
Their rapt attention made their emotions as clear as blue ice
to Sira, and she became aware that this moment of music
was restful for them, a brief respite from their constant work
and struggle. Their thoughts intruded on hers; this one was
worried about mold on the grain crop, that there would be
no grain for the *keftet*; another one was grieving for some
older woman, perhaps his mother, whose joints pained her
unendingly in the cold; Ober himself was fearful for
someone who had gone out to hunt that very morning,
worried that he might be caught by the darkness.

Sira drew a deep breath. Never had she felt these things
while singing or playing. How could Theo bear it? She must
make sure he learned to shield his mind when he performed
the *quirunha*, or the distraction would affect his work.

The tune came to an end, and Theo put his *filla* in his lap
and smiled at the little gathering. Light now filled this part
of the nursery gardens, revealing the drooping grain, the
sagging tops of the root vegetables, the black soil faithfully

turned and tended by the gardeners. Sira looked up and saw that the limeglass roof was kept as clean as possible, but Theo's *quiru* could reach only part of this space. It was warm and bright here, where they stood, and Sira had felt him stretch it as far as he was able, perhaps a bit farther with her involuntary help. Still the corners and the furthest part of the nursery gardens lay in misty gloom.

"Thank you, Singer," Ober said. Sira was glad not to feel his fear anymore, and the worries of these others. Their emotions tired her, made her feel as if she were carrying a heavy load not her own. She was thoughtful and silent as she followed Theo from the nursery.

You see their need, Theo sent.

More than that, Sira replied. *I felt their need. That has not happened to me before.*

It can be painful to sense the emotions of others, was all Theo sent in return, and they turned toward the kitchens.

A young woman hurried up to them in the hallway. "Singer!" she cried, ignoring Sira's presence. "There will be a revel! You must come to the great room, now!" She turned and ran off down the hall, too excited for simple walking.

"Lise, wait!" Theo called after her, laughing. "What do you mean, a revel? What is that?"

Lise stopped and stared at him. "Don't you know? There was a sighting last night. The Watchers!"

Theo shook his head helplessly and shrugged. Lise gestured down the hall. "There was a sighting, Singer. Now we celebrate! Come on, hurry. We don't want to miss anything."

Sira and Theo followed the girl, smiling and surprised at her enthusiasm. Hers was the happiest face they had seen in months. They encountered the other members of the House streaming into the great room from the hall, all of them looking as if they had put on their best tunics and brushed and bound their hair. Even the children were unusually neat and clean. They looked exactly like a crowd at Conservatory going into the Cantoris, Sira thought. Something important must be happening.

Small cups of wine were arranged on the long tables, and the company stood beside them, growing quiet, waiting for something. Their attention was on the center table, which was empty at the moment except for the winecups. The excitement in the air made Sira uncomfortable, and she shielded her mind strongly to shut out the intensity of emotion.

Have you any idea what is happening? she sent to Theo.

I can only guess, he responded, *and if I am right, it is beyond belief.*

Pol made a sudden and dramatic appearance in the doorway to the great room, with two men beside him. All three looked tired but triumphant, and Pol cast Sira a significant look as he strode to the center table. He picked up his winecup with much ceremony. The entire assembled company picked up their cups as Pol did, and held them high in the air, still waiting. Even the children seemed to know what to do, with their parents helping them so the wine would not spill.

"Revel!" Pol cried in his hoarse voice. "The Watchers saw the lights last night, moving swiftly across the sky. The Ship comes closer!"

A cheer rose up, and Sira was stunned by the energy and jubilance. These dour people were transformed by . . . by what? *What actually happened?* she asked Theo in bewilderment.

They saw something, I would guess, he sent back dryly. *Or they claimed to see something.*

Pol believes it, Sira sent.

Theo nodded, and they watched as the two men came forward and gave their testimony.

"It was like a star, only moving very swiftly and in a very straight line," one said, and the assembled people hung on his words. "It came from the west and disappeared into the east as we watched."

"Then it returned," said the other, "and went in the opposite direction, very fast. It lasted only moments, but it was glorious."

Another cheer went up when the brief description was over, and Sira had the distinct impression, even with her mind shielded, that this was a familiar experience for these people. *They have done this before,* she sent to Theo.

Oh, yes, he replied, *this is well-rehearsed.* He narrowed his eyes for a moment, as if listening, and then sent, *They are nevertheless sincere, I think.*

Are you not shielded? Sira asked him.

He grinned at her. *I am now,* he sent, *and I think I know a camp story when I hear one. But the people believe this. Absolutely.*

I know. Sira looked around her at the smiling faces, now recognizing the gardeners, who had hastily brushed dirt from their tunics, and Lise, who was at their table.

With a single motion the winecups were drained, even those of the children, and a group of the kitchen workers came out with plates of grain bread and small sweets. These were parceled out with great care so that each member of the House should receive an equal share. Everyone sat, or moved freely around the room greeting each other, slapping backs and laughing. The difference in their demeanor was more than Sira could take in just yet.

She herself sat, although she did not touch the winecup at her plate. She noticed that Theo watched her, and when she did not drink, he pushed his own cup away. Pol came from the crowd and stood across the table from them.

"You see," he said, looking at Sira. "We have even more reason."

"Because of lights in the sky?" she asked. "The sky is full of lights, Pol."

"Not like these lights," he said with satisfaction. "These are the signs that they are coming."

"How often have you seen them?" Theo asked.

"They appear perhaps once every summer," Pol said. "Sometimes less. Sometimes more." He waved his arm grandly around him. "Can all these people be wrong?" he asked. He said something more, but his words were drowned out by the song that rose spontaneously from the crowd.

> "We will Watch for the Ship to come
> To come and carry us home.
> We will Watch until the watching is over,
> A hundred summers,
> A thousand summers,
> For the Ship to carry us home."

Like the lullaby, Sira sent to Theo. *And they are like children, they believe every word.*

Under the table he touched her hand lightly. She did not draw away. *Still we serve them,* he sent, and she saw that his face was grave. *Even if they are like children. Perhaps especially if they are like children.* He turned his head to her. *Unshield your mind, Sira, for just a moment.*

Now she did draw back, and frowned deeply. *The emotions are too strong,* she sent. *They disturb me.*

Allow yourself to be disturbed. He reached for her hand again under the table and held her long fingers in his. *Allow yourself to feel them. Just for a moment.*

Sira breathed uneasily. She looked into Theo's eyes, gone dark violet like the twilight in the Marik Mountains, and she nodded slightly and returned the pressure of his hand. Warily, she unshielded her mind, and the tide of emotions from the people in the great room flooded into her. She gripped his hand as she felt herself inundated by their undisciplined feelings.

There was joy, the more acute because of the pain which preceded it. There was triumph, as long-held beliefs seemed vindicated. There was grief, because some beloved member of the House had gone beyond the stars before this occasion. And there was the most painful, the most poignant, of all the emotions: a terrible, desperate hope, an emotion Sira herself had felt not long before.

Sira bore it for as long as she felt she could, and then the shield of her mind sprang up almost as a reflex. She looked around her at the people of Observatory, and at this moment she saw individuals, families, personalities, not nameless, faceless victims. Her eyes were wide when she turned back to Theo.

How do you tolerate it? she asked.

This is what life is, was his response.

Sira shook her head, as if to rid herself of the memory of those moments. *This is not my life,* she sent. *I could not bear to live with the burden of those thoughts.*

Theo squeezed her hand and released it. *I shield myself most of the time,* he sent. *But there are advantages to being open.*

Sira looked around her again. *They are so pitiful,* she sent.

Theo watched her as she rose from her seat. *They are no more pitiful than other people,* he sent. *Perhaps if they knew my feelings, they would pity me. Or you.*

Sira looked down at him for a long moment. Then she turned and hurried from the great room, unable to bear the scene anymore. Theo sat very still as he watched her tall, slender form move away from him.

CHAPTER
TWENTY-EIGHT

✳ IT WAS NOT THE SIGHTING OF THE LIGHTS IN THE SKY THAT caused Sira to sing at Observatory. In the end, it was Theo.

Some weeks after the revel, three hunters who had left the House five hours before came galloping back with terrible news. One of the *hruss* had slipped on the narrow cliff path and plunged into the great canyon. Its rider had been scraped from the saddle by an outcropping of rock, and was now trapped, injured but alive, on a ledge overhanging the abyss. The hunters were desperate to save him, but they knew it would not be easy, and could not be accomplished quickly. One courageous rider had stayed with the injured man, talking to him over the edge of the cliff, and the others had made their way back as swiftly as they could.

Pol himself came in search of Theo, and grated out a few words of explanation.

"I will go, of course," Theo said, reaching for his furs even as he spoke. "But you will have to trust the Cantoris to the Singer Jon by himself."

Pol nodded sharply. "Yes, but if the Spirit allows, they will be able to get Emil back up to the path before dark, and then you can all return tomorrow. It is a risk we must take, in my judgment."

Theo followed Pol out of the House and into the stables.

His alarm over the fate of the injured Emil was almost overridden by his relief at being outside for the moment. He breathed deeply of the clear cold mountain air, and squinted up into the pale blue of the sky. As a *hruss* was saddled for him, he tied back his long hair with a bit of thong, and sent an explanation to Sira.

With good luck we will return tomorrow, he sent.

Be careful, Theo, Sira responded. *The Spirit of Stars go with you.*

He sensed the shield she kept over her feelings, but nevertheless he recognized her anxiety. He would feel the same, he thought, if their positions were reversed, but he would also not try to stop her from doing her duty.

The feel of the saddle under him and the reins in his hand was familiar and gratifying after months of being inside. He lifted his face to the sun, taking pleasure in its pale rays, and sniffed the old familiar smell of snowpack.

Pol spoke a few words to the riders, and they were off. Theo was startled to sense Pol's envy, and he quickly shielded his mind so as not to intrude on the man's private thoughts. Nevertheless, it was curious to think that Pol would rather have ridden out on this frantic attempt to save a life than stay safely behind in the House. He certainly does his duty as he sees it, Theo thought, and admired him for it.

The party of three riders and Theo traveled for two hours before they came to the narrow passage that he remembered from his trip up to Observatory. His legs scraped the rock once again as he and the *hruss* pressed through the crevice and came out onto the dizzying height of the cliff path. Here the riders went more slowly and carefully. The rocks were rimed with ice that had more than likely caused the accident. Theo's heart beat faster when he peered over the edge into the chasm below. The cliff path was no wider than a man's height, and the canyon gaped below into darkness, as if it had no bottom.

"Now that is not a trip I'd like to make," Theo muttered, and the rider just in front of him laughed shortly.

"I'd think not, Singer," he said. "Hard to come back from."

At the site of the accident, the hunter who had stayed behind was lying on his stomach, toes planted securely behind a tongue of rock, only his shoulders and head over the edge of the cliff, keeping an eye on the injured Emil below.

The riders came up quietly, and dismounted on the cliffside with great care. Theo found he was holding his breath. Hours' ride below this treacherous foothold he saw the north to south sweep of Ogre Pass, and he drank in the view like a thirsty man. It had been more than a year since he had seen it. For a moment, he understood Sira's craving to be away from Observatory. It was hard to think of never traveling through the Pass again, never riding south into the Southern Timberlands, or east to the Frozen Sea.

But now was not a time for contemplation. Gingerly, Theo made his way around the *hruss* to the edge of the precipice where the other riders were gathered. He was here to protect them from the cold, of course, and to help with Emil's injuries, but any extra hand might be useful.

"He stopped talking an hour ago," said the one who had stayed with Emil. "I'm afraid he's dead," he added wearily. Theo closed his eyes and reached out with his psi to find Emil's own mind, and found it blank and gray with pain.

"He's not dead. He's unconscious," he said with relief.

"How do you know that, Singer?" asked Baru, a big, older man with hardened features.

Theo shrugged, not knowing how to explain to these people who knew so little of Cantors and Cantrixes. "I can hear him," was all he said. The others nodded as if Theo had said something very wise. He wished he had something wise to offer. He leaned over carefully and looked down the steep drop.

The unconscious man was limp, and he was in danger of slipping off the narrow ledge. It was only a jagged outcropping in the wall of rock, and Theo could not see how the man had escaped plunging all the way down the abyss. "Only the Spirit could have put Emil on that shelf," muttered one of the riders, and the others nodded.

"We're going to need to hurry," Theo said. "He's not holding on to anything, and it's not long till nightfall."

Ropes had been brought out, but it was clear someone would have to be lowered to bring Emil up. There was little purchase on the narrow, slippery path, and the men discussed the problem.

"We could tie the ropes to one of the *hruss*," someone suggested.

Theo shook his head. "I don't think that's the best way," he said. "A *hruss* has slipped already, and we don't want to lose another man along with this one." The men nodded, pale and grim and accepting of the terrible risk. Theo was impressed by the fierce loyalty to their own Houseman that brought them to this juncture. He looked up at the sky, which was beginning its shade of violet. There was no time to lose. He looked around the group, assessing the men.

"Baru and I, we're the heaviest," he said. "We should tie the rope around ourselves, and Stfan here, who is so light, should go down."

Stfan was the youngest of the group. Theo saw his throat work as he swallowed, but he nodded stoutly.

"Good man," murmured Theo. "These two others will help to hold the rope. We won't let you fall."

In moments, a rope harness had been fashioned by one of the hunters for Stfan to put around the unconscious Emil. Stfan's own harness Theo checked and rechecked himself.

Swiftly, Theo and Baru tied themselves securely into the web of ropes, and Stfan put his legs over the edge of the cliff.

Below, the last of the daylight was reflected on the far wall of the chasm. The near side was already in shade. Stfan looked back at Theo with eyes stretched wide.

"We must hurry," Theo said again. "We've got you, my friend." He and Baru began to pay out the rope.

Stfan used his legs to brace himself as Theo, Baru, and the others gradually lowered him toward Emil's ledge. Before any one of them let the rope slip a few grudging inches through his hands, he confirmed that the others had a firm grip.

Theo opened his mind to follow Stfan. The youngster was terrified, but absolutely silent and determined to serve his House, to die if he must. Theo smiled to himself. This is what bravery is, he thought, going on in spite of fear. He took a tighter grip on his section of the long rope.

With his mind open, he suddenly heard, *Be careful, Theo.*

Sira? he sent in amazement, even as his leg muscles trembled with the effort of holding Stfan steady. *Can you follow me so far?*

Maestra Lu could go even farther, she sent. *When you return, I will tell you the story.*

I can hardly wait, Theo sent back to her.

The pressure on the rope suddenly eased, and the men stood straight, flexing and shaking out their leg muscles. Stfan called up from below.

"It's so dark," he said, "I'm afraid I can't tie the harness properly."

Theo leaned to look down. It was true, the encroaching darkness had engulfed the ledge. He could only barely make out the top of Stfan's head.

"Can't you do it by touch?" asked Baru.

"I can try, but . . ." Theo caught the wave of doubt that came from Stfan.

"Wait," he said. He reached inside his furs and found his *filla*. "Let me see how far I can extend a *quiru*. If I can make it far enough . . . Well, let me try."

Dark was coming quickly over the cliff path. The chasm had become a yawning black void, and the *hruss* were growing restive and nervous. Theo began quickly, in *Iridu*, without embellishment.

The *quiru* around Theo sprang up quickly, strong and warm and wider than any he had ever created before in the outdoors. With his mind he reached, stretched, trying to extend the circle of light many feet below to poor Stfan and Emil. It was so far, and so difficult. He wished he had the *filhata*. With the stringed instrument, and his voice, he thought he could make his *quiru* reach, but now . . . He struggled, pushing his psi with all his strength.

Never force, came Sira's calm voice in his mind. *Always release, like releasing your breath.*

Suddenly Theo felt his own psi lifted and strengthened, as if Sira's hand were under his. His *quiru* leaped outward, almost reaching the opposite wall of the chasm, easily extending downward to the two men, and enveloping the *hruss* with room to spare. There was an appreciative murmur from the waiting men, and Theo put his *filla* down.

Thank you, my dear, he sent gratefully.

I am waiting for you, Sira sent, and then released the thread of their contact.

Theo turned to the task of helping pull up Stfan, and then the injured Emil. It was only hours later, after he had made Emil as comfortable as he knew how, that he realized Sira had broken her own tabu. She had sung for the Watchers.

CHAPTER
TWENTY-NINE

★ SIRA PUT DOWN THE *FILHATA* AFTER BREAKING HER CON-
tact with Theo. "I see now," she whispered to the
memory of Maestra Lu, "how you could reach so far. It was
love that made it possible, love and fear."

Slowly, she wrapped the *filhata* and restored it to its shelf.
Her mind felt vulnerable, sensitive as skin scraped raw on
stone. She felt lonely in a way she had never known before.
Around her, despite her mental shielding, she sensed the
feelings and emotions of the House members, and she did
not pull away. If Theo had the courage to face the barrage
of thoughts coming from unGifted ones, so must she. She
straightened her tunic and ran her fingers through her short
hair before she stepped out of her room and into the dark
corridors of Observatory.

She went first to the *ubanyix* and found several women
there in the tepid water, the darkness and cold making it an
uninviting place. One of the strange little lamps smoked in
one corner, but it only slightly dispelled the gloom, and
clouded the air with foul-smelling smoke. The women
looked up at her blankly as she came in.

"Excuse me," she said, and then she hesitated. Their eyes
on her were neither friendly nor unfriendly, but waiting. Of
course they had seen her in the great room with Theo, and
would recognize her by her height if nothing else. She

wondered if Pol had told other House members his guesses about her.

"I would like to warm the water," she said.

One of the women snickered. "How are you going to do that, build a fire with the benches?"

"Of course not," Sira protested, not seeing the joke. "If we began that, the House would be gutted within days."

The woman shook her head as if despairing of Sira's foolishness. Still they watched her, wondering where her behavior would lead. Perhaps, Sira thought, she was at least offering them some diversion.

She reached in her tunic and brought out her *filla*. It seemed best simply to begin, and let them understand about her in their own time.

She sat down cross-legged on the stone floor and began to play. Her *Doryu* melody was plaintive and sweet, springing out of her longing for Theo and her fear for him. The light grew gradually, first in a warm circle where she sat, then expanding to fill the *ubanyix*. The water seemed to grow clearer as it warmed, and the entire room took on a different aspect. Sira knew she had played long enough when one of the women exclaimed at the warmth. Another stood up, dripping and naked, and pointed at Sira where she sat.

"You're a Singer, too!" she cried out.

The group of women stared at Sira, their silence stretching into long moments. Then the one standing, her hair in long sodden strands about her, burst out angrily, "All this time you could have been warming this great cold horrible pond, and you sat in your room listening to the Singer Theo play all by himself!"

Sira's face was a frozen mask with its white-slashed eyebrow raised. This was how it must have seemed to them, that Theo came to her room to play, and she listened. They would not know, even Pol could not know for certain, what she was. And now, instead of gratitude for warming the *ubanyix*, she received anger. She received just what she would have given had she been in their place.

Sira smiled, a big smile, almost equal to Theo's merry grin.

"You are quite right, Housewoman," she said, and she laughed aloud. "I have stayed in my room listening to the Singer, and now I am out of my room. Make of it what you will!"

What a surprise she had for these people, she thought as she got to her feet. Not these poor, or pitiful, people, but these spirited, stubborn, hard-minded people. Perhaps she did not have to like them to admire them. And perhaps she did not have to agree with them to serve them.

Without taking time for a bath of her own, she left the *ubanyix* and hurried to her own room to fetch the *filhata*. Not since she and Theo had begun work on it had it left her room. Now she carried it in the old way, tucked gracefully under one arm, as she strode to the Cantoris.

She had avoided the Cantoris and its bitter implications since her arrival, and it seemed little more to her than a strange, high-ceilinged, empty space. It was neither elegantly spare, like that of Conservatory, nor ornately decorated like the Cantoris of Bariken. Theo and Jon did not use the dais, it appeared, but sat together on two carved chairs in the aisle between the benches. As Sira stepped up on the dais and took her seat, her furred boots left light prints in the accumulated dust.

Her work with Theo had kept Sira in practice, and her fingers were sure and deft on the strings of the old, refurbished instrument. She tuned the C, and as a melody came to her mind, it was as if her last *quirunha* had been only yesterday instead of half a summer ago. If only there were a junior beside her, she thought, and then smiled to herself. There could be, of course, when Theo returned. He was almost ready.

But this task she could handle alone without difficulty. She began in *Aiodu*, first just with the *filhata*, and then, when her psi was clearly focused on the House, she began to sing as well. The two together provided the energy her psi needed. As she modulated smoothly to *Iridu*, the rise in pitch was accompanied by a steep rise in the temperature of the House. She forgot that Observatory's *quiru* had to fade in the hours of darkness. She forgot that she was a prisoner, and she almost forgot that her beloved Theo was working on a narrow rocky path above a terrifying gorge. Sira lost herself in doing what she was born and trained to do, and Observatory began to come alive.

One by one, and then in small groups, the House members were drawn to the Cantoris. The music was strange to them, but the glow and the warmth of the *quiru* was hypnotic, and they straggled in with eyes and mouths wide with wonder. The *quiru* billowed out from the Cantoris, through the corridors and into the family apartments. The nursery gardens came alive as if summer had burst upon them all at once, and the dark abattoir brightened as if the sun had reached past the stone walls and into its noisome interior. Pol was among the first to come, and he stood in unabashed triumph at the back of the Cantoris as Sira, his captive Cantrix, played the swiftest and strongest *quirunha* of her life.

In the mountains, two hours' ride southeast from Observatory, Stfan looked up from where they all huddled on the narrow path around the injured Emil. "What is that?" he cried, his voice cracking like that of the boy that he really was.

They all looked up, past the crags around them, to the

peak which was home to Observatory. Theo grinned and slapped his thigh as he recognized the halo of light that bloomed brightly on the far side of the peak, a radiance like all those that rose above the Continent and served as beacons to travelers.

"That, my friends," he said, "is Cantrix Sira v'Conservatory at work." He laughed heartily, hardly able to contain himself on the perilous perch where they had so carefully arranged themselves to spend the night. "That is the result of a real *quirunha* performed by a Conservatory-trained Cantrix. And no one will Watch at Observatory on this night!"

Sira finished her music, and looked up to see that the Cantoris had filled with people. Some stood, others sat on the benches, and all but one stared at her in utter mystification. Unsmiling now, she stood and bowed to them all.

"I am Sira v'Conservatory," she said in her deep voice, feeling the resonance of the Cantoris answer her. "I warn you that I will not stay at Observatory any longer than I must. But while I am here, I will serve."

Defiantly, although she knew it was strange to them, and perhaps even offensive, she chanted the closing prayer of the *quirunha*:

> "Smile on us,
> O Spirit of Stars,
> Send us the summer to warm the world,
> Until the suns will shine always together."

She tucked the *filhata* under her arm once again and stepped off the dais. The people watched her as she went, and Sira, her mind still feeling bare and sensitive, sensed a lightening of their worries and griefs. She sensed their hope, and that was almost too painful. She pressed her lips together and strode out of the Cantoris.

Pol caught up with her in the hall.

"A marvelous *quirunha,* Cantrix," he began, looking sideways and up at her as he matched her stride.

Sira threw him a look. "Just Singer," she said firmly, and Pol chuckled.

"You may choose your title as you wish," he said. "But please remember in the future that at Observatory we require darkness at night."

Sira stopped, thunderstruck at his arrogance. He stopped with her, and his small eyes glittered savagely in the brilliance of her *quiru.* "I'm sure you can manage that," he added, and his wooden features almost softened into a smile. "I doubt there's a more talented . . . mmm, Singer . . . on the Continent." He turned and marched away from Sira, wearing his satisfaction like a fur wrapped around him.

Sira took a deep breath. If she had expected gratitude, or effusive compliments, she thought, they were not forthcoming. She started to laugh again, a bittersweet amusement. In truth, these people were more like herself than she had ever wanted to believe.

Baru knelt beside Theo, watching in silence until the Singer sat back wearily to rest a moment. "Will he live?" Baru asked roughly.

Theo shrugged. "I wish I could say," he replied. "I am doing all I know how to do."

The others were sleeping, each snuggled close against the cliff face, as far from the edge of the precipice as possible. Stfan moaned in his sleep, and Theo and Baru turned to look at him. All was well, however, in the oversize *quiru* that still stretched along the cliff face and down into the chasm to the ledge where Emil had lain.

Emil's injuries were grave. Theo had spent the long hours of darkness on the cliff path trying desperately to stop the bleeding that threatened the man's life. He knew Sira was with him—he could feel her presence, although she was silent—and he had no time to spare for conversation.

Emil was bleeding deep inside his body as well as from lacerations of his belly and chest. Theo figured he had been lucky not to plunge into the canyon with his *hruss*, and he had undoubtedly bounced against the steep cliff face more than once before landing on the ledge from which they had rescued him.

There had been no need to use the first mode, as Emil was still unconscious. It was *Aiodu* that Theo used, and he had to reach deep inside the torn tissues to nudge them together, to stanch the worst of the bleeding. He knew from experience that if Emil wakened, the pain from the blood that filled his belly would be intense.

He played a slow, searching melody as he followed the path of the bleeding. Here, he thought, must be the worst of it, and he applied precise and gentle touches of psi that pressed on the source of the blood. And there, he told himself, there is another, and he did the same, the slow music and Sira's energy making him stronger, more accurate, more powerful than he had ever been.

It went on for hours, with Theo unaware of his own body, only of the torn one he was trying to mend. When at last he thought he had done all he could, he put down his *filla* and found that he was trembling with fatigue. Sira spoke to him then, over the distance which she had bridged by using her *filhata* throughout the night.

Well done, Singer, she sent. *Emil is lucky to have you for his healer.*

Thank you. Theo felt the contact dissolve, and he looked around him for the first time in hours.

The high mountain sun glimmered over the eastern peaks, and the overlarge *quiru* was pale and diffuse in its light. The unconscious man had faint color in his cheeks now, and Theo thought he might wake before long. Now the problem was to transport him.

The path was too narrow to use a *pukuru*, but Baru had prepared a litter of *caeru* hides and softwood poles to be carried by hand back up the cliff path. The sheen of ice on the rocks reflected the rising sun. The men knew it would be a treacherous passage until they had made it through the crevice to the broad road above the canyon. Stfan led the extra *hruss* on long tethers held loosely in his hand; if one of them slipped, he wanted to be able to let go of its rein immediately. Theo rode in front of him, watching his patient and trying not to look down to his right into the depths of the chasm. Ahead, Baru and one of the riders walked slowly, the litter slung between them, feeling their way cautiously and trying not to disturb Emil. It was a silent and tense group of travelers.

When they were perhaps a quarter of an hour from the narrow opening, Emil began to wake from the stuporous sleep that had held him all night, and he began to move about in the litter, putting Baru and the other man who carried him at risk of slipping.

"Put him down gently," Theo called with some urgency. They did so gingerly, mindful of their footing on the icy path. Slowly and carefully Theo dismounted and pulled out his *filla*. He knelt in an impossibly small space by the litter and played a melody in *Iridu* this time, to induce his patient to sleep. Emil's pain had begun to rise, and he tossed deliriously and groaned. Theo put his hand on the injured man's forehead, and the sensation of Emil's pain made him catch his own breath. Not knowing what else he could do to help the man, he cast about for an idea.

Theo, Sira sent. *You will need a sleep* cantrip *for him.*

I do not know one, Theo sent back to her helplessly.

Then I will help you, she sent.

At this distance?

We must try, was the answer. *Be as open to me as you can, Theo. I will give you the* cantrip. *It will come from me, but you will be the instrument.*

Theo took a deep breath, set down his *filla*, and closed his eyes, putting himself in Sira's hands. He felt her psi, so strong, so incredibly sure, join with his own as if they were one person. Almost without knowing the source of his song, he began to sing the words that came into his mind, and he allowed Sira's psi to lift his own. His voice was neither so cultured nor so disciplined as Sira's, but the *cantrip* was effective just the same. Emil's restlessness ceased, and he lay quiet and still, only his breath showing that he lived. Somehow, Theo thought, I must learn that skill from Sira.

Shortly afterward, the party was on its way once again, with Emil soundly sleeping in his litter. The *pukuru* was waiting beyond the cliff path, and when they had squeezed themselves and the *hruss* through the crevice, Baru hitched the *pukuru* to his own *hruss* and tied Emil securely into it. He looked up at Theo.

"I don't know how you did it, Singer," he said, "but you've saved this man's life. His family will be grateful, and so are we."

"Better thank the Spirit," Theo said, smiling through his exhaustion. "I hardly know how it happened myself."

The party was safe at Observatory two hours later. They were welcomed into a warm, brilliantly lighted House, and went to bathe in very hot water in the *ubanyor*. Mates and children greeted them with excited cries, and the injured man was put to bed in his family apartment. Sira insisted that Theo bathe and sleep, and promised that she would treat Emil's pain if he wakened.

I could not have stopped his bleeding, she sent to Theo in a private moment, *but I can ease his pain.*

I think you would be surprised at how much your healing skills have grown, Theo sent to her tiredly. *But we can discuss it later.*

She smiled a little at him. *Indeed. Sleep now, dear. I will be here when you waken.*

In his fatigue, Theo pushed away the question that came to his mind. She would be here when he woke this time, but for how much longer? It was not a question he could deal with now. He kept his thoughts low so as not to disturb Sira with them. He fell into his cot then and slept for hours without moving and without dreams.

CHAPTER
THIRTY

WHAT ARE YOU THINKING OF, SIRA?

I am remembering Isbel. You knew Isbel, did you not?

Theo grinned across the table. They were at the evening meal, enjoying the vegetable-laden *keftet* that now graced the table at Observatory. Sira was delighted to see Theo's brown cheeks smooth again, his hair bouncing energetically around his shoulders. Her own hair she kept severely cropped, but she too was less gaunt and the patchiness of her skin was long gone.

Isbel with the dimples, who loved to tell stories, Theo sent. *She should be Cantrix of Amric now.*

So she should, Sira answered. *For almost three years.*

Theo nodded. *And what were you remembering?*

Sira traced the grain in the ironwood of the table with her long forefinger. *Isbel's mother withdrew from Isbel as soon as her Gift made itself known. I never understood why that pained my friend so much, even when she had only three summers. And now . . .* Sira lifted her head and looked around her. *Now I believe I do.*

Around them were the members of Observatory, the fullness of family life that Sira had failed to see at Bariken. She knew them now, their names, their histories. She had helped Theo heal many a small ailment and a few serious ones. She had eased the pain of the dying and of women in childbirth, and had learned from Theo to allow their feelings to penetrate her mental shielding. If she did not love them, she at least understood that they loved each other, and therefore she understood why Isbel had suffered from her mother's abandonment.

Together Sira and Theo left the great room. Many House members called out to Theo, and he answered them all, smiling. Annet, Jon's mate, said "Good night, Cantrix Sira." Sira nodded to her with her usual gravity. One or two other House members bowed to her, and then she saw Pol in conversation near the door. He looked up, and she met his gaze, her eyes dark and cool.

I am sure he thinks you are a gift to him straight from the Spirit, Theo sent.

Sira turned her eyes on Theo now. The time was at hand when she must speak to him of her intentions. It would not be easy.

There is something else I am remembering, Sira sent. *A very young boy, Gifted but untrained. His mother had been an itinerant, but she died. His father refused to have the boy—Zakri was his name—tested for Conservatory. He was troubled when I met him, even desperate.*

This can be a cruel world, Theo sent. *Do you know what they say in the Southern Timberlands?*

Sira smiled in anticipation of a proverb.

They say, sent Theo with a wink, *that a wezel with too many kits is feeding the ferrel.*

What does that mean?

It means you shouldn't take on more tasks than you can reasonably accomplish.

But, you see, Theo, the shortage of Singers is growing very serious on the Continent.

Theo shook his head. *No, Sira, I think the shortage is of*

Cantors and Cantrixes. *The Gift still appears. It has appeared here, at Observatory.*

What do you mean?

I think Lise's child—she is two—is Gifted. We will have a student.

Sira looked up swiftly. *But, Theo—perhaps she should go to Conservatory.*

Theo shook his head again. *No, Sira, I do not think so. I think that Lise's child, and any other Gifted ones born to Observatory, should be trained at home. There must be a reason why the Gift appeared now, when you and I are here.*

Sira was quiet. Change was desperately needed on Nevya, and change was coming. She could feel it as clearly as she and other Nevyans felt the coming of the summer. Something profound and essential was in the making, and in some way only the Spirit could understand, she knew she was part of it. She struggled to understand.

Theo smiled gently at her. *I think the way we treat the Gift must change, Sira*, he sent. *The price must not be too high, or the Gift will be suppressed.*

Sira sighed. *And if the Gift is suppressed, the people pay the price.* They lapsed into silence as they walked.

The summer was very near. From the aerie that was Observatory, the people could see the lightening of the sky that marked the beginning of the long-awaited warm season. Before long, the Visitor would appear, low on the horizon, and when its warmth reached Nevya the snow would melt even here, at what felt to Sira like the top of the world. Sira felt her destiny pull at her, in a way she could neither define nor resist.

Theo took her hand when they were alone in the corridor. *You are very thoughtful tonight*, he sent. *Shall we walk, or do you prefer to be alone?*

Sira gave him a slight smile, and sent, *Let us walk in the nursery gardens.*

Done, he sent, and pulled her after him in a half run that made her laugh as she tried to keep up. She pulled her hand away and slowed to a dignified pace when they encountered one or two House members in the hall.

The *quiru* light in the nursery gardens had begun to dim just a little from its daytime brilliance. Sira and Theo held their *quirunha* very early, before the morning meal, to diminish before full night fell, at least to fade enough for the Watchers to see the night sky. There had been no more sightings by the rotating teams of two Watchers, and no revel had been held, but the centuries-old tradition carried on as always. Here in the gardens now the plants grew strong and high, and the effluvium of offal had been replaced by the rich smell of compost and damp warm air. The gardeners smiled and called to the two Singers when they came in.

For some minutes they strolled arm in arm. Sometimes Sira pinched some of the dark dirt between her fingers, or Theo bent his face to a plant to breathe in its fragrance. Finally Sira indicated a bench under a sapling in one distant corner of the nursery, and they sat side by side.

Theo looked up at the slender branches with tentative buds just beginning to show. *There may be fruit here one day,* he sent. He looked back at Sira, and his eyes were dark, almost violet, his smile absent. *Or perhaps not.*

There will be fruit, Sira said. *Because I think you want to stay here.*

And you do not.

Sira closed her eyes as if in pain. *My dearest dear,* she began, and then felt Theo's big hand on her shoulder.

I know, Sira. I know your thoughts and I believe I know your heart.

Sira opened her eyes to look at Theo's face, the lines of laughter around his mouth and the vivid color of his eyes. She touched his hair, his face, his arm. For her it was a most demonstrative gesture, and it was his turn to close his eyes.

Theo, I cannot explain, but I have work to do. I hardly know how to begin it, but it is of the greatest importance.

He was silent, catching her hand in his and pressing her fingers to his lips. When he opened his eyes his face wore only a ghost of his usual smile. *Do you think Pol will let you go?* he asked.

He must, she said, *because I have given Observatory their own Cantor.*

Theo shook his head, but Sira insisted. *So I have,* she went on, *but only if you agree. I think a Cantor must serve willingly. He must choose the work. He must understand its cost.*

All my life I have wanted my own House, Theo sent, *but I never dreamed of my own Cantoris. I am not sure even now that it is possible.*

Sira leaned close to him, her eyes shining. *You are as Gifted a Cantor as any I have known,* she sent, *except Maestra Lu.*

There was a long pause as they looked at each other, knowing each other's joy, and unable to avoid the deep pain that would come. Then Theo slowly, tenderly, put his hands on either side of Sira's narrow face and kissed her fully on the lips. She did not pull back, although at the unaccustomed contact her stomach contracted strangely. His mouth was smooth and cool on hers, and she tried to remember the moment perfectly. It was an indulgence that would not be soon repeated.

Come back to me, my dear, Theo sent to her, *as soon as you can.*

I will. I promise.

Theo's sudden grin was as merry and brave as any she had seen from him. *I will serve you nursery fruit on your return!*

Sira found Pol in his apartments, and when she asked to speak with him, he led her through the varied clutter to the room with the long table on which he had shown her the artifact.

"I am going to leave Observatory when the summer is here," she told him without preamble. "Please arrange a guide for me, and when he has brought me to Ogre Pass he can return home."

Pol watched her through narrowed eyes for a moment. "I'm not going to let you do that," he rasped, with an air of finality.

"Your House has the Singer Theo now," Sira said, "and I trained him for you. You owe this to me."

"My people have grown to like having a warm House. I don't know that the Singer Theo, fine though he is, can manage alone."

Sira stared at Pol. She was not inclined to waste time arguing. "Then we will show you."

"The only way you can do that is for you to leave, Cantrix Sira," Pol said heavily. "And I have told you, I will not allow it. I'm sorry," he added surprisingly. "I see no choice."

The air around Sira began to sparkle dangerously and her jaw grew tight with her anger. She rose to leave the room, only looking back at him when she had reached the door. "I knew if I sang for you, you would think you had defeated me. You were wrong. I sang because of Theo, because his Gift is worth any sacrifice.

"You can never control me, Pol, any more than the Magistral Committee of Nevya could. I strongly recommend you seek a truce with the Committee. Your House members never need to live in the cold and dark again. You need a succession of Cantors and Cantrixes who are properly trained, and for that you need to rejoin the Nevyan community."

Pol, his face no less hard than the cliffs that surrounded Observatory, folded his arms and watched Sira leave in silence.

The next morning Theo mounted the dais of the Cantoris alone. The sleepy House members who faithfully attended the early morning *quirunha* were already seated on the benches, and Pol was in the back of the room, watching as he always did. He stepped forward before Theo could begin.

"Where is Cantrix Sira?" he grated. The audience looked back and forth, from him to Theo, curious and alarmed. Theo felt the current of apprehension from them. He grinned.

"There is no need for concern," he said to the people, ignoring Pol. He bowed, formally, to the assembly, and took his seat as calmly as he had been doing each morning for months. He began in *Iridu*, modulated to *Aiodu*, and began to sing. The warmth and light billowed out on the tide of his psi, and the room began to glow, as always. The people smiled, comforted, and then closed their eyes and listened.

Before the *quirunha* was finished, Pol offended all courtesy by stamping out of the Cantoris. Theo's concentration was so complete that he was unaware of Pol's departure, and the *quirunha* was unaffected by the disruption.

When he stood to chant the final prayer, and bowed, receiving the answering bows of his audience, Theo looked around and realized Pol had left. He smiled to himself. Let him look, he thought. Let him turn Observatory upside down. He will never find her.

*   *   *

For three days, Theo maintained the House *quiru* alone.
Pol, stubborn and proud, kept silent. He prowled the
corridors, and asked questions of all the House members,
and minutely examined the stables to see if *hruss* or tack
were missing. All were accounted for. Even Sira's own
saddle still hung on its ironwood peg, awaiting the day when
she could use it again.

At evening of the third day, beside himself with rage and
frustration, Pol pounded on Theo's door when he was
practicing alone. Theo put the *filhata* aside, taking ample
time to wrap it meticulously in its fur before opening the
door.

"By the Six Stars, Singer, you will tell me where she is!
Surely you would not let her commit suicide by trying to
find the Pass on her own?"

Theo grinned hugely at Pol. "Shall I sing for you, maybe
a little something in the first mode, help you relax, Pol? I
don't think so much excitement can be good for you."

Pol controlled his temper with visible effort. His small
eyes snapped with anger, but his rough voice was even.
"Just tell me. I don't want her to die."

"She won't die. You have no need to fear on her account."

"I sent a rider after her, to the canyon, but he didn't find
her." Pol slumped slightly, and leaned against the doorjamb.
Theo took pity on him.

"Has the House been cold, Pol?" Pol shook his head.
"Dark?" Another shake of the head. "You're going to have
to let her go."

Pol straightened again, and came into Theo's small room,
looking around absently at its sparse furnishings. "It's true,
Singer. The House has been as warm as ever. It has never
been in such good care." He turned and looked up at Theo,
and a small smile lightened his craggy features. "The

Cantrix has given us a great deal in addition to giving us you. I want her to be safe."

Theo gestured to the door. "Come with me," he said, "and I'll show you where she is."

He led Pol down the corridors to the back of the House, where the abattoir doors opened onto the waste drop. A broad path lay within the reach of the House *quiru*, which was just beginning to fade for the hours of darkness. The two men stepped out onto the path, and Theo pointed up the mountain behind Observatory.

A small blossom of yellow light lay on a ledge of the mountain, perhaps an hour's ride away.

Pol looked at it and began to laugh, not his usual sardonic bark, but a rumble of mirth that took years from his appearance and infected Theo, too. Together they looked at Cantrix Sira's camp *quiru* and laughed into the violet evening of the high mountains. Only when the House *quiru* began to noticeably diminish and the cold to slip past it, did they step back in through the abattoir to the House itself.

Theo sent then to Sira, *You can come home now. All is well.*

And Sira sent back, *I will come home. I will be there for your quirunha in the morning.*

CHAPTER
THIRTY-ONE

SIRA DID ATTEND THE *QUIRUNHA* THE NEXT DAY. SHE made her way down the slippery talus slope from her campsite in the first light of morning, seeing in the distance the beginning glow of the Visitor as it appeared above the crags. She walked into the Cantoris just as Theo began with the ritual, formal bow, and she and the other members of the audience bowed in response, and sat down.

Sira closed her eyes and listened as Theo played and sang. His technique was quite satisfactory, she thought. His voice was pleasant, lacking the polish that early training might have given it, but always true in pitch and inflection. His *quiru* had a strength and quickness seldom equalled anywhere on the Continent. Observatory would be well served.

When the closing prayer was said, which the members of Observatory had learned to recite in unison, the *quirunha* was complete. Sira stood where she was and spoke aloud before Theo could leave the dais.

"Members of Observatory," she began, and surprised faces turned to her—Theo's questioning, Pol's ironic. She walked forward, down the aisle between the benches.

The House members at Observatory had grown used to Sira's silence. Only rarely had she spoken aloud in public. Now they stared at her as she stepped up on the dais beside

Theo, moving uneasily in their seats, some murmuring among themselves.

"Forgive me for interrupting your *quirunha*," she said aloud to Theo, and she included the House members in her glance. "At Conservatory, where I trained, the day of departure from the House was the day on which a Singer became a full Cantor or Cantrix." Her voice, deep and ringing, reached every ear without effort. Others heard her and came in from the great room, and the Cantoris seemed quite full.

"Here at Observatory, the ceremony is reversed. The Singer Theo has come to stay, and so it is on this day that I pronounce him to be a full Cantor. He is fully qualified, and already has proven himself in ways that other Cantors have not. From this day, he is Cantor Theo v'Observatory, and as such, is to be accorded all the respect due his position and title."

Formally, Sira turned and bowed to Theo, and privately, she sent, *Congratulations, Cantor.*

Thank you, Maestra, he sent back with a wink, *and do not argue with me. You are my maestra, I have no other.*

With no further ceremony, Sira stepped down and away from the dais, leaving Cantor Theo to receive the congratulations and good wishes of the House members. She turned back and watched from the doorway, and Pol approached her there.

"I'm glad to see you back," he said.

"The summer is here," she responded. "There is a party in Ogre Pass, looking for the route to Observatory. I want to go down to meet them."

He looked up at her, his intelligent ugly face resigned to her decision. "How do you know that?" was all he said.

"I have seen their *quiru* these past two nights."

Pol nodded. "You're right. Our hunters spotted them

yesterday." He bowed slightly to Sira. "I will arrange a guide for you, then, to take you down to them. Your *hruss* is healthy, and your tack is ready."

"Have you considered my suggestion about renewing your ties to the Magistral Committee?"

"I have, Cantrix," he said. "I will suggest to your guide that he bring the traveling party here to talk. I would appreciate your recommendation to them on Observatory's behalf."

Sira measured Pol with a long look. She smiled a little, and then she bowed, deeply and formally. "It will be my honor," she said. "Magister Pol."

Pol laughed, but he bowed stiffly to her in return. "Thank you, Cantrix Sira."

Sira looked back to the front of the Cantoris, and saw Theo coming up the aisle. "When can I leave?" she asked Pol shortly, feeling a sudden bitter ache in her throat.

"Today," he answered, "if you wish."

"So I do," she responded softly. Pol turned away to make the arrangements, and Sira waited in the doorway for Theo to join her. Together they walked slowly down the corridor toward her room, and although they were in perfect accord, they neither touched nor conversed. Sira thought her chest would burst with her love, and she feared Theo must feel the same. Still in silence, they went inside and began to collect her few possessions.

It took only an hour for Sira to prepare. Morys, one of Observatory's riders, came by to announce that her *hruss* was saddled and ready, and that he would be her guide, ready to depart at her convenience.

"Thank you," she said, and then found she was unable to speak further, to give instructions. The purpose that had been driving her these past days suddenly was lost in a wave of grief. She hung her head in helpless misery. Theo stepped forward.

"The Singer will be ready in about half an hour," he told Morys. "We will meet you in the courtyard." The man nodded, and disappeared. Heavily, Sira sat down on her cot.

This is so very hard, she sent.

Theo sat next to her, but he did not touch her, and she knew it was a sacrifice for him. *How can I ever thank you?* he sent.

You have already, in a thousand ways, she answered. She hardly dared lift her head for fear she would lose her composure. *I will miss you terribly,* she sent, looking at her long fingers twined tightly in her lap.

I will be with you each moment, Theo sent, and when she breathed deeply and looked into his eyes at last, they were warm and reassuring.

There was nothing left for them to do, and after a time they rose to go to the courtyard. At the last moment, Theo pressed something small into Sira's hand. *For later,* he sent, and she nodded.

The *hruss* stood ready for Sira, its saddlepacks stuffed full of dried meat and grain. The two suns had begun their slow dance across the cloudless blue sky, and Sira stood in the courtyard with the reins in her hand to say farewell to Observatory. She pushed back her furs and felt the mountain air chill her burning cheeks. The full warmth of summer had not yet reached the peak which was home to Observatory.

She was surprised to find that Pol and a sizable contingent of House members had assembled on the steps, steps that were now smooth and straight and solid, to say goodbye to her, in unconscious imitation of a Conservatory farewell.

Sira could think of nothing to say to them. She had been an unwilling guest in their House, and yet had worked hard and long to improve their lives. It was an unspoken and yet acknowledged gift she had given them. Several of the House members, particularly one or two young women, had tears in their eyes. Sira saw those tears, and accepted them as gifts.

Pol rasped, "Until you return, be well, Singer."

Sira bowed. There was a moment's pause, and then at a signal from Pol, the House members retreated inside the double doors, leaving only Theo on the steps.

His grin was as bright as ever as he looked at her, but she was as sure of his feelings as she was of the destiny that was tearing her away from him. For long moments they stood in utter silence, the early summer suns glancing off the shrinking firn on the crags above them. Then Theo, ever faithful, broke the mood.

Your guide will be waiting, he sent. Sira nodded, and pulled herself up into the *hruss*'s high saddle.

I will be waiting, too, Theo added, and Sira turned her face quickly away from him, to hide the tears that slipped down her cheeks. He saw, and took a step toward her, but she held up her narrow hand.

I cannot bear it, she sent, and he stopped.

Sira, he sent one more time, *remember that I love you. Go with the Spirit.*

She wiped her cheeks with her hands, and then turned back to Theo. *Goodbye, my dear friend,* she sent. Her face felt stiff and ugly with pain. Theo's smile faded for just a moment, and Sira saw the blue of his eyes suspiciously bright, but he held his composure.

Be safe, he sent at last. *And come back.*

I promise, she responded, and turned the *hruss* away. She did not look back at Theo as she rode out of the courtyard to join Morys, who waited among the trees. She could feel his presence, though, strong and calm, watching her go. *What am I doing?* she asked herself in a moment of panic.

Only what you need to do, Theo sent to her, and she realized he had read even that thought of hers.

Yes, my dearest dear, she sent back to him, much comforted. Morys rode out to meet her, and led the way through the trees to the path down the mountain. *Goodbye, my Theo,* Sira sent.

Goodbye, my love, came the answer, and Theo held the contact for as long as he could while Sira rode away from him down the side of the mountain. She could feel the warmth in his thought even after the contact was broken and she was alone again.

Only then did she look into her hand at the small object he had placed in it. It was a fragment of metal, strung on a thong, polished and imprinted with strange incomprehensible glyphs. It was Theo's necklace, which had been his mother's, and her father's before that. It was Theo's talisman, and now Sira's.

Sira placed the thong around her own neck, tucking the metal down inside her tunic over her heart. It was cold at first, and then it grew warm against her skin, and she pressed her fingers against it as she rode after Morys down the mountain. It seemed almost to vibrate with Theo's essence, from his soul to hers. *Thank you,* she sent, not sure if he could hear her, but sending anyway. *Thank you.*

AUTHOR'S NOTE

The Nevyan clef symbol is a C clef, indicating the one pitch all Singers must be able to remember and reproduce accurately. Both the *filla* and the *filhata* are tuned to C. The *filhata*'s central, deepest string is the bass C; from top to bottom, the *filhata* is tuned thusly: E-B-F-C-G-D-A. The *filla* is tuned with no stops on C.

The modes are natural scales of whole and half-steps; alterations, or accidentals, are considered variations and are used as embellishments, and can be half- or quarter-tones. Even those Singers without absolute pitch are required to memorize the pitch C early in their training.

The modes are employed customarily in the following ways:

First mode, *Iridu: quirus,* inducing sleep
Second mode, *Aiodu: quirus,* healing
Third mode, *Doryu:* warming water, treating infections
Fourth mode, *Lidya:* entertainment, relaxation
Fifth mode, *Mu-Lidya:* entertainment, relaxation

GLOSSARY

caeru	Fur-bearing animal; a source of meat and hides
carwal	Sea animal living mostly in the water
ferrel	Large predatory bird
filhata	Stringed instrument similar to a lute, used exclusively by Cantors and Cantrixes
filla	Small, flutelike instrument used by Singers
hruss	Large, shaggy animal used for riding and carrying, or pulling the *pukuru*
keftet	Traditional dish of meat and grain
obis knife	A knife made of slender long metal pieces, used in conjunction with psi to carve stone and ironwood
pukuru	Sled of varying size, with bone runners
quiru	Area of heat and light created by the psi of Gifted Singers
quirunha	Ceremony that creates a *quiru* large enough to heat and light an entire House
tkir	Great mountain cat with long, serrated tusks
urbear	Silvery-gray, very large coastal animal
wezel	Thin, rodentlike animal, native to Nevya